THE FAIRHAVEN CHRONICLES
BOOK 4

A THORNY PATH

THE FAIRHAVEN
CHRONICLES
BOOK 4

A THORNY PATH

SHARON DOWNING JARVIS

DESERET
BOOK
Salt Lake City, Utah

THE FAIRHAVEN CHRONICLES

Book 1: A Fresh Start in Fairhaven

Book 2: Mercies and Miracles

Book 3: Through Cloud and Sunshine

Library of Congress Cataloging-in-Publication Data

Jarvis, Sharon Downing, 1940–
    A thorny path / Sharon Downing Jarvis.
        p. cm. — (The Fairhaven chronicles ; bk. 4)
    ISBN-10 1-59038-612-4 (pbk.)
    ISBN-13 978-1-59038-612-5 (pbk.)
    1. Mormons—Fiction. 2. Bishops—Fiction. 3. Southern States—Fiction.
I. Title. II. Series: Jarvis, Sharon Downing, 1940– Fairhaven chronicles ; bk. 4.
    PS3560.A64T47 2006
    813'.54—dc22   2006009843

Printed in the United States of America
Malloy Lithographing Incorporated, Ann Arbor, MI

10   9   8   7   6   5   4   3   2   1

*For all who find themselves
treading a thorny path of
whatever kind*

CHAPTER ONE

"ARISE, YE SAINTS, AND SET THEM FREE!"

He enjoyed the fragrance of summer rain. More especially, he enjoyed the fragrance of summer rain falling on cement and filtered through a screened door as he breathed it now, watching from his family room the drops splashing on the uncovered portion of the patio behind his house.

"Smells good," Bishop James Shepherd remarked. "Takes me back to my childhood." He turned back into the room, where his wife, Trish, four months pregnant, lay curled on the sofa.

"Makes me sleepy," she replied, not opening her eyes. "Low pressure always does, especially when I'm pregnant. I get lazy."

"Rest while you can," he advised. "Nobody expects you to keep up your normal pace right now, least of all me. What can I do to help?"

"Nothing, at the moment. You deserve to relax, too. When you can, you might want to sort through your clothes for the trip, decide what you're taking, and see if anything needs washing or cleaning."

"We'll only be gone four or five days. I won't need much. How about Jamie? Can I help get his gear ready?"

"I've already packed his and Mallory's, with strict instructions that they are not to open their bags until we get to the first motel. In fact, I stashed them in the trunk already, so they won't be tempted."

He chuckled. "Good thinking."

Trish yawned. "I just hope nothing happens to keep us from going on this trip."

"In the ward, you mean?"

"Mmm. Seems like something always comes up."

"I know. But I have two good counselors, and they'll both be in town. Besides, this trip is almost mandated, you might say, by President Walker. I do believe he's got me off my duff at last, genealogically speaking."

His stake president, President Walker, had announced a year-long emphasis on family history and temple work, requesting the bishops to set the example for ward members by making a concentrated effort to expand their knowledge of their own ancestral lines and provide temple ordinances for as many deceased relatives as possible. On the other side of the coin, he had also gotten the younger generation involved, both in learning to do research and in doing baptisms for the dead. Several young people from the ward had participated, including the bishop's daughter Tiffani and Thomas (T-Rex) Rexford, who was still experiencing residual dizziness from the head injury he had sustained in a motorcycle accident the previous Christmas.

"I cain't take that constant dunkin', Bishop," T-Rex had told him. "It makes my head swim. How 'bout I just sit there and be confirmed? I mean, I'd purely hate to puke in the baptism font!"

The bishop had agreed. He would purely hate to have that happen, too.

Following his priesthood leader's request, Bishop Shepherd and Trish had prayerfully examined his family records and identified his mother's paternal line as the one that needed the most research. His grandfather, Benjamin Rice, had lived in a small town in southwestern Georgia and had died a young man, leaving his small family to fend for themselves until the widow remarried—and that was pretty much the extent of the bishop's knowledge about the Rice connection. His mother, who had taken her stepfather's name, had never known much about them, and he remembered her saying that her stepfather didn't like her mother to tell the two older girls about their real father, feeling that it caused a division in the family and undermined his authority and claim to their affection.

He had tried to search for Benjamin Rice on the Internet, but with no success. True, there were numerous people by that name, but none of them was the right one. Finally, he and Trish had determined to make a short family vacation out of traveling to southwestern Georgia and searching out in person whatever might be found concerning Benjamin and his forebears. They had also promised the children that they would have some fun along the way and stay at nice motels with swimming pools whenever possible. The bishop himself wasn't very interested in the prospect of swimming, which could be done any day except Sunday in the Fairhaven Community Pool, but he found he was excited to track down Benjamin—could hardly wait, in fact, to get going.

"Dad," his six-year-old daughter said, in an uncharacteristic whining tone, "I don't want to go away and leave Samantha. Can't she go with us? I'm scared that lady'll get her again."

He turned to see Mallory with her arms full of a purring but squirming Siamese cat. "Oh, we'll make sure that doesn't happen, Mal," he reassured her. "Mom's got that all taken care of, don't you, hon?"

"M-hmm. I told Muzzie all about what happened, and she and the girls know to keep a close eye on Samantha when they come to feed her. She'll be fine."

"Well, I don't care if Mar-greet wants to pet her, but I don't want that lady to even see her."

"That lady" to whom Mallory referred was Mrs. Maxine Lowell, a next-door neighbor who the previous winter had captured Mallory's beloved pet and secretly dropped her off at an animal shelter.

Marguerite, the Lowells' adult daughter, seemed fond of both Mallory and Samantha, but the bishop had to admit to himself that he and his family had made little progress in befriending the parents in the months since the Lowells had moved in on the corner and disturbed what had heretofore been a comfortable, tolerant, and friendly neighborhood. Mrs. Lowell, in particular, had taken exception to the notion that Mormons—members of The Church of Jesus Christ of Latter-day Saints—had the right to call themselves Christians and to live in peace and harmony with their fine neighbors of all religious persuasions. To the bishop's mind, her behavior left a good deal to be desired in a person who, herself, claimed to worship the Lord and to have taken His name upon her.

It had become a source of some concern to him to set a good example for his family regarding how to behave in the face of persecution and how to get along with antagonistic folks. He had to admit, however, that he hadn't exactly scored any resounding successes in that department. It wasn't such a problem for him to deal with her snipes at him personally, but when she attacked his wife and children and tried to turn other neighbors against them, he found it difficult to maintain a very high level of love and tolerance. Not only that, he didn't care for the uneasy feeling he seemed to have so much of the time when he was at home, as if some malevolent force had taken possession of the house next door and was waiting to spring out upon him and his loved ones at an unguarded moment. He chided himself for such childish fantasizing, and he continued to pray for the ability to love and forgive the Lowells, but so far, he couldn't see much progress in himself.

Y

"So, Dad—you said we're coming back Saturday afternoon, right? What time?"

"I don't know exactly, Tiff—I reckon it'll depend on where our search takes us, and where we are when we start back. We're kind of playing this whole trip by ear, if that makes sense. And I sure hope it'll be harmonious!"

"Cute pun. But, see, the thing is—if we get back early enough that I have time to shower and get ready, I can go out with Billy. Or even better, if we could possibly make it home on Friday afternoon, then he and I could double with Claire and Ricky to the square dance at the Community Center. Wouldn't that be cool?" Tiffani gave her father a raised-eyebrow look of hopeful pleading.

He didn't yield. "No promises, Tiffi. This trip is for a special purpose, as you know, and I just can't tell ahead of time how things will go. Plus, it's probably the only family vacation we'll get this summer, and I don't want to cut it any shorter than we have to."

Tiffani sighed. "I know. It's just—if we don't make it on time on Saturday, at least, it'll be a whole week until Billy can go out again. He's only allowed to date on Friday and Saturday."

"You and Billy seem to be getting pretty close."

"What do you mean? We're just friends."

He could see her hackles beginning to rise. Of late, Tiffani had grown defensive about her friendship with Billy Newton. He liked Billy—liked him a lot, in fact—but he was uneasy having the two young people spending too much time together. Tiffani was only sixteen and Billy not much older.

"Billy's working construction this summer, isn't he?"

"Uh-huh. His uncle's a contractor, down in Birmingham."

"You know, construction's really exhausting work, especially in the heat. I expect by Friday night, Billy's ready to kick back and go to sleep watching TV."

"No, he's not! Dad, he's the one who asked me to go to the square dance. Doesn't sound to me like he'd be too tired, if he wants to do that!"

"Well, he may just have to do-si-do with somebody else this time around," he replied, and immediately could have bitten his tongue.

"Exactly—and he probably will, too!" Tiffani said, and pounded up the stairs to her room. "And don't tell me about how absence makes the heart grow fonder!" she yelled over the banister. He could hear the latent tears in her voice and then the slam of her door.

"Open mouth, insert all four feet," her father muttered to himself. "Way to go, Dad."

"First one to say 'Are we there, yet?' will be the last one in the pool!" the bishop announced cheerfully as they left the Fairhaven city limits and headed southward. Jamie and Mallory immediately clapped their hands over their mouths, but Tiffani drawled in a bored tone, "Are we there, yet?"

"Tiffi's last in the pool!" Mallory crowed.

"I think she wants to be, silly," said her brother.

"Like I care," Tiffani said. "Who needs green hair from all the chlorine they dump in those pools to kill everybody's germs?"

"Oh, cool!" Jamie said. "Mom, does your hair really turn green?"

"Never fear. I brought our special shampoo that gets chlorine out," Trish said patiently. "And our sunblock. And our beach towels. And Mallory's water wings. And our suits. And . . ."

"Shoot," said Jamie. "I thought green hair'd be rad."

"Are we there, yet?" asked Mallory, giggling.

"Ha-ha! Mal's last in the pool!"

"Nuh-uh. Daddy said *first* person to say that. I was second."

"Did I remember to set the sprinkling system?" Trish wondered.

"Nope, but I did," her husband replied, reaching to cover her hand with his. "And the doors are locked, and I saw you give Muzzie a key. And the stove is off, and you put the iron away, and you left a light in the downstairs hall, and I have my cell phone and its charger and my razor and toothbrush and camera and my notebook on Benjamin—and we're on our way at last. Whoop-de-doo! The Shepherds are on vacation together!"

"Whoop-de-doo," he heard Tiffani echo under her breath from the backseat. "What could be more exciting? Just can't wait to get to those courthouses and graveyards."

He smiled to himself. It was exciting enough for him.

Y

They picnicked in a park for lunch, swam at the motel pool, and relaxed in the cool of their room while they consumed a pizza for dinner. While the children watched TV and Trish indulged in a lengthy shower, the bishop sat at a round table by the window and pored over maps and notes. They would hit the courthouse first thing in the morning, to look for land records and for a record of Benjamin's marriage to Annie Josephine Burke. Dying so young, Benjamin would likely not have left a will—the bishop wasn't sure if, in fact, he had even owned the land he was reputed to have farmed—but the deeds should tell him that. Why, he wondered, had he not been able to find him on the on-line census records? He wasn't sure of the dates of his grandfather's life, but it was reasonable to assume he should appear as a boy with his parents in 1900 and 1910, and possibly as a young married man in 1920. But no appropriate Benjamin Rice had turned up in those census years in Georgia—and the bishop had searched for him as Benjamin, Ben, Benj., Bennie, and B. It was perplexing. His mother had seemed certain that her dad had been a Georgia boy, and a farmer, though she knew little else about him.

"Dad, can I borrow your cell phone?" Tiffani asked. "And is it okay if I sit out by the pool for a while, to make a couple of calls?"

He wondered why she needed to contact her friends so soon; it had been less than twenty-four hours since her last visit with them.

"Sure, honey," he told her, handing over his phone. "Just don't let it go swimming."

After she left, he opened the drapes a bit so that he had a view of the pool area. A dad couldn't be too careful, these days.

Y

The next morning, after a quick breakfast in the lobby, they piled into the car for a short drive to the county seat and courthouse.

"Now, guys, this is where it gets interesting for me and kind of dull for you," he advised, as he parked the car in a shaded slot.

"I know it's warm out here, and I'll try to be as quick as I can. Maybe no one will mind if you and Mal play under these trees, Jamie, and Mom and Tiff can take turns watching you and helping me, inside. Now—who's on research duty first?"

"I'll go first," Tiffani said with an air of pained boredom. "I'll get my half hour over with. Maybe," she added, brightening, "there won't be any stuff you need, here."

"Sounds like you're hoping that's the case."

"Not really. It just all sounds so deadly dry and boring."

"Hmm. These folks have been dead for a while, true—I expect they're just dry bones by now."

She giggled. "That's not what I meant, and you know it!"

They ventured into the office of the county clerk and explained their mission.

"Well, now, our staff doesn't have the time to look up family history for folks, if that's what ya'll want," the clerk behind the counter drawled. "And you should know that our courthouse has suffered three burnings in its history—one during the Civil War, one in 1891, and another in 1917. So we've had a lot of record loss."

"Wow," said the bishop. "That's really unfortunate. What we were hoping to find here was the marriage record of my grandparents, and any land records that might be in my grandfather's name. We don't expect anyone to do the searching for us, but if you allow it and can just point us in the right direction, we'll be happy to look for ourselves."

"Marriage records are right here in this office, those that we have. They're pretty sketchy. What year were your people married?"

"I'm not totally sure. I'd guess between 1912 and 1918."

The woman looked doubtful. "Most of those years were

destroyed in that 1917 fire. We can look, but I can't promise any success. What was the groom's name?"

"Benjamin Rice."

She took down a smallish, blackened ledger with ragged edges. Fire had eaten away about half of each page.

"You see what I mean," she said, displaying the volume. "This is our index to the marriage records from 1892 to 1917." She set the book carefully on the counter and opened it gingerly. The binding made an ominous cracking sound. Using the tip of a retracted ballpoint pen, she carefully turned to the page containing grooms whose surnames began with "R."

"You'll notice they didn't index them alphabetically except for the first letter. They just listed chronologically all the 'R' grooms as they took out licenses. Let's see . . ."

She turned the book so that the bishop and his daughter could see the page with her. "I don't see anyone named Rice. But that doesn't mean he wasn't listed. His name could have been on the half of the page that got scorched and crumbled away."

The bishop leaned close, scanning the names listed. He couldn't find a Rice, either. He felt an unexpectedly strong surge of disappointment.

"What was the bride's maiden name?" asked their helper.

"Um—Burke. Annie Josephine Burke."

Gingerly she moved to the back half of the volume. "There's a reverse index, by bride's name," she explained. "Maybe we'll be luckier, here, let's see. Well, looky here! This might be her. It says 'Annie J. Bur . . . , but the rest of the name and the page number are gone. That's still a clue that the marriage probably took place in this county. Of course, the name might have been Burns or Burwell or something—there's really no way to tell. Did she have any sisters? Let's see if there are any other Burkes."

"One sister, I think. I heard of an Aunt Lily Burke, but my impression is that she never married."

"How about brothers?"

"Two. Um—Everett and Jesse."

The clerk turned back to the grooms' section again, to the "B" page, and found an entry for a Jesse Burke.

"Well, I know it's not much, but it's some evidence that your grandmother's family probably lived here during that time period."

The bishop copied the entry about Jesse into his notebook. "What about the records themselves? Did anything survive except the index?"

"Not from about 1900 through 1917. We can look at the 1918 index and see if maybe they're listed there, but I'll be surprised. I'll bet that Annie J. we found was your lady."

He sighed. "Likely so."

They examined the 1918 index, to no avail. There were no Burkes or Rices listed.

"What about birth certificates for these people?" Tiffani asked. "Can't we just look at those and get their parents' names and stuff?"

"Oh, honey, birth certificates in Georgia didn't get going good until 1927 or '28," the clerk explained. "Good thought, though. Now, if ya'll want to look at deeds, the old ones are down the hall in Room 105."

They thanked her and went to that office. The bishop found fairly complete indexes for the time period in question, but was puzzled to find no land records at all listed under the name of Rice. There were a number of Burke deeds, and he obtained copies of them, but he already knew a good bit about the Burke line, and he wasn't sure that these deeds would add much to his knowledge, although he was glad to have them. It was the Rice family he was after on this trip. Time for Plan B.

He found a playground at a shady park for Jamie and Mallory to run off some energy while he and Trish pondered what to do next, and Tiffani stretched out with her book. For lunch, they came across a place on the highway that advertised "Real Smokepit BBQ" and that exuded mouthwatering smells. Trish ate sparingly, being well aware of what all the fat, spice, buttered biscuits, and coleslaw dressing could do to her presently delicate digestion. She tried to warn her husband that he, too, might suffer, but he waved away her concern.

"I'm on vacation," he said, lifting his oversized barbecued beef sandwich from its basket of fries. "Besides, a genealogist needs his nutrition. I've decided this is hard work!"

They ate at a rustic picnic table in a vast, dim dining room only slightly cooled by high ceiling fans. He used the time to peruse the Burke deeds he had collected, fighting his way through the legalese to get to the facts on each document.

"You know," he said at last, "all these deeds show that the Burkes owned land in a little town called Winns Corner. If the Burkes lived there, chances are the Rices did, too. Let's go have a look around, there."

"Cemeteries?" Tiffani asked darkly.

"Wonderful idea!" her father agreed. "Thanks, Tiff."

"It's Mom's turn to do research," she said. "I'm going to read my book."

"GENERATIONS GONE BEFORE"

The area known as Winns Corner seemed to consist of little more than a corner—an intersection of two country roads that boasted a dilapidated gas station and what appeared to be a general store on the southwest quadrant. A battered pickup nosed up against the side of the building, but there seemed to be no customers at present. The bishop and his family got out of their air-conditioned car and stretched in the sleepy heat and silence that was broken only by the occasional buzz of an insect. Green farmlands stretched in all directions as far as they could see, with periodic clumps of trees that might or might not be sheltering houses and outbuildings.

"Let's all go in," the bishop suggested. "Bound to be cooler inside."

They trooped in through the squeaky screened door, their presence announced by the jangling of a bell, and paused while their eyes adjusted to the dimness. A counter ran along about six feet of the left wall, and a radio softly played country-western music. Tables were piled with merchandise, offering everything from folded children's clothing in front to tires and automotive parts in the rear. One table held school supplies, another, used paperback books. Several racks against the wall offered bread and canned goods—Spam, tuna, pork and beans, hash, and boiled peanuts—and two chest-style coolers stood adjacent to the counter, the first containing bags of ice, ice-cream bars, cans of beer and soft drinks, and wrapped meat—the second with milk, butter, and eggs. Bushel baskets of produce—potatoes, green beans, beets, and onions—sat on the floor, and, most appealing to the bishop, a couple of washtubs filled with ice water offered huge, striped watermelons or sweet corn.

"This place is so cool," whispered Jamie, as if the peace and quiet of the store demanded reverence. "They got everything. Look, Mal—they even got a couple of Barbies! And the same kind of transformers I used to have."

"Is this a store or a museum?" Tiffani wondered aloud, standing still with her arms folded around her middle. Her mother was looking through the infant clothing.

"Hello-o," called the bishop. "Anybody here?"

No one replied.

"I bet aliens came and captured the people," Jamie advised. "And it happened five years ago, and there's a spell on the place, so everything's stayed just the same."

"Interesting theory," his mother told him with a fond smile. "More likely, though, the proprietor stepped out for a minute, or went home for a bite of lunch."

"Would he leave the store open like this?" Tiffani wondered. "I mean, even here in the back of beyond? Anybody could come in and steal anything they wanted."

"Cool," Jamie was saying. "Look, Mom, they've got Ninja Turtles comic books!"

"They're used, aren't they? They look pretty beat up."

"S'okay, they're still good. Can I get some?"

"Up to you, Jamie, how you spend your vacation money," his mother said. "But remember that you might want something else, somewhere along the line."

The bell on the front door jangled again, and they all turned toward it. A woman of about fifty came in, wearing a plaid house dress, sandals, and white socks. Her hair was caught up in a hairnet the likes of which the bishop hadn't seen since his grandmother had died, and her face was red from the heat.

"Hey," she greeted. "Harvey around?"

"We haven't seen anybody. We called, but nobody seems to be minding the store," the bishop replied.

"Oh. Well, reckon I know where he is," she said, moving purposefully toward the back of the building. "This is the slow time of day around here, and I just bet he's takin' him a nap. He's got him a little room back here with an air-conditioner, and he prob'ly ain't heard ya'll come in." She pounded on a door in the back wall. "Harvey! Harve, you got customers, boy! Where you at?"

After a moment, the door opened, and the "boy," of about sixty years of age, shuffled through, stifling a yawn.

"Hey, how ya'll?" he said. "Sorry 'bout that—reckon the heat got to me. That and the fact that I was up early this mornin', pickin' beans and corn 'fore it heated up. Now what can I do for you folks? Bet ya'll young 'uns could do with an ice-cream bar, couldn't you? No charge, of course." He handed each a bar, for which he was politely thanked.

"We mostly stopped for information," the bishop explained. "We're down here from Alabama searching out my grandfather's history, and we know he and his wife lived in Winns Corner when they were first married. Her folks—the Burkes—came from around here, and we suspect his did, too, but we don't know much of anything about them."

"What was your granddaddy's name?" Harvey asked.

"Benjamin Rice," the bishop replied. "He died young. His wife was Annie Josephine Burke. We wondered if you could point us toward some cemeteries around here that we could search."

Harvey scratched his head, then smoothed the sparse gray hair over it. "I know there used to was a Burke family had a farm about five mile north of here," he said. "Seems like it was their daughter got the place when they died, and she married a Winn. This town was named for her husband's people," he explained.

The bishop could barely hear Tiffani's cynical comment, "This is a *town?*" He hoped Harvey didn't hear it.

"Don't recall nobody named Rice, though," the man continued. "May? You know anybody around here named Rice? Back a generation or two, most likely?"

May heaved a twenty-pound sack of sugar onto the counter. "Rice? Don't ring a bell with me. Miss Susie might know; she's been here nigh onto forever, and she's eighty-some-odd years old. Here—I can give you directions to her place."

"Thanks, we'll appreciate that. And are there any cemeteries in the area?" Jim asked.

"There's two—three old ones," May answered. "When'd your grandpa die?"

"We think around 1919."

"Oh, that ain't so old—he might could be in the Baptist cemetery. Was he a Baptist?"

The bishop shook his head. "We don't know, but we'd sure appreciate some directions to that one and any others you might know about."

Harvey and May regarded each other.

"Let's see," Harvey said. "'Course, there's King's Chapel. That's out on Highway 32, and off into the woods, past the old tobaccy barn. Bower family used to have a big old tobaccy plantation, till old man Bower got religion and decided smokin' was of the devil," he explained. "Or so I heard," he added with a grin. "Anyhow, the dryin' barn's still standin', and you go past it for a little ways, and the buryin' ground's on the left. It ain't kept up too good, though, so watch out for snakes and all. Me, reckon I'd start with the Baptist cemetery. It's got perpetual care."

"Okay. Where's that?"

"Oh, it's right by the First Freewill Baptist Church, on the road to Dawson. You cain't miss it. The Freewill folks donated the land, but they take all Baptist burials—Primitive, Missionary, Hardshell, Southern, Baptist Temple, and so on. It's about fifteen—sixteen miles from here."

May added, "Then there's the old Methodist graveyard, out towards Eads. Church is gone, now, but the cemetery's still there, of course—I mean, reckon it ain't goin' anywheres, is it?" May laughed at herself. "I think it's still used once in a while, in fact. I know the Methodist ladies go out ever' Memorial Day and make a project of cleanin' it up. But these days, lots of people like to be buried in the city cemeteries, like in Albany or Bainbridge."

"Thank you," said the bishop, scribbling down directions to compare with his atlas in the car. "Any others?"

"Well, you know—just folks who used to bury their dead on their own places, though by the time you're lookin' at, most people were usin' the reg'lar cemeteries. I'm not sure when the law started about that, but nobody does it, no more. Not openly, anyhow." May smiled. She told them how to get to "Miss Susie's" place, and they prepared to take their leave, with Mallory gleefully clutching a dusty Barbie box and Jamie a handful of comic books. Tiffani had found a couple of paperbacks that interested her, and Trish had purchased a little pair of hand-crocheted baby booties. The bishop wistfully eyed the chilled watermelons.

"If we get back this way by evening, I'm going to have to have one of those," he told Harvey, who chuckled.

"I tell you what, they're mighty fine," he promised. "Good old-fashioned Georgia rattlesnakes."

The bishop carried the twenty-pound sack of sugar to May's car for her.

"Well, I thank you, sir—you're a real gentleman."

"What do you plan to do with all that sugar?" Trish asked pleasantly. "Are you canning?"

"Oh, hon—I got me a ton of blackberries on my place," May responded. "I'll make up several batches of jam and jelly, and a few pies, and Harvey'll sell 'em here for me. A little later, I'll do some crabapple. Makes me a little extra spendin' money. Comes in handy 'round Christmas time."

"Sounds yummy. Thanks for your help with the cemeteries and Miss Susie."

"No problem. Good luck findin' Grandpa." She started to get into her car, then turned and asked, "Where y'all stayin' at?"

The bishop responded. "Last night we were at the Southern Belle Motel, about thirty miles south of here. Do you happen to know of a nice place closer around here, since this seems to be our point of interest right now?"

May smiled. "Not around close, but to tell you the truth, I was thinkin' of my place. Got me a big old shady farmhouse, and all my young 'uns are gone. I could give you as many bedrooms as you want, plus supper and breakfast, for about thirty dollars. The young 'uns might enjoy my critters—I got goats, and a donkey, and a dog and cats and chickens. Got me one air-conditioned bedroom besides my own, and the other rooms have fans. I'd be plumb tickled to have ya'll stay."

The bishop didn't know what to say. He looked at Trish, who seemed intrigued, and he could see his children weighing the advantages of swimming pool and air-conditioning versus a farm-yard full of animals to play with. For Mallory, at least, the choice was clear: she smiled hopefully and teetered on her tiptoes to exert whatever influence she could on her parents. Tiffani, on the other hand, frowned, and Jamie looked interested but neu-tral. Their dad thought back to childhood visits to Shepherd's Pass, and to his Uncle Ben's farm as a boy.

"I think that'd be fun, for all of us," he said, relieved that Trish nodded.

"We hate to put you out, though," she added. "That's a lot of work, to put us all up and prepare meals too, when it sounds like you already have your work cut out for you."

"Oh, hon, it'll be my pleasure. I like to keep folks whenever I can. I don't advertise like a fancy bed and breakfast, but ever' now and then I get a referral, or a call from somebody who's got family coming and nowhere to put 'em. I just rattle around in that big house and talk to my animals all day long till I think I'm goin' crazy! I'll enjoy havin' somebody around who talks back." She laughed, and winked at Mallory. "The animals do answer me, mind you, it's just we don't speak the same language."

"Well, we'll look forward to it. Now, how do we find your place?" the bishop asked.

"So are ya'll headed to see Miss Susie first? If you are, my house is just off the road on the way to hers, and you can foller me and see where I turn off. My house'll be in the first clump of trees you come to. Hers is further along the highway about twelve miles or so. It's a pink Victorian on the left. You won't miss it."

They thanked her again and climbed into their car.

"Dad," Tiffani said, as soon as their doors were closed, "you don't know what kind of place that woman has, or if it's even clean! Or if she's a good cook, or her beds are comfortable, or her animals are friendly to kids, or—"

"I know, Tiff—all those thoughts went through my mind, too," her dad soothed. "But I just have a good feeling about taking her up on her offer. I'm not sure why, to tell the truth. It's not just the price, though that's way beyond generous. Even if we pay her more than she's asking, it'll be much less than a night at the Southern Belle and two restaurant meals. I think it sounds like fun."

"I do, too," Trish agreed. "I mean, every detail might not be just as we'd like it, but, hey—for one night, we should be fine. We'll be sure to find another place with a nice pool before we head home, right, Jim?"

"Sure thing. Let's just take things as they come, okay, guys? That's part of the fun of this kind of trip."

Tiffani's look said she seriously doubted her parents' judgment, but she sat back and opened her book.

May was right about Miss Susie's pink Victorian—it would have been hard to miss. Trimmed with white "gingerbread" and a veranda that stretched halfway around the house, it stood in serene, ladylike splendor against a backdrop of azaleas and live oaks.

"Oh, my," breathed Trish. "It's exquisite."

"It looks like it popped out of my Candyland game," offered Mallory.

"Yeah, it does," Jamie agreed, his voice awed.

Even Tiffani was intrigued. "Now, I wouldn't mind spending the night here," she announced.

"Let's go see if Miss Susie's receiving callers," the bishop suggested.

The door chimes were answered by a slender black woman in a pink uniform with a frilly white apron.

"Good afternoon," she said in a soft voice. "May I help y'all?"

"Hello," the bishop responded. "We've come to see Miss Susie. Is she available?"

"Is she expecting you? May I give her your name?"

He shook his head. "We're the Shepherd family, from Alabama, but she won't have heard of us," he explained. "A couple of neighbors have told us that she knows a great deal about local family history, and my grandparents were from this area, so we were hoping she might be able to tell us something about them."

"I see. Would ya'll mind waiting here while I check with her?"

The bishop agreed, and she closed the door quietly.

"I get the impression Miss Susie appreciates her peace and quiet," he whispered. "Let's be sure and not disturb that for her, okay?"

The woman in the pink uniform returned. "Please step into the parlor," she invited, standing back and holding the door for them, her left hand indicating the arched entrance to the parlor. "Ya'll just make yourselves comfortable. Miss Susie'll be just a moment."

They perched on the edges of dainty chairs upholstered in a brocade featuring pink roses. Climbing roses adorned the wallpaper as well—and the painted glass lampshade—and the Persian carpet on the gleaming hardwood floor was in shades of rose, green, and gold. A faint scent of—what else? the bishop thought—rose potpourri perfumed the air.

"Welcome to Roseacre," came a voice from the archway. They all instinctively rose and turned to face the elderly lady who spoke in a distinct, carefully modulated voice. "I am Susie Throckmorton."

Miss Susie appeared to have once been rather tall, the bishop noted, but age had shrunk and bowed her by several inches. She held her head erect, however, and the hand that grasped a cane was steady and bedecked with rings—several diamonds and one oval, rose-colored stone that he couldn't identify. She wore a lightweight floral print dress, nylon stockings, and white shoes, and her silver hair was perfectly waved. Her dark eyes held a glint of amusement.

"Please, sit down, so that I can," she invited. "Arlene says you are the Shepherd family. Is that correct?"

"We are," the bishop replied. "Thank you for seeing us like this, with no notice," he added.

She peered at Jamie and Mallory. "Arlene?" she called over her shoulder. "I rather expect these little ones would enjoy a sip of lemonade in the arbor. We'll no doubt be speaking of things that would bore them to tears."

"Yes, ma'am," Arlene said, again holding out one hand to indicate which way the children should go. Tiffani looked at Trish, uncertain of whether she was included with the "little ones" or not.

Trish nodded and whispered, "Keep an eye on them. Thanks, honey."

As the children exited, Miss Susie sank onto a straight-backed chair. "When Arlene returns, I'll have her bring us some iced tea. It's a warm afternoon."

"It is that," the bishop agreed with a nod. "But no tea for us, thank you. Water would be fine."

Miss Susie's sharp gaze moved from the bishop's face to that of his wife. "You're Mormons," she announced. "Three nice, clean children, expecting another, interested in genealogy, and you don't drink iced tea in weather like this! I hope you have nothing against lemonade."

Trish smiled at her. "Nothing at all. And you're very astute, Miss Susie—or rather, I should say, Miss Throckmorton. Excuse me."

That lady waved a hand. "Everyone calls me Miss Susie. Always have. Who recommended me to you?"

The bishop replied. "A fellow named Harvey, down at the store at Winns Corner, and a lady called May, who was shopping there."

"Oh, May Hinton? Good woman, May. Now, Harvey Kickliter, he's another story. Well-intentioned, but rather lazy, that one. Who is it you're searching for? I must tell you, to be honest, I don't hold with what you folks do in your temples, trying to turn everyone who ever lived into Mormons, but I figure that's your business, and you have as much right to know about your people as anyone does."

"Um—thank you," the bishop said. "My grandfather was Benjamin Rice, who married Annie Josephine Burke."

She frowned. "I've known a number of Burkes. I seem to recall that Homer Burke had a daughter named Annie."

"Yes, Homer's my great-grandfather. That's the right line."

"But I don't recall—I'll have Arlene pull the files—but I don't recall that Annie married a Rice. Seems like she married a fellow from over by Quitman. A Mitchell, wasn't he?"

"Your memory is excellent, and you're right again. But Robert Lee Mitchell was Annie's second husband. She married him after Benjamin Rice died and left her with two little girls. Then they moved up into Alabama, just south of Birmingham, where she and Robert had three more children. But my mother was Annie's eldest child, and she and her sister were originally Rices. Grandpa Mitchell adopted them."

"And I suppose your mother's gone?"

"She's living, but she suffered a stroke a few years ago that has impaired her speech. But I remember her saying that she knew virtually nothing about her real father and his people. That's why we've come looking for him. I'm hoping to find a gravestone for him around here."

"Hmm. I suppose that's possible, all right. Oh, here you are, Arlene. Two things, if you will, and then I'll let you relax for a bit. Iced tea for me, lemonade for these folks, and then if you would pull the Burke file for me? Thank you."

Arlene brought the file first, along with a portable table to place in front of Miss Susie so that she wouldn't have to balance the thick, unwieldy packet of papers on her lap.

"You must be quite a researcher," Trish remarked, eyeing the bulk of the file.

"I never intended to become one, to tell the truth," Miss Susie told her. "But before Father passed, he entrusted me with our family records, and as I perused them, I found some gaps that I wanted to close, and then I became interested in the families that connected with ours, and they all intermarried with other old families in the county, so it became a hobby to research many of the early families in the area.

"I have to tell you, it's been the strangest thing—I've never had a hobby that so totally engrossed my time and my interest! I absolutely couldn't put it down for more than a day or two at a time without feeling almost compelled to get back to it. I've never been an obsessive-type personality—I prefer doing everything in moderation—but I surely was obsessed by this work. Now, of course, I can't get to the courthouse much to search the records—not that we have such good ones, anyway, being a burnt county—but I still write letters and have even learned to use the Internet, and Arlene is helping me compile my work into a book about our first families. It simply amazes me, the volume of information I've collected over the years! And I wasn't even a very enthusiastic history student in school. I majored in English literature, if you can imagine—for all the good I thought that would do me!"

The bishop and his wife exchanged knowing glances. They knew exactly why Miss Susie had developed such an interest in genealogy, even if she did not.

"It's a wonderful thing to investigate our histories," he told her. "It gives us perspective and wisdom, and appreciation for those who gave us what we have, today."

"Yes, and I find that more than that, it gives one a feeling of connectedness, of family, that one loses when one has grown older without spouse or child to continue the line, as I have done."

She smiled, a deprecating, heartbreaking little smile. "I could have married, you know, several times. But the young men I brought home never sufficiently impressed Papa, and once I left school and came home to live, I simply didn't have many opportunities to meet anyone interesting. Then one by one, my family died out. My brother was killed in World War Two, before he had a chance to marry. My older sister died childless. My younger sister had one daughter, who herself died in childbirth, along with the baby. So I am the last of the Throckmorton line, and I cling to my memories and my records—and hope to recognize my dear ones when we meet in heaven—assuming, of course, that I qualify for that blessed place! Now, why am I telling you all this? You didn't come here to learn my history! I do apologize. Let's see what I have in my files about your Annie Burke."

Arlene brought their drinks and a plate of small sandwiches. The bishop sipped gratefully, his outsized barbecue lunch having made him thirsty, and Trish nibbled at a couple of sandwiches. They sat quietly, so as not to disturb Miss Susie in her search.

"Well, here we are," she said at last. "I'm afraid the only reference I find here to your grandmother, Annie, is that she was a war widow when she married Mr. Mitchell."

"Really? That's more than we knew," the bishop said excitedly. "So Benjamin must have been killed in World War One!"

"Yes—and that should open up some good opportunities for you to search his military records," said Miss Susie. "I've seen draft records on the Internet—actual images of the forms the boys filled out when they registered."

"I'll look into that as soon as I can," he promised. "Miss Susie, you may not think that's much, but to me, you're a goldmine."

"Well, you're kind. Others have shared with me, so why should I not share with you?" She shook an arthritic finger at him. "Mind you, most researchers are glad to share. A few are not. I know one woman who answered my query with the remark, 'I spent my time and money to discover this information, and if you want it, you can do the same.' So I did. And, I rather suspect, more thoroughly than she! Now, I have a copier in my study, and I'm going to select the records I have that pertain to your branch of the Burkes, just in case I have something you don't."

Trish spoke. "We'll be more than happy to reimburse you for the copies."

Miss Susie raised both hands and looked around her. "Oh, my dear! Do I look as if I need to be reimbursed for a few sheets of paper and some ink? My money, my house, and my precious records are all I have in life. If I can share something useful with you, my day is complete. However," she added, pulling a blank pedigree chart and family group form from the back of her file, "I will ask you to fill out all you can on these, while I make the copies. And I'll add you to my Burke file, where you belong. And when your little one arrives, send me an announcement, and I'll make sure he or she is included, as well."

Trish smiled as she accepted the sheets. "I'm not worried about your place in heaven," she said.

CHAPTER THREE

"MY WEARY, WAND'RING STEPS
HE LEADS . . ."

O kay, Mom," Tiffani announced as they drove away from Roseacre, "that backyard was gorgeous! You would—"

"Yeah, if you like pink," interrupted Jamie. "Even the lemonade was pink."

Tiffani laughed. "I know. But, Mom—seriously, you'd have loved what she called the arbor. Except it was really a—what do you call those little houses made of crisscrossed white wood?"

"A gazebo?"

"Yeah, right. Except it had like a little hallway leading out of opposite sides, covered with arched wood, with rosebushes and some other vine growing all over it, and the hallways circled around and met, and in the middle of everything was a rose garden. There wasn't much blooming now, but it'd be so pretty when there was."

"I'll bet it would. It's a little hot right now for roses. But obviously Miss Susie sees to it that the house lives up to its name."

"I guess! She was awesome. Dad, did she know anything about your grandpa?"

"Well, I did learn one new thing, Tiff. Grandpa Rice evidently died in World War One, because his wife was referred to as a war widow in Miss Susie's records. Plus, she copied some things for me on the Burke line. It wasn't much, regarding Grandpa, but I'm stoked to know that much! Hey, gang—we've got time to hit a cemetery or two. Who's game? Trish, you're navigator. Which one are we closest to?"

Trish consulted her map and the notes they'd made. "I think the nearest one must be the one that Harvey fellow talked about—King's Chapel. I know we crossed Highway 32 on our way here, and from the direction he pointed, I'd say we need to turn right at the intersection."

"Are you okay, Trish, for a little further adventure? I know it's hot, and I don't want you to overdo."

"Oh, I'm fine, after that lemonade—and especially after Miss Susie invited us to use her 'facilities,' as she called them. I was afraid I was going to have to find a friendly bush."

"What for, Mommy?" queried Mallory.

"To go pee behind, Mal," her brother whispered. "What do you think?"

"Mommy! We're not s'posed to do that outside, 'member? You yelled at Jamie the last time he—"

"I never—" Jamie began, and Trish interrupted.

"I know, sweetie. That's why I'm glad we had a nice bathroom to use. Oh, here comes Route 32, Jim. Now, kids, watch for a big old barn on the left with a road going by it."

They passed farm after farm, field after field—some fallow, some burgeoning with green rows. The bishop recognized beans, potatoes, peanuts, and of course, corn. There were barns here and there, but none had roads beside them until they spotted a huge, looming old structure on the left, with a narrow road beside it that led into a tunnel of dappled green shade. The bishop was reminded of his favorite stretch of road on the way to his ancestral home, Shepherd's Pass. As he always did there, he slowed the car here as they passed under the canopy of over-arching trees.

"This is nice," Trish remarked. "I bet it's ten degrees cooler under here."

"Which should bring the temperature down to about a hundred and five," said Tiffani wryly.

"Ah, Tiff, you're a cynic," her father teased. "And riding in an air-conditioned car. Look at this—it's beautiful!"

"What'd be cool would be riding a horse through here," she said. "Or maybe driving, so that I could see it all better—please?"

Her dad chuckled. "Maybe on the way back to Mrs. Hinton's," he promised. "If you don't complain too much about the cemetery, that is—because I see it now, and it's pretty grown over. Oh, boy."

"It really is, Jim," Trish said. "I don't know if we should have the kids roaming around in there. I'm thinking snakes, poison ivy, poison oak, ticks, chiggers, sandspurs—and Jamie and Mal have shorts on, and Tiff's wearing sandals."

"The place really could use a good mowing—or maybe a machete," he agreed. "Tell you what—you guys stay here and keep the air-conditioning going for a few minutes while I go poke around the newest-looking tombstones. I'm hoping I can tell from the dates whether there's any chance that Grandpa could have been buried here."

"You be careful," Trish advised, as he left the road and picked up a small fallen tree limb. He stripped the twigs away and pounded the stick on the ground a few times, continuing to do so as he made his way into the cemetery. There were a number of old, lichen-rimmed stones, and far to one side he sensed as much as saw the foundation of a fallen building. That, he supposed, might have been the King's Chapel for which the cemetery had been named. Did "King's" indicate that the congregation who had worshiped here had been Church of England, or was the chapel named for a King family who had donated the land for it to be built? Had the worshipers built a more modern church to accommodate their needs, or had the congregation dwindled until all had died off or moved away? From the condition of the cemetery, he had to assume the second because it was obvious it had been many years since anyone had been here to clear the undergrowth. Fairly mature trees had sprung up in several places that he was pretty sure, from the layout of the gravestones, had once been pathways between them.

The silence was deep in this place, and the inhabitants slept soundly in the sun. Using the branch as a snake-scaring device, he thumped it on the ground, then moved it back and forth before him like a blind man with a cane as he worked his way toward the whitest and most modern-looking of the markers. Small scrabbling or slithering sounds headed away from his intrusion.

Heavenly Father, he prayed silently, *if my grandfather Benjamin Rice is buried here, please help me find his marker. I know it's Thy work that we seek our kindred dead and provide ordinances for them, and I pray for guidance and success in doing so. I thank Thee most sincerely for the assistance we've been given thus far. May all who help us be richly blessed.*

He closed his prayer and began to read the gravestones, noting the death dates, none of which seemed later than the eighteen-eighties, even on the newest-looking stones, and he soon returned to the car.

"You know," he said, as Trish opened her window, "these all seem a little early for Benjamin, though I realize that some of his people might be buried here. But I don't want to take the time right now to tramp through all this. It occurs to me that maybe somebody, somewhere, has transcribed all these markers, and published their work. That'd be so much easier to check than physically hacking my way through the brush, though I'm willing to, if need be. What do you think, babe?"

"Well, who would know? Maybe Miss Susie—and she gave us her phone number. Why don't you check with her on that?"

"I will. Although it seems like she would've mentioned such a thing, when we talked about finding gravestones."

Trish nodded. "Call her anyway. Maybe it just slipped her mind."

"I'll do that this evening. I think I'm ready to relax a while, how about you guys? Tiff, your turn at the wheel."

Tiffani successfully navigated the country roads and delivered them safely to the home of May Hinton just as the afternoon sun was beginning to sink behind the stand of trees, sending long shadows across the landscape. While the Hinton homestead in no way compared to the grandiosity of Miss Susie's, it was large and seemed welcoming—a two-story farmhouse with peeling paint and window boxes of colorful petunias across the front. A small lawn of close-cropped grass set off the front porch, but most of the yard was hard-packed clay. A barn and two other outbuildings could be seen behind the house, plus a pen with a couple of black-and-white goats who crowded against each other like competitive children, rearing up to peer through their fence to see who was coming.

The family unfolded themselves from the car and

approached the house. The bishop imagined that they all felt a little strange, as did he, showing up for bed and board at the home of a virtual stranger, even though they had been cordially invited.

A brown dog wagged its way around the corner of the house and headed straight for Jamie and Mallory, bounding around them in obvious delight and announcing their presence in a hoarse "Arp!" that resembled the bark of a seal. At the sound, the unmistakable bray of a donkey began from somewhere out back, and the front door opened with a bang, emitting a smiling May Hinton.

"Well, y'all did come! I'm so glad—I've had fun gettin' ready for you. Did you find Miss Susie all right? Ain't she somethin'? Come on in, and might's well bring your things with you and get 'em tucked away upstairs while supper's finishin'. Hey, there, you old hound, leave them young 'uns be! He's lonesome for somebody to play with since Luther, my youngest, up and joined the Navy last year. The donkey misses him, too. She's Luther's special pet, and I don't know what I'm supposed to do with her. Ya'll come on in, now!"

Obediently they got their overnight bags and followed her into the house. The high-ceilinged living room with its faded wallpaper and dark red plush-covered chairs reminded the bishop mightily of his grandmother's house—as did the aroma of supper cooking and the window fan that was wedged into one long dining room window to suck the hot air out of the house.

The house was old and shabby but spotlessly clean enough to appease even Tiffani's worries. They followed May up the staircase and into the bedrooms she indicated. A front bedroom was air-cooled and furnished with a four-poster bed that the bishop knew his wife was admiring, and it was there that May indicated that they should sleep. Next door was a room with twin beds and a box of toys.

"This here's where my grandbabies sleep when they come," May told them, "so I figgered ya'll young 'uns might take to it, too. Right now, that window fan's suckin' out the warm air, but after while, when it's cooled off a bit outside, I'll reverse it so it blows air in. Same in here, honey," she added to Tiffani. "This was my girl Selma's room. She's married now with two of her own. Lives in Atlanta. The bed's real comfy."

"Thank you," Tiffani said. "It's really pretty."

"Well, Selma was always the frilly type. She ordered her spread and curtains from the Sears catalog we used to get, and paid for 'em with money she saved up sellin' eggs and produce. You should see the place she's got, now! So fancy a body cain't even relax in it. But it's purty to look at."

She stood in the middle of the hallway and looked around. "Oh—bathroom's right through there, and you're all welcome to a bath or shower, though you might want to space 'em out a little, 'count of my hot water heater's kinda old, and takes a while to fill up. Well, y'all make yourselves at home, inside or out. I'll be in the kitchen for just a few more minutes. Onliest thing, y'all kids—don't let the goats out of their pen or I'll never get 'em back tonight! They're friendly, though, and you can pet 'em and feed 'em through the fence. They'll eat handfuls of grass or weeds or whatever. And there's some little-bitty kittens in the barn. If you're real soft with 'em, I reckon their mama'll let you hold 'em. She's a sweet-natured cat. Now, can I get y'all anything? Ice water? Iced tea?"

"We're fine, thanks. We had ice water with us in the car. We'll just freshen up and be down in a minute," Trish told her. "Thanks so much for preparing all this for us."

"My pleasure, honey. I've got pork chops, applesauce,

mashed potato, pole beans, and fresh tomato and cucumber and hot biscuit and gravy, if y'all can make a meal offa that."

"Boy! Can we ever," the bishop responded with enthusiasm. "Sounds great."

The children wandered outside, with Mallory predictably making a beeline for the barn and the kittens. The bishop and Trish followed, enjoying the peaceful close of a fine day, watching their children get acquainted with the livestock, and feeling that life was, indeed, very good.

While they waited for dinner, the bishop made a few calls on his cell phone. He spoke with his counselor, Sam Wright, and learned that so far, things hadn't fallen apart in their absence.

"I hear Sister Hildy ain't feelin' so well," Sam told him. "You know how she's just fadin' away since she lost Roscoe, bless her heart. I don't reckon we'll have her with us too many more months. Ida Lou keeps a close eye on her, thank goodness. Oh, and I saw Ralph Jernigan, and he says he's got somethin' to tell you. Wouldn't breathe a word of it to me, of course. All hush-hush. You know how Ralph is."

"I do," the bishop agreed, smiling. Indeed, he did.

"And I b'lieve Sister Winslow wants to be released from the Activities Committee. Don't know why."

The bishop winced. Not only did LaThea Winslow do a bang-up job on that committee, but it would be a challenge to find another appropriate place for her to serve. Although, he reflected, she had humbled herself appreciably of late, and maybe she would be willing to teach a class of youth somewhere. He would ponder and pray on the matter, and he asked Sam to do the same.

"So how's the ancestor hunt goin'?" Sam asked.

"I'm having a blast," the bishop admitted, "but I'm beginning to see what Sister Collins meant when she said research is time-consuming. I've been to the courthouse, a cemetery, and to visit a lady genealogist who seems to know everything about everybody in the county, but I've only uncovered two little-bitty facts about my grandpa, one of which I already figured to be true. The other is that he apparently died in World War One, which is news to me."

"Well, maybe more'll turn up. I wish you luck."

He said goodbye and shared the information about Hilda with Trish, who nodded sympathetically.

"She's such a sweet lady, and she must be desperately lonely, with all her family in the next world."

He agreed. "Never complains a word, though, does she? And thank heaven for Ida Lou. They've become real close."

They strolled toward the barn to check on Mallory, just as she emerged cuddling a tiny black kitten to her chest.

"Look, Daddy—she's so little! But she purrs real big."

He stroked the tiny back with one finger and felt the vibration.

"Yep, she's got a good motor, doesn't she? Hard to believe Samantha was once that small."

"I miss Samantha. Can we call Chloe and Marie and make sure she's okay?"

"Their mom has our number, honey," Trish told her. "If there's any problem, I'm sure they'll let us know."

"I know, but I'm scared that lady'll get her, like before!"

"Okay," her dad said. "Tomorrow morning we'll call Muzzie and the girls to make sure, all right? But I need to charge my phone before I make many more calls, and there's one more I need to make tonight."

"Okay," Mallory agreed with a sigh. "Come on, baby kitty. Let's put you back to bed."

Her parents exchanged smiles, her father thinking how early

the mothering instinct surfaced in little girls. Mallory had been cuddling dolls and animals, dressing and wrapping them in little blankets, since she'd been a very small child. Samantha, the Siamese, took exception to that brand of nurturing, but she was still partial to her young owner, obviously able to discern the little girl's devotion to her.

They watched Jamie and Tiffani as they leaned over a fence, offering grass to the two goats, who capered around before bounding back for more. The bishop walked over to the donkey and rubbed its coarse-haired nose, which silenced its raucous calls for the moment. His wife went to relax in the shade of some magnificent old trees. The bishop pulled his small notebook from his shirt pocket and found the phone number Miss Susie had given him.

When she answered, he apologized for calling at what might be her meal time, and then put his question to her about whether the local cemeteries had ever been catalogued.

"Well," she said reluctantly, "in fact, several have been transcribed, but I don't know whether you'll be allowed to see the results."

He frowned. "Why is that?"

"They're in a private collection. The county Historical Society has begged, pleaded, and offered to pay good money for copies of the inventories, but the woman who spearheaded the work has, so far, declined."

"Wow. That seems kind of selfish." He paused. "Do you happen to know her name or phone number? I figure I have nothing to lose by asking."

"Mmm. Do you recall, when we spoke this afternoon, that I mentioned the researcher who refused to share information with me, saying that she had put in the effort and expense to acquire it, and I could do the same?"

"Uh-oh. Same person, is it?"

"One and the same. I can direct you to her, but I'm afraid you're likely to find her no more accommodating than anyone else has."

"I expect you're right, but I'd appreciate the chance to be rebuffed!"

"Her name is Leanore St. John," Miss Susie told him. "She lives just outside Whitchurch, which is east of Winns Corner by about fourteen miles. If you turn right by the American Farmers Seed and Feed Company store, and then right again on State Road Four, you'll soon come to her place. It's red brick with white columns, and she likes to pretend it's antebellum, but I happen to know it wasn't built until after the war. She fancies her ancestors to be among the early planters in the area, but they didn't arrive until the mid-eighties. Eighteen-eighties, that is. One moment, and I'll get the phone number for you."

"Thank you." The bishop smiled to himself, amused at the obvious rivalry between the two genealogists. Miss Susie came back with the number, which he duly copied into his notebook, and for which he thanked her.

"Don't bother letting her know I referred you to her," Miss Susie said wryly. "She wouldn't regard that as much of a reference. And good luck to you!"

He slipped the phone and notebook into his pocket just as May Hinton opened her back door and announced supper.

The cliché of a table groaning under a bounteous spread had new meaning for Bishop Jim Shepherd as he and his family gathered around the one in May's dining room.

"Now if ya'll don't mind, I always say grace before meals," May announced, glancing around to get their reaction.

"Please do," the bishop encouraged, and all bowed their heads. When May's simple prayer of gratitude for blessings was ended, they echoed her "amen."

"Well!" she said with a surprised smile. "How nice! Y'all just all start with whatever's in front of you, then pass to your left. I'll get the hot biscuit."

"Mrs. Hinton, I'm afraid you've worked far too hard for us," Trish told her. "This is like a holiday dinner!"

"I'll tell you the truth," May replied, pausing at the kitchen door, "it gives me a reason to whip up some favorite dishes that I don't bother to fix for just me. Not that I'd want to cook a big meal ever' night of the week, like I used to do when my husband and kids were all here, not at my age—but I do love the chance to do it now and again."

"I understand that. I like to cook for people, too," Trish agreed.

"On Sundays, me and a couple of other widows and single ladies get together and take turns makin' dinner for each other. Sometimes we invite a family from church to join us, to make it all worthwhile. Makes us feel useful again. Good thing, to feel useful. Ya'll eat up, now!"

They ate with dedication for a while, and then May passed a little glass dish of blackberry jam.

"This is for the leftover biscuit," she told them. "Part of what I put up today. I made us a pie, too, but I gotta confess—when I thought about the way you was eyein' that old Georgia rattle-snake, Mr. Shepherd, I went back and got us one. See, that's another thing—how can one solitary woman justify buyin' a big old watermelon? So you gave me a good excuse for that, too! We'll have us some a little later on."

"How come they call them rattlesnakes?" Mallory asked. "That sounds yucky."

"I reckon it's 'cause of their markings, honey, and how they like to hide in the melon patch under all the leaves, like a snake. And I've been told snakes like 'em, though I couldn't swear to that. I'm also told bees'll sting 'em, 'cause they smell so sweet, though I don't know how much stock to put in that, neither. I do know snakes like blackberries, on account of I've run 'em off from my berry patches, and I'm always real careful when I'm out pickin'."

"How many children and grandchildren do you have, Mrs. Hinton?" Trish asked.

"Six children livin' and two in heaven, died as babies. Thirteen grandchildren—but do I get to spoil 'em rotten, like I want to? No, sir-ee. Some lives in Atlanta, some in Columbus, some in Flomaton, Alabama, and one way off in Albuquerque, New Mexico. Nary a one's close around here. None of the kids wanted to work this land, so I rent most of it out. They all went off to college and got different degrees. One's a dentist, two girls are teachers, and one's an attorney. One boy's an electrician, and like I said, Luther, the youngest, is doin' a stint in the Navy. I sure hope he don't get sent anywhere near where the fightin's goin' on—but he says he hopes he does—so there you are." She sighed. "So, hey—did y'all have any luck findin' your grandpa?"

The bishop told her what had transpired, concluding with their plan to visit Leanore St. John in the morning.

"Is that right? Well. I went to school with Leanore—Leanore Caldwell, she used to be. I shouldn't say it, but she was prissy then, and the years haven't improved her. Well, I mean, she's smart and all, and good at just about anything she sets her hand to, but she's not what you'd call a friendly woman. I hope she'll be nice to y'all."

The bishop hoped so, too. "All we can do is try, I reckon. I'm told she spearheaded a project to transcribe all the tombstone inscriptions in the local cemeteries, but that she's pretty selective about who she lets see her work."

"Sounds 'bout right. Reputation for bein' stingy. Tell you what—I'll send along a jar of my blackberry preserves with my greeting to her, in case that'll help. No guarantees, though!" She laughed. "We never did get along real good, so she might just dump 'em down the sink and run you off her land!"

"Mrs. Hinton, your preserves are sweet enough to melt the heart of a witch," the bishop declared.

She laughed again. "They might have to be!"

CHAPTER FOUR

"... How good to those who seek"

B y the time Bishop Jim Shepherd and his wife emerged rested and showered the next morning, their two youngest were nowhere to be seen. Tiffani, on the other hand, slumbered on as only a teenager can, on her stomach with one arm flung off the edge of the bed, several books beside her on the floor—her own and a couple from the small bookcase that had been Selma's.

"Looks like our bookworm read herself to sleep," her father whispered as they tiptoed toward the stairs.

"I hope it wasn't too late, or she'll be grumpy today," her mother replied. "And a grumpy Tiff is no fun to travel with. No patience with the little ones."

The dining table was set for breakfast. May Hinton had told them to sleep as long as they desired, that she could pull breakfast together at any time with no trouble. They wandered through the empty kitchen and out the backdoor. Jamie was perched atop the fence, talking to the donkey, who bobbed its head as if in complete agreement with whatever he was telling her. Mallory and May came from the direction of the henhouse, where conversation between the chickens sounded less amicable. Mallory held a cardboard egg carton carefully before her, while May carried a more substantial box with several cushioned layers of eggs.

"Mommy! Look, I found eggs for our breakfast. It's like hunting Easter eggs!"

"All right!" said Trish, bending to kiss her daughter's face.

"She's such a good helper," May praised. "I let her find the ones at her level, and where the hens had already left to go feed," she explained. "Some of them old Mama chickens are kinda grouchy, aren't they, honey?"

"Yeah," Mallory agreed. "Some of 'em try to peck you. They think you're kidnapping their eggs. Eggs can grow up to be baby chicks, if they stay with their Mamas," she advised wisely. "But Sister Hinton doesn't need lots more chickens, so she uses the extra eggs."

The bishop smiled at the *Sister* appellation, but May Hinton leaned over and whispered, "She's plumb precious. So's the boy. He's so cute with the animals, it puts me in mind of Luther."

"Thanks," their father replied. "Um—we call everybody brother and sister in our church, so that's where that came from."

May nodded. "I figgered as much. I can tell y'all are a good Christian family. Well, I'll go to work on breakfast and scramble up these special eggs Miss Mallory found."

"Can I help?" Trish asked.

"Land, no, honey—you take it easy while you can! I won't be no time."

"Dad, look! She likes me," Jamie called, as the donkey rubbed her head against the leg of his jeans.

"I'm not a bit surprised," his dad said, as they walked toward him. "She knows you like her. Animals can tell."

"Cool. So, what're we doing, today?"

"Well, this morning we're going to visit another lady who studies family history, to see if she can tell us anything about where Grandpa's buried. And I guess our next step will depend on what she tells us."

Jamie made a face. "Wish I could stay here. I'm kinda tired of visiting family history ladies."

His mother laughed. "We've only been to see one," she reminded him.

"Yeah, but—you know. She was kinda a lot. Even if she was nice, I mean."

"I know what you mean, bud," his dad agreed. "And the one today might not be quite as nice, from what I hear."

"Please, can't I stay here? I wouldn't be any trouble, and you could just pick me up, after."

"Well, now—we can't ask Mrs. Hinton to look after you, kiddo, after all she's done for us," the bishop stated.

"But no, Dad—she's the one who said! She said she wished us kids could just spend the day with her—that it was like having her grandkids here. Ask her if she didn't!"

"I'm sure she did," Trish soothed. "We'll see, okay? Right now, though, it'd probably be a good idea if you were to go wash your hands really good, before breakfast. And see if Tiffi's up, all right? Tell her breakfast is almost ready."

"Okay." Jamie gave the donkey one last pat and hopped down from the fence.

"Coward," the bishop teased gently, as he and Trish turned back toward the house. "You just didn't want to brave a sleepy Tiffani!"

"You've got that right," she agreed, leaning against him.

"I feel kind of lazy, myself. Can I stay here, too, while you go see the not-so-nice lady?"

"Not a chance, matey. I take courage from you. Besides, you're the class part of our act. Mrs. Leanore—whoever—St. John will be so impressed with your innate quality that she'll fall all over herself offering us information!"

Trish bumped her hip against his. "Oh, yeah—I'm just so sure," she said, her voice echoing Tiffani's at its most cynical.

He hadn't thought he'd even be hungry for breakfast, after the supper and subsequent watermelon of the night before, but he found himself happily working his way through fried ham, grits with red-eye gravy, hot biscuits, and scrambled eggs. The fragrance of coffee wafted through the house, and May Hinton was surprised when no one accepted a cup.

"Well, y'all are likely better off," she opined, "but lands! I don't see how you make it through the day 'thout it. Don't know as I could."

"You get used to it," the bishop explained. "Some folks have a headache for two or three days, but that's all. I reckon it always smells good, though. It even smells good to me, and I've never been a coffee-drinker."

"And that's part of y'all's religion, is it?"

"It is," Trish replied. "We avoid anything addictive—alcohol, coffee and tea, tobacco, and of course street drugs. It's like a law of health, and we feel that we're blessed for obeying it."

"And I expect you are. Now, how about it—can I keep the young 'uns here with me, while ya'll go visit Leanore? I kinda think it might work better. Leanore's not real big on kids. But I am," she added, winking at Mallory. "I can think of all kinds of fun things to do."

The bishop and his wife exchanged glances. Trish turned to Tiffani.

"Tiff—could you keep an eye on Jamie and Mal? We don't want to impose on Mrs. Hinton's kind nature."

"Sure," Tiff replied, yawning. "Besides, I want to finish one of her books that I started last night. Plus, I haven't had my shower, yet. But I'll watch them, too," she added. "Don't worry."

So it was that the bishop and his wife set off together to find Leanore St. John. First, of course, they'd had to call Muzzie, as promised, to be sure all was well with Samantha and the house. Reassured that there had been no abduction attempts by "that lady," Mallory was content to stay behind and play with the kittens and her new Barbie. Jamie had been elated.

The bishop had taken a few moments to himself to walk off under the shade of the live oaks and commune with his Heavenly Father, asking Him to soften the heart of Leanore St. John, so that she might provide them with any available knowledge that would be of use. Thus fortified, he enjoyed the drive with Trish to Leanore's home.

"I could just about believe the antebellum part," Trish whispered as they walked up the wide approach to the columned porch. "It feels really old, but it's beautifully kept."

"Even if it wasn't built before the war," he reminded her, "it's still over a century old. That's pretty respectable, historically speaking."

"I wonder who had the money to build this, soon after the war. I thought everybody was pretty much financially devastated for a long time."

"Maybe she'll tell us."

Leanore herself answered the bell. She was a slightly plump woman with an erect carriage, imperious expression, and graying hair piled on her head in a complicated-looking arrangement.

"Yes?" she asked briskly. "If ya'll are missionaries, or selling anything, I'm not interested."

"We're neither," the bishop assured her, with a smile. "We're Jim and Trish Shepherd from Fairhaven, Alabama, and we're here researching a part of our family history. A couple of folks have told us that you're one of the most knowledgeable people in the county on that subject, and we've come hoping you might have a few minutes to discuss it with us. Oh, and one of the people who spoke of you is Mrs. May Hinton of Winns Corner. She said she was a classmate of yours and sent you these preserves, with her greeting." He held out the jar. Leanore St. John took it cautiously and slowly turned it over in her hand.

"May Hinton made these?" she asked.

"Indeed she did—just yesterday. She said some really nice things about you. She told us you were a very smart lady and that you always did a good job at whatever you set your hand to. We took that as an excellent reference and presumed to call on you and get acquainted." Both he and Trish were smiling hopefully.

Leanore stared at him for a long moment. "Are ya'll related to May, or to her husband?"

"Actually, neither, as far as we know. We just met her yesterday, for the first time. My grandparents were from around here. Benjamin Rice and Annie Josephine Burke."

She shook her head. "Must be the wrong one. The Annie Burke from around here married a Mitchell."

He nodded, feeling a pang of sorrow for his grandfather, Benjamin, whose memory seemed to have been so thoroughly expunged from the annals of county lore by the brevity of his life. "That's the one. Benjamin Rice was her first husband," he explained patiently. "He apparently died in the First World War, leaving Annie with two little daughters. She then married Robert Lee Mitchell, and they moved to Alabama, where they had several more children. But we're trying to find more about Benjamin and his family—the Rices."

Leanore looked at him again for a long, silent pause, as if she expected him to break under pressure and admit his mistake.

"Come in," she finally reluctantly invited, and showed them into a parlor that rivaled that of Miss Susie, though not in flower-motif. This one was furnished in pale greens, with stands of ferns and smaller replicas of famous statuary scattered between the dainty chairs with curving, carved legs, the name of which style he couldn't recall, but he was sure Trish did. He could all but feel her, next to him, avidly absorbing details to relate to Muzzie later. A large, blocky, very old piano stood against one wall, its top draped with a fringed shawl between two shaded oil lamps.

"Sit down," indicated their hostess, "and tell me what it is you want from me."

Trish spoke up. "Your home is absolutely lovely, by the way," she began. "It must be a treasure, historically, in your family as well as to the whole area. But as to what we're hoping to learn— we've been told that at one point, you spearheaded an effort to transcribe the tombstone inscriptions in local cemeteries. Is that true?"

"It is."

"What a job that must have been!" commented the bishop. "I've only barely looked into one of them—King's Chapel—and it's so grown-over that it's daunting. I'm really impressed that you'd take on such a challenge."

She shrugged slightly. "It needed doing."

"That's certainly true," Trish agreed. "Inscriptions wear away, stones crumble, and precious information is lost forever. But what a service for you to undertake! Who helped you with it?"

Leanore raised her eyebrows wearily. "I hired some history

students from the University of Georgia, but I found that I had to recheck their work so frequently that I finally let them go and simply finished the job myself. It took longer, of course, but at least I knew it was done right. It's very important to me to be accurate."

The bishop nodded. "Integrity in research certainly is important. Have you published your work?"

"I have not."

"I see. So you use it for your private research? Do you take clients?"

"Occasionally. If it's worth my while."

"How much would you charge to search for Benjamin Rice? Or to let us search for him?"

She was silent again, looking back and forth from one of them to the other. Finally she asked, "Do you want his whole family tree run, or are you just interested in where he's buried?"

"We're interested in everything about him and his family," the bishop replied, "but we'd like to do as much of the research ourselves as possible. We're just beginners, though—and we'll surely need some guidance and suggestions along the way. Plus, there may be some records that we just don't know how to find or interpret correctly, and we'll need professional help there."

"At least you recognize your ignorance," Leanore allowed. "You'd be surprised how many bull-in-the-china-shop genealogy enthusiasts there are, making wild guesses and creating chaos out of perfectly good information, twisting facts and ignoring dates and running lines that are worse than fictional. I won't be a party to that."

"We're not at all interested in that kind of genealogy, either," Trish said gently. "We want to be as careful as we can to draw correct conclusions and avoid guesswork. Our reason for coming to see you is the hope that you can save us valuable time. If

Benjamin is buried in one of the local cemeteries, we could visit and photograph his grave, see if any other relatives are buried close by, and move on to other possibilities. But if we have to spend our limited time here looking for his grave, we wouldn't get nearly as far along in our search. I assume there isn't a sexton's record for King's Chapel, is there?"

"Not that I've ever seen. And at the Methodist Cemetery, the current ministers kept records of the burials, but the records moved on with them. Some of the earlier ones might have found their way to Methodist repositories when the ministers died or retired, but I'm not aware of where that might be, as there are several. The new Baptist Cemetery does have a man who serves as sexton, but I'm practically certain he won't be likely to help you. He's very staunch against Mormonism. Ya'll are Mormons, aren't you?"

The bishop nodded. "We are."

"Thought so. I've had occasion to use your church's family history centers and Web site. The volunteers in the centers were mostly rather ignorant of advanced research methods, but they were as helpful as they knew how to be, and very patient. For that reason, I'll allow you to search my cemetery transcriptions here in my home. Come with me."

The bishop and his wife exchanged looks of anticipation as they rose to follow.

Leanore St. John ushered them into a study that would have done credit to any of the Family History Centers she had mentioned. Books lined the walls wherever windows were not, two computers and a copier sat against one wall, and a sturdy table with four chairs stood in the center of the room.

"Sit down," she directed. "Please use pencils, not pens, and please turn the pages carefully. If you have any questions, ring the bell and I'll come. I'll be attending to some things in the kitchen. Here are the three cemetery books. The names are alphabetized, and there is a number assigned each, which corresponds to a series of charts in the back of the book, so that you can locate the grave of anyone you may find. Good luck."

"Thank you so much, Mrs. St. John," the bishop said. "This will be such a help to us."

She shrugged again. "Perhaps," she agreed. "But what makes you think your grandfather's body ever made it home to be buried here? So many did not."

The bishop stared at her. Why had he never thought of that possibility? Of course it could be so! "Do you happen to know," he asked slowly, "if there's a list anywhere of the men who served from this county? Or those who died?"

She nodded. "There's a memorial in the park across from the courthouse. I don't know how complete it is, and some of the dates are missing, but you could look." She turned without waiting for a response and left them to their work.

"Wow, do you think he could be buried overseas?" he asked his wife, who nodded.

"It's a thought, isn't it? First, let's see if we find him here. I'll take this book—you get the Methodist one."

Finally they leaned back and regarded each other wearily. There was nothing written in their notebook. There hadn't been a Rice in the whole collection.

"What now?" the bishop asked his wife.

She shook her head. "Mrs. St. John must be right. He must be buried somewhere overseas."

He tapped his pencil on the table, frowning in thought. "Funny, though, that we don't find anyone at all by that name, don't you think? He didn't just appear out of nowhere!"

"Do you think he might have changed his name?"

"No idea. Don't know why he'd do that."

"Or maybe he was an orphan, or something, and didn't know his family. Maybe he was a foundling and they named him Rice at the orphanage because they were having rice for dinner the day he was found."

"Oh, man—that'd stop us in our tracks, wouldn't it?"

"Well, it's probably something much simpler than that. Shall we see if Mrs. St. John has any ideas for us?"

They summoned their hostess by use of the bell provided and confessed their lack of success.

She shrugged. "Well. I expect he was buried overseas, then. So many were. Or maybe his body was never even recovered."

"We just wonder why we can't find any of his relatives around here, either," the bishop explained.

"What makes you so sure he was from this county? Maybe his people lived in one of the adjoining counties, or even farther away."

"Well, he married here, and I just assumed—"

"One of the first laws of geometry and genealogy is 'Never assume,'" she said severely. "We work from the known to the unknown, using facts as our stepping-stones. Assumptions are dangerous. The fact that your grandfather married in this county means only that. He may well have come here from elsewhere." She reached across the table and pulled the bound typescript books toward her, leafing through them one at a time. On the second volume, that of the Methodist cemetery, she paused, gazing at the page. "I wonder," she said, and moved quickly to a shelf, from which she retrieved a tall, thin book.

"What is it?" Trish dared to ask. The bishop, having been previously rebuked for his assumptions, merely watched in interest.

"I wonder if he changed the spelling of his name," Mrs. St. John said. "I find there are some people named 'R-H-Y-S' buried at the Methodist cemetery," she added, raising her eyebrows at them. "I would have thought that would be pronounced like 'Reese,' but perhaps not. I'm checking now to see if they owned any property in the county in 1877. I have a copy of the plat book for that year, and I've indexed it. Let's see . . . yes, Rhys, page twenty-nine, C-19."

She turned to that page and perused it silently. Then she made some notes on a slip of paper and handed it to the bishop.

"If you care to check into it, it appears that a couple of Rhys families owned some property in the northeast corner of the county in the year 1877, along a stream known as the Horsepen Branch of the Hatchacoonee River. Whether their name ever became 'R-I-C-E,' I cannot tell you. Sometimes part of a family would spell a name one way, and another part insist it should be different. I have a line where half of them call themselves Johnson and the other half add a 't' and call themselves Johnston. I don't know whether any of the Rhys family still live there, but it's a lead I would follow if I were you. Look for Five-Mile Road—they seemed to be concentrated along there."

"Thanks very much," the bishop told her. "We certainly will follow up on it. Now, what can we pay you to compensate your time and the use of your materials?"

"Not to mention your expertise," Trish added, smiling.

Leanore St. John gazed past them out the window at the green and gold day. "It's been my pleasure," she said abruptly. "However, should you decide that you require my services, I charge $45.00 per hour plus expenses. And you might mention to May Hinton, if you see her again, that an occasional visit from an old classmate is surely not too much to expect."

"We'll be glad to tell her that," the bishop agreed. "I expect she'd be happy to come. I think she gets lonely."

"Not surprised. I stay far too busy to be lonely, but I will say that those with whom I spend most of my time are not very talk-ative." Her lips pressed together, and the bishop realized she had made a small joke.

"Very quiet friends," he said, nodding at the books around the walls. "And yet, I'd imagine that in some cases, you know more about most of these folks than their friends and family did when they were alive."

Her eyebrows rose again, but she didn't disagree. "It's sur-prising the secrets the records can yield, when you know how to read them," she agreed, as she showed them to the front door. "By the way, 'R-H-Y-S' is a Welsh name. If you're related to them, then no doubt you have some Welsh ancestry. Many people do, and don't know it. Common names like Jones, Evans, Davis, Meredith—all Welsh names."

"Really? That's interesting," Trish commented. "Thank you so very much for your help, today."

"Here's my card. Let me know if I can be of assistance."

They got into their car and sat and looked at each other while the motor purred and the air conditioner labored to dispel the built-up heat. Finally the bishop spoke.

"Wow."

"I know. You did a good job, Jimmy. A little sincere flattery, a little praise—and it worked. We got to see her lists, and I was doubtful of that happening. And this 'R-H-Y-S' business might just be the clue you need."

"It might. I about blew it all with my stupid assumptions, though," he said, easing the car into drive.

Trish chuckled. "She was probably delighted to have an excuse to scold you a little."

He grinned. "Oh, well. I wasn't very good at geometry, either."

CHAPTER FIVE

" . . . May you seek until you find them"

Bishop Shepherd felt a definite need of sustenance after his encounter with Leanore St. John, so when he and Trish came across a small drive-in at an intersection of two highways, he convinced her to stop and have lunch. Over his bacon cheeseburger (approved by his wife only because they were on vacation), he perused the paper Mrs. St. John had given him, showing the coordinates and directions to the general vicinity of Horsepen Branch, erstwhile home of the Rhys family.

"You know," he said, "in the record of Benjamin and Annie's wedding—or, at least, the index to it—there was no R-I-C-E entry. But now I wonder if we ought to look again, under this spelling." He flicked the paper with one finger.

"It wouldn't hurt, would it? Jim, are you sure your grand-father spelled his name like the rice we eat? Where have you ever seen it written down?"

He frowned, trying to remember. "You know," he said slowly, "now that you mention it, I think I've only seen it written down in my own handwriting, or my mother's—and she may not have known the difference, either. I mean, if it was pronounced 'Rice,' why would she have thought to spell it differently? And you know, babe—this may be exactly why we never were successful at finding any of the family in the census!"

Trish nodded, and took a long sip of her fresh lime drink. "We may have success there, too, with the new spelling. I'm getting excited to look!"

He checked his watch. "We've got time to hustle back down to the courthouse and that war monument Ms. St. John mentioned. Let's do it."

"And if the R-H-Y-S folks do turn out to be yours, we can check the cemetery for them, too. They were listed in the Methodist cemetery, weren't they? Ms. St. John didn't give us the names from that list, but we should be able to find them. She said the Methodist cemetery is in good condition, at least."

"You're right. Boy, I hope this is the breakthrough we need!"

"Would you look at that, Trish!" he exulted, as they leaned over to peer at a name on a bronze war memorial in the park across from the courthouse. It read, "Pvt. Benjamin Rhys, 1895–1917."

"That's got to be him, honey," she whispered. "Bless his heart. So young."

The bishop snapped a couple of photos of the inscription, and Trish copied it into their notebook, after which they hurried up the steps of the courthouse once again. They had no luck with the marriage index, but there were several deeds under the name *Rhys*, which they copied and took with them for study at their leisure, stopping only to ask in which part of the county the land had been located—unsurprised to discover it was in the northeast quadrant. A quick perusal of the deeds yielded a couple of references to "Horsepen Branch of the Hatchacoonee River."

They next located the Methodist cemetery and divided it in half, each walking between the rows of markers and watching for Rhys names. After about twenty minutes, Trish called out, "Jimmy! Paydirt." He made a note of where he had stopped looking and jogged over to her side.

"Well, look at that. 'Robert B. Rhys, born January 13, 1871, died November 2, 1925.' You know what, hon—he's about the right age to have been Benjamin's father!"

"Maybe the initial 'B' stands for Benjamin, and your grandfather was named for him," Trish offered. "And look—this is his wife: 'Edna Putnam Rhys, born 25 October 1874, died April 10, 1931.' These people just might be your ancestors, Jim."

He photographed the stones and once again Trish copied the information into the notebook. They finished surveying the rest of the markers, but with no further discoveries.

"I finally feel that we're beginning to get somewhere," he said with a deeply satisfied sigh as they headed back toward May Hinton's.

Y

"Now, ya'll might just as well stay on over another night," May told them as they relaxed in her living room with the fans cooling them after their exertions. "I've made us a chicken pie, and I thought I'd fry up some okry and slice some more of them good ripe tomaters. Ya'll will, won't you?"

They nodded happily, having already agreed that if asked, they would stay.

"One more night," the bishop told her, smiling. "Mrs. Hinton, you could list your home in a Bed and Breakfast catalog and do a good business."

"Oh, I don't want to do it that steady," she replied. "Just a few guests now and again. Besides, it's not like there's a lot right around here for folks to see and do—just farmland."

"Exactly," the bishop agreed. "That's what's so restful. It's so quiet—well, except for the chickens and the donkey, of course, but they add to the charm. Anyway, we're grateful for the offer. Thank you. Oh—and we have a message for you from Ms. St. John."

He delivered that lady's request for a visit from her old schoolmate, in her own words.

"Hmph!" snorted May Hinton. "Makes it sound like an invitation to see the queen, don't she?" She laughed.

"It did sound kind of like a royal summons," Trish agreed, fanning her flushed face and Mallory's with a magazine. "But I really do think she's lonely. She made a little joke about how the people she spends her time with don't talk much."

"Well, I reckon I'll have to mosey on down and see her," May said reluctantly. "It's just she's a mite hard to visit with, if you know what I mean. You say something, and she just stares at you with those little beady eyes, like you talked Russian or something. Then she says something that you think might be insulting, but you're not sure. It's hard to know how to take her."

Trish nodded. "Jim called that stare her 'schoolmarm look.'"

"Exactly," he said. "Felt like I was back in seventh grade, being whittled down to size by my math teacher."

"But she is smart, and she knows a lot about family history," Trish added. "She gave us some really helpful tips."

"So what'd you find out?" Tiffani asked. "Did you find Benjamin?"

While May headed back toward the kitchen, the bishop caught Tiffani up on the new developments in the research, and

Trish herded the two younger children up the stairs to have their baths before dinner.

"Mom, we made blackberry ice cream for dessert," Jamie told her as they approached the stairs. "But, man! It was an old-timey churn, and I had to turn the thing by hand. I thought my arm was gonna fall off!"

"You'll be a stronger and a sorer man," Trish advised him. The bishop smiled in thanksgiving for the good things of life.

The next morning, they bade May Hinton farewell and continued their journey. May shook hands with Jamie and his father and hugged all the girls.

"I don't know when I've ever enjoyed any comp'ny as much as I have you folks," she told them. "I just had a good feelin' about y'all when I saw you down to Harvey's store. And you've got about the cutest family ever. Stay sweet now, y'hear?"

"We'll try, and you take care, Mrs. Hinton. You've been a joy and a blessing to us, as well," the bishop told her, and everyone waved as they drove away.

"I like that lady," Mallory said in a small voice. "I wish *she* lived next door to us."

Her parents exchanged glances. They were entertaining similar thoughts.

They drove the highways and back roads of the upper county, crossing and re-crossing the sleepy brown waterway known as Horsepen Branch, checking names on mailboxes and looking vainly for someone—anyone—to ask the location of Five-Mile Road. They pulled into driveways and knocked on doors that were open except for the screens; they heard a radio playing in one house, and a television was on in the open front room of another home that had laundry hanging on lines behind the house. A truck stood in the drive. But no one came to the door.

"Okay, this is getting spooky," Tiffani said, when her dad came back from knocking and calling at the fourth house that appeared to have people at home but offered no response.

"I told you," Jamie said nonchalantly. "It's aliens. They come and collect the people and study them, then bring 'em back and erase their memories. Randy Timmons did a book report about it at school."

"I'm almost ready to believe that theory," his dad muttered, backing the car to head down the road again. After a few more miles of interminable green, they approached another intersection of farm roads.

"Which way should I go?" the bishop asked. "Have we been down this road before?"

"Who knows?" asked Tiffani in disgust. "They all look exactly alike!"

"Go straight," Trish advised. "I see a little house down there on the right. Maybe someone's home there."

"Don't know why they would be," her husband said with a grin. "Everyone's still busy being alienated."

"Whoa, Dad, there's a live one, on the porch! Don't let him get away," Jamie cried, leaning over the seat and pointing.

"Well, sure enough, look at that," his dad agreed, pulling the car off the road in front of a very small house with a porch across the front. An elderly man in an undershirt and pajama bottoms rocked in a chair on the porch. He raised one hand in greeting as the bishop got out of his car.

"Hello, there," the bishop called. "How're you, today?"

"Well, I'm right toler'ble, how you be?" replied the man.

"We're fine, thanks. But I wonder if you could answer a question for us? I think we're kind of lost."

The elderly man chuckled. "Where you tryin' to git to?"

The bishop rested one foot on the top step and leaned forward. "We're looking for Five-Mile Road," he confided. "We're down here looking up some of my people, and a lady told us some of them might still live on Five-Mile Road, but we haven't seen a road sign."

"Who's yer people?"

"It's my grandfather's family. The name is R-H-Y-S, but we're not sure if they pronounced it like Reese or Rice."

The man pulled his head up and searched the bishop's face.

"You a half-blood Rhys or a full-blood?" he inquired, giving it the "Reese" pronunciation.

The bishop straightened. "Excuse me?"

"Half-blood or full-blood?" the man repeated. "Me, I'm a full-blood."

"You? You're a—Rhys?"

"My daddy called it like Reese, but I got cousins that say it Rice. Spelt the same, though, so hit don't matter."

"Okay. Wow. Now, I'm sorry to be ignorant, but I don't get the half-blood, full-blood thing."

Trish got out of the car and went to stand beside her husband, and the children followed.

The man nodded politely in their direction. "Well, see—I'm a full-blood Rhys because my mama and daddy was both Rhys descendants. They was second cousins."

"Oh, I see. Well, tell the truth, I don't know for sure on that. All I know is that my grandfather was Benjamin Rhys. He died in World War One, after he had married a girl from Winns Corner—Annie Burke."

Mr. Rhys, who seemed practically toothless, appeared liter-ally to chew on this bit of information, then spat a brownish stream a surprising distance out onto his scraggly lawn. Tiffani took a step back behind her mother, but Jamie whistled softly.

"Whew! Wish I could spit that far," he whispered.

"Wal, I reckon we'd be cousins, like as not," Mr. Rhys allowed. "My daddy was Ezra Rhys—an' I'm Ezra too, named for him. I go by 'Junior,' though. My grandaddy was Arthur Rhys, and he married Eliza Lanier. My mama, though—she was Martha Ann Dowdy—and her mama was Ethlyn Rhys Dowdy. Now, I don't rightly recollect a Benjamin, but iffen he was from around here, he's bound to be kin."

"Mr. Rhys, I'm Jim Shepherd, and this is my wife, Trish, and our children Tiffani, Jamie, and Mallory. If you wouldn't mind going through that again, so that we can get it down on paper, I think it'll make more sense to me."

"How-do," Junior Rhys said politely in the direction of Trish and the children. "It's gettin' a mite warm out here now the sun's movin' around thisaway. Iffen ya'll don't mind a mess, we can go inside for a spell. I got an electric fan in yonder."

He rose creakily from his rocker, pausing briefly halfway up to be sure he had his balance, then led the way inside his home, which appeared to consist of two rooms—a front room that held a double bed, a dresser and a couple of chairs, and beyond that, a kitchen with a free-standing sink, a table with a hotplate, and an ancient refrigerator. There were apparently no shelves or cab-inets; a small stack of plates and cups shared a tabletop with a skillet and a battered saucepan and a collection of canned goods. He turned on the small fan that stood on the dresser. It rattled and whirred, but stirred the air.

"Y'all sit you down," Junior invited. "Sorry I ain't got more chairs, though. Maybe y'all young 'uns can sit on them boxes."

He indicated a pile of several cardboard boxes sitting in the middle of a worn linoleum floor. "I'm fixin' to move tomorry—that's what all that conglomeration's about," he explained. "Goin' to the old folks' home," he added. "Reckon it's time. I ain't gettin' no younger, and I got nobody to look after me when I get down. Kinda hate to see it come to that. I'll miss my place here, but it's air-conditioned where I'm goin', and the cookin' ain't half-bad—I been to visit there and tried it. Then I reckon, too, I'll have folks my age to visit with, which beats talkin' to my lonesome day and night!" He cackled good-naturedly.

"How old are you, Mr. Rhys?" the bishop inquired.

"Call me Junior, son. 'Mr. Rhys' sounds like my daddy. Wal, let's see—reckon I must be nigh onto ninety—maybe ninety-one."

"You've done very well to live alone and take care of yourself this long," Trish told him.

"Wal—had my wife, Pauline, till about three years ago, then she left me. Passed away, I mean. Had a real sudden pneumonia come on her in the winter, and time I could contact somebody and get her to the doctor, she was well-nigh gone. Didn't last the night." He sighed. "Then it was just me and Blackie—my old dog—and even he's went and died on me. Pauline and me, we married late, never did have no young 'uns. But we sure used to enjoy growin' our garden, and ever' now and then we'd take off and go fishin'. Times, we'd camp overnight and go froggin'. Whoo-ee, them frog legs is good eatin'! She was a good woman, Pauline."

The bishop thought she must have been a saint, to have lived in such primitive circumstances with her husband. He became aware of Mallory whispering insistently to Trish, and looked at her.

"She needs a bathroom," Trish said apologetically.

"Wal, sure thing! The privy's right out back, there—and it's stocked with toilet paper," Junior announced proudly. "Ya'll ladies go right ahead."

Trish gave a questioning glance at Tiffani, who sat primly on a box with her arms wrapped around her knees. The girl gave a small but definite shake of her head.

The bishop stifled a smile as Trish ushered Mallory outside. He picked up his notebook and began to draw out of Junior again the names of his family and to plot their relationships in a crude pedigree chart.

"So you don't remember a Benjamin Rhys, hmm?" he finally asked, and Junior shook his head.

"Reckon I don't—but I ain't sayin' I knew all my cousins and such. They spread all around, and over into Lee County, too. Ain't so many of us left with the name of Rhys, any more. Some boys moved on to other parts, and o' course most of the girls married and changed their names. But it's a big clan, iffen you could just find 'em all."

"Well, I sure appreciate all you've given us. Do you happen to know who—let's see—Robert B. Rhys and Edna Putnam Rhys were? We found their graves in the Methodist cemetery."

"Yessir, I had an Uncle Bobby and Aunt Edny. They was good people. A bit better off, somehow, than most of us, and real generous to ever'body. Aunt Edny made the best chicken and dumplin's I ever et."

"Did they have any children?" Jim asked, half-hopeful that Junior would suddenly recall that they had a son called Benjamin.

Junior nodded. "They had three girls—Zora, Lena, and Barbara. Lena was the purtiest thang I ever did see. I was mighty sweet on her, all through school, but o' course I didn't never say so. Zora and Lena growed up and married and moved away—I lost track of whereto—and little old Barbara made a secatary—worked in some big office up in A'lanta and never did marry, I don't think. Don't know if she's still livin' or not. Hard to keep track."

"It would be," the bishop agreed. "I'll have to see what I can find out about everybody, once I figure out where I fit in."

"You say your granddaddy was kilt in the First World War?"

"That's right. We don't know if he was buried somewhere overseas or shipped back here."

"Pity. I didn't serve—the Army didn't like the sound of my lungs." He laughed. "But they're still a-breathin'—done outlasted most of them Army fellers."

"Junior, do you happen to know if anybody kept a family Bible record or anything like that?"

Junior spat discreetly into a small teacup. "S'cuse me. Wal, I do know there was a family Bible, all right—my great-granddaddy had one. It was a handsome thing."

"Do you have any idea who might have it now?"

"I had it for a long time. Then after Pauline died, my sister Dovie Jane come and took it away—said it oughter stay with a more stable part of the family, one that had kids to pass it on to. I reckon I could see her point, but I shore hated to see it go."

"I'd surely love to see that Bible," the bishop said wistfully. "Where does Dovie Jane live?"

"She passed on last April, and I swear I don't know who got the Bible. She had four young 'uns, and they all scattered to the four winds when they married. Their names was Ezra-Ann—she was named for me and my dad, then Eleanor, then Jake, and Albert."

"What's their last name—who did Dovie Jane marry?" the bishop prodded.

"She married a man by the name of Whitlow, from over in Moultrie. Al Whitlow, he was. He died back in seventy-seven."

The bishop diligently made notes, planning to track the Whitlow family for all he was worth, to try to find that family Bible.

"Do you know the married names of Ezra-Ann and Eleanor?"

"Ezra-Ann married her a sailor-boy, name of Messick. I don't r'collect Eleanor's husband. She watn't never very friendly to me. I don't recall that we even got an invite when she got married."

"That's too bad," the bishop sympathized. He could hear protests from Mallory outside and knew that his family's patience with this visit was probably running low. He stood up.

"Junior, it's been a real pleasure to visit with you," he told the old man sincerely. "I know we must be cousins of some kind or other, and you're the first Rhys I've met. Thanks so much for your help. Now tell me the name of the home you're moving into, so I can keep in touch."

Junior's delight was a joy to see. He stood up and took a card down from a shelf above his bed and handed it to his new friend. The bishop wrote the name and address of the place into his notebook and shook Junior's hand, then gave him a hug. Jamie and Tiffani also shook hands with him and trooped back outside, where Mallory stood with her arms folded, a mutinous expression on her face.

"All right, then," Trish whispered to her. "We'll just have to find you a bush. Get in the car."

Mallory complied, slamming the door with unaccustomed ferocity. The bishop winked at his wife, who rolled her eyes in amused exasperation. He took a picture of Junior, and they took their leave. The bishop felt the beginnings of a lump in his throat as Junior stood on his porch, smiling and waving as they pulled away.

Everyone was silent for a few moments, and then Tiffani spoke softly. "Dad? You know what just happened, don't you?"

"What's that, Tiff?"

"You know why none of those people down the road answered the door, don't you?"

He smiled. "Reckon I do know, honey—and I'm grateful."

"Why?" asked Jamie.

"Well, it wasn't aliens, little brother," Tiffani explained. "It was so that we could find the one person in this area who's related to us, who could tell us about the family. See, if anybody else had been around, we would've asked them where Five-Mile Road is, and they'd have told us, and we wouldn't even have known about Mr. Rhys. It's like a miracle."

"What—like all those people were struck deaf or something?" he asked.

"Something," the bishop replied, profoundly grateful not only that such a thing had happened in their behalf, but that his eldest daughter recognized it for what it was.

CHAPTER SIX

"... And signs shall follow living faith"

L et's take a little time off, shall we?" Bishop Shepherd asked his family. "Trish, why don't you check your list of motels and find us a nice one with a good pool? I believe our loyal employees here deserve some splash time."

"Yay!" agreed Jamie.

"And see if you can find one in a real town," Tiffani added. "I'm getting pretty tired of bean and cornfields."

"Boy—good thing I didn't decide to follow my ancestors' career of farming," her dad remarked with a grin.

"That's for sure," Tiffani agreed. "I mean, it was kind of fun to stay at Mrs. Hinton's place for a couple of nights, but that was enough farm life for me."

"I liked it," Jamie said. "I liked the donkey and the goats, most of all."

"And the baby kitties," put in Mallory, restored to good humor after her dad found her a service station with a reasonably clean rest room. She hadn't been about to use Junior's privy.

Trish consulted the atlas and the printout of potential places to stay she had downloaded from the Internet before they left home.

"Here's a nice-sounding place in Albany," she reported. "It's only about thirty miles from here, and Tiff, I believe Albany's the biggest city in the area. This place has two pools, a spa and exercise room, and an attached restaurant. It's more expensive than the Southern Belle, but then we've saved quite a bit, staying with Mrs. Hinton."

"Go for it," her husband suggested, handing her his cell phone. "See if they can accommodate us."

They could and did, and the family spent a pleasant afternoon alternately playing in the pool and relaxing in the coolness of their room. After a refreshing swim, the bishop took the opportunity to study the deeds he had copied, poring over the formal wordiness and cramped handwriting of the documents until he had isolated and extracted the pertinent facts from them.

"So what'd you learn?" Trish asked quietly as he stretched out beside her on one of the beds. Tiffani and Jamie were watching a video across the room, and Mallory had fallen asleep curled on the other bed.

"Well, what I did was try to figure out any relationships mentioned in the deeds, and there are some—and I kind of traced who owned which pieces of land through the years, according to the description given. It's pretty interesting. But here are the relationships I found." He passed her the notebook, in which he had listed names of married couples and, where noted in the deed, any names of children or heirs.

"Okay, so here's the Robert and Edna we found in the cemetery," Trish said. "I suppose they weren't your great-grandparents after all, from what Junior said—that they just had the three daughters. So, what does this mean—are these their girls?"

"Well, I'm sure no expert, as you know, but it looks like after Robert and Edna died, one of the girls, Zora Daynes, bought out the interest of her sisters, Lena Potter and Barbara Rhys, in the property their folks left to them."

"Interesting. Now who are Arthur and David E. Rhys, who sold land together in 1867—any idea?"

"I'm thinking they were probably brothers. And it looks like they also had a brother named Robert, since it mentions that he had retained his interest in the estate of Robert Rhys, Sr., deceased, but they were both selling theirs."

"Well, didn't Junior say his dad's name was Arthur?"

"Um—flip back a page. No, Arthur was his grandfather, remember, because he's Ezra *Junior*, named for his father."

"Oh, that's right. It gets so confusing. But then, so Arthur, David E., and Robert were sons of another Robert? And if the Robert Jr. had only daughters, then he's not your direct ancestor. Do we know what children Arthur had, except for Ezra Sr.? Or maybe you're descended from this David E."

"Maybe. Unless I'm from a totally different branch of the family that we don't even know about yet."

"Possible, I guess. But since your Benjamin was listed as being from the county on the War memorial, I'd suspect he lived somewhere around Horsepen Branch."

"Likely. Although he was already married to a local girl when he went off to war, so maybe it just means he moved there when they married. Ahh. Man, I'm tired. Too many questions and too few answers. And I don't have a clue where to turn, next."

"Why don't you give it a break and just relax for the rest of the evening? Maybe something will occur to you."

He grinned. "If it doesn't, then Tiffi might get her wish to see her friends on Friday instead of Saturday."

He put through a call to his counselor Robert Patrenko and learned that apart from the little Arnaud boy having broken his arm, all seemed on a fairly steady course in the Fairhaven Ward. After the children were tucked in bed and Trish was heading to the shower, he told her where he was going, carefully locked the door to their room behind him, and went out to the car, where he sat enjoying the night sounds of frogs and crickets from a nearby wooded area and taking advantage of the solitude to ponder and pray for guidance and understanding in his search for his kindred dead. He expressed gratitude for all who had helped him so far and reminded the Lord that he had only one more day available on this journey and wanted to use it to best advantage, if only he could know what that might be. He also prayed for his ward—for the several individuals who had ongoing sorrows or problems—and for his family. He prayed for the missionaries and the servicemen and the leaders of the Church, both general and local. Finally he closed his prayer and leaned back, growing drowsy. He tried to stay awake in case an answer to his question was forthcoming, but after falling asleep twice, he locked his car and went back to the room, where he slept more-or-less soundly all night, despite the fact that the mattress was firm enough to make the term "pressure points" take on a whole new meaning.

Y

"Where are we going today, Dad?" Jamie asked as they ate breakfast at a nearby pancake house.

"Home, right?" asked Tiffani brightly. "If we leave like right after breakfast, I'll have plenty of time to get ready for the square dance."

He smiled at her regretfully. "Well, I'll tell you," he said slowly. "I have a feeling we need to go back and visit Mr. Junior Rhys one more time."

"What? Why?" demanded Tiffani. "He already told you everything he knows!"

"Yeah, Dad, I don't want to go back there," Jamie said. "His place was kind of creepy, and smelly."

"And he doesn't even have a bathroom!" Mallory added.

Their dad nodded. "I know. I don't particularly want to go back, either, although I enjoyed meeting him. But I really feel I should. Sorry, guys."

"Do you have any idea why you feel that way, Jim?" Trish asked.

He shook his head. "Woke up this morning with that impression, and it was pretty strong. I don't know what good it can do, but I figure when you pray for direction, and direction comes, you should follow it."

"I think you'd better," Trish agreed, and all three children responded with groans of disappointment.

"Well," Trish reminded them, "remember yesterday when we all agreed that we were led to Junior's place, because we were apparently invisible and inaudible to everybody else in the neighborhood? He's obviously related to Dad, and he must know something important that he hasn't told us yet."

"But why couldn't Heavenly Father have prompted him to remember whatever it is, yesterday when we were there?" Tiffani's voice was dangerously close to a whine.

Trish shook her head. "No idea, honey," she said with a sympathetic smile. "You'll have to take that up with the Lord."

"Maybe it won't take long," her dad suggested. "Maybe we can still get home today—although if you'll recall, Tiff, I didn't promise we would."

"We won't," Tiffani grumbled. "I already know that."

The bishop was tempted to reiterate his feeling that Tiffani should only go out with Billy Newton once a week, if that, but he held his peace. He wanted the remainder of their trip to go as smoothly as possible, and Tiffani had been pretty cooperative for a teenager who was cooped up with parents and younger siblings for over four days. Of course, he credited a lot of her cooperation to the relative freedom of the time spent at May Hinton's—a genuine blessing, in his book.

They wound through the countryside again, trying to retrace the route to Junior's house, with all absorbed in their own thoughts. Jamie played a traveling game, Mallory whispered to her Barbie, and Tiffani buried herself in a book, emerging only once to say, "You know Junior's supposed to be taken to a rest home today, Dad. He'll probably already be gone when we get there."

The bishop held up his notebook with the address of the home in it. "If need be, we'll follow him there," he said, and she subsided with an annoyed sigh. Trish reached over and patted his knee in wifely empathy, and he sent her a wink.

Junior had not yet departed the premises. He was dragging his cardboard boxes out onto the front porch when they pulled up, tugging to get them over the threshold. The bishop sprang from his car and went forward to help.

"Hey, there, Junior, let me get those—I'm a couple of years younger than you!"

Junior turned and squinted in the sunlight. "Well, hey, there, young man," he responded, and once again spat a brown stream into the dirt.

"Mom, how come he spits all the time? And why's his spit brown?" Jamie asked.

"I believe he uses snuff, honey," she told him, as she prepared to get out of the car.

"That is unbelievably gross," Tiffani stated. "I can't believe Dad's related to somebody who uses snuff!"

"What's snuff?" Mallory asked.

"It's kind of like powdered tobacco," Trish explained. "It's dangerous to use, but a lot of elderly folks use it, especially in the country. And some young people, too."

"Yuck," said Jamie. "I wouldn't want to be spitting out tobacco all the time. Not even if I was a baseball player. I'd chew gum."

"It's a pretty disgusting habit, all right. Be glad your parents and your church teach you better."

"Didn't nobody teach Mr. Junior better?" Mallory inquired.

"Probably not, sweetie."

"Maybe I'll tell him."

"Um—maybe you'd better not," advised Tiffani. "He's old enough to be your great-grandpa, and it wouldn't be good manners."

"What's a great-grandpa?"

"That's your grandpa's daddy," Tiffani told her.

"Does Papa have a daddy?" she asked, referring to the only grandpa she knew—her mother's father.

"Of course he had one, honey—everybody has a mother and father," Trish said, reaching for her hand. "But Papa's father died a long time before you were born."

"Well, that's not fair. I wanted to see him!"

Trish exchanged a smile with her two elder children and turned toward the little house. Tiffani shook her head and chose to stay in the car, but Jamie went to sit on the steps.

"There we go," Junior said, as the last box was deposited on the porch, ready for pick-up. "I thank you, sir. And I'm sure proud to see y'all folks again. I been thinkin' on things, since you was here yestiddy, and somethin' come to me. Remember how you was askin' me about the family Bible?"

"I sure do," the bishop said. "Have you thought who might have it?"

"Naw. I sure wisht I knew. I'd be plumb tickled for y'all to see it. But what I recalled was that before Dovie Jane come and got the Bible, I took out some loose pages from the middle of it. You know how folks write their birthdays and such on special pages in some Bibles?"

The bishop held his breath and nodded encouragingly.

"Well, I don't rightly know why I done it—reckon it was orn'ry of me—but I kept them pages for my own self. They're right in that box, yonder, if ya'll want to see 'em. I put 'em in a vanilla envelope that come from the insurance comp'ny."

The bishop didn't know whether to laugh or cry. He did neither, but carefully opened the box Junior had indicated and began to look through it, feeling a burning and a quivering beginning in his midsection, which was definitely not heartburn from breakfast.

About a third of the way into the assorted items Junior had packed to take with him, he located the "vanilla" envelope and drew it out. His hands were trembling as he opened the clasp and carefully peered inside. There were three pages with writing on both sides. He sat down quickly on the edge of the porch, mostly because he didn't trust his legs to hold him upright much longer. Trish perched beside him.

"Oh, my—look at that beautiful handwriting!" she exclaimed.

"Ain't it purty?" Junior agreed. "See, my great-granddaddy was a school teacher. And he taught my granddaddy to write real nice, too—but time it got down to daddy and me, there was so much farm work to do that we didn't get much time for school, so I barely just scrawl, nothin' like that!" He nodded toward the pages, which the bishop was scanning eagerly. There were two pages each of births, marriages, and deaths.

"Look," the bishop said. "Here's a Robert Rhys, and it says he 'passed from this life on Monday, June the 11th, in the year of our Lord eighteen sixty-five.' Wow. That was during the Civil War."

"Yep, that'd be my great-granddaddy. It was his Bible. He wrote in his wife and kids, then my granddaddy took over and wrote in the time when he died."

The bishop turned to a page of marriages and squinted at the tiny but elegant script. "Robert Rhys and—what's this name, Trish?"

She examined the entry. "Looks like an R. Um—I think it says 'Rhiannon.' 'Robert Rhys and Rhiannon Meredith was married on January the first,' I think it is—it says 1th—'in the year of our Lord one thousand eight hundred and fifty-six.' That's so cool, Jimmy—it even gives her maiden name!"

He turned to the births page to look for a list of Robert and Rhiannon's children, and found five listed—Arthur Christian, Robert Benjamin, David Evan, Christine, and Gwyneth—all with their respective dates, including the day of the week on which each had been born. Scanning further, he found Robert Jr.'s three daughters and Arthur's grandsons, Ernest and Ezra, and their sister, Dovie Jane. Then, in a different hand—not nearly so fancy, but still legible—he read "Caroline Mary Rhys, daughter of David E. Rhys and Marian Rose Walters, born March 22, 1890. Benjamin Evan Rhys, son of David E. Rhys and Marian Rose Walters, born October 30, 1895."

"Trish!" he whispered urgently, pointing a shaking finger at the entry. "There he is."

Trish clapped one hand over her mouth, and her eyes filled

with tears. "Oh, Jimmy, it is! It has to be—born in 1895, just like it said on the War memorial!"

"I think I found him, Junior," he told the old man, who smiled widely.

"That so?"

"I'm sure it is—it's my grandfather, Benjamin. It says he was the son of David Evan Rhys and Marian Rose Walters."

"Wal, could be. I never knowed much about them, and I'd plumb fergot their names. But you know, I b'lieve they might've lived over in Lee County. I recall hearin' my daddy talk about havin' some kin over there, but we didn't visit back and forth, not that I can call to mind. Well. That's mighty fine. I'm sure glad ya'll come back this mornin'!"

"Oh, so am I, Junior! So am I. Now, I wonder if I dare ask you a really big favor? And if you say no, I'll surely understand. But I wonder if there's any way you could trust us to take these pages and have copies made? I'd send them back to you right away, at the care center you're going to."

Junior puckered his face and consulted the sky. The bishop breathed a silent prayer and knew that Trish was doing the same.

When Junior spoke, it was in a low voice, as if he were talking to himself. "Dovie Jane's done gone to her reward. I don't never hear from none of her young 'uns. Ernie's so far gone it's like he ain't even hisself no more. I got neither chick nor child to leave these to. I tell you what," he added, his voice louder. "I'd like to have these records to look at, onc't I get settled at the home, but I could do that just as well with copies, if you can get good ones made. I b'lieve I'd like y'all to have these. Reckon you care more about the fam'ly and all than anybody else I can think of, and I b'lieve you'd take good care of 'em."

"Junior, I assure you I would take excellent care of these—

they're priceless. And I'd be more than happy to make copies for you. But are you sure you want to let us keep the originals?"

The old man considered again, then slowly nodded. "Cain't say exactly why, but yessir, I b'lieve that'd be the best thang. Tell you what, though—you write down your name and address and put it with them copies, so's if anybody comes lookin', I can tell 'em where the pages have got to."

The bishop nodded deeply, and momentarily unable to speak, reached to clasp the old man's hand in both of his. Tiffani had wandered up, her book in hand, to see what had been found, and Trish showed her Benjamin's name. Mallory, mean-time, had taken Jamie around back to view the offensive privy.

Just then, a blue van with a flowery sign painted on the side that read "Restful Years Retirement Center" pulled up behind the bishop's car, and a young woman got out.

"Mr. Rhys?" she asked, pronouncing it like "Rice."

"It's Rhys," Junior said loudly, correcting the mistake. "Junior Rhys is my name. What's yours, young lady?"

"I'm Jennifer, from Restful Years. It looks like you're all packed up and ready to go, is that right? Is this your family?"

Junior looked them over. "Wal, yes, I reckon they are," he said proudly.

"We're his cousins," the bishop said. "Visiting from Alabama. We're glad we found Junior here before he moved."

"Well, how nice. Next time, you'll have to come see him at the center. We welcome visitors. They're good for the residents' morale."

"We'd love to," the bishop said firmly. "We'll pop in when-ever we can."

"So are you ready, Mr. er—Rhys? Are these the things you're taking?" Jennifer asked.

"I'll help you move them," the bishop said, and lifted a box while the young woman went to open the back door to the van.

The bishop stacked the boxes in the vehicle, while Junior stood to one side and looked over his land and his little home.

"Is that everything then, Mr. Rhys?" asked Jennifer. "We want to be sure and get there in time for lunch today. We're having fried catfish. Do you like catfish?"

He ignored her, and stumped back inside his house, emerging a moment later, stuffing a small snuff can in his shirt pocket. He turned a key in the door and slipped the key under a rag rug on the porch.

"Don't you want to take the key, Mr. Rhys?" asked Jennifer.

"What fer? I won't have need of it at the home."

"But someone might get in and cause trouble!"

"Around here? It'll be two weeks afore anybody realizes they ain't seen me lately! And nobody never bothers nothin', anyway. Never have. Besides . . ." his voice grew quieter. "Reckon one day soon the real estate lady'll want to go inside and have a look, and I'll just tell her where to find the key."

"All right, then—if you're sure. Now—ready to go get some catfish?"

The bishop hadn't known Junior Rhys for long, but he knew him well enough to sense the mixed emotions the old man was experiencing in leaving his home.

"Junior, good luck to you," he said, enveloping the old man in a hug. "God bless you for your kindness. Keep well."

"Yessir, I'll try to do that," Junior said. "Ya'll have a good safe trip, you hear?"

"Junior, it's been a pleasure," Trish said, kissing the bristly cheek. "We're glad you're part of our family."

"Well, now. I thank you for that. Y'all young 'uns be good, now! I gotta go. Miss Jennifer here says I've got fried catfish waitin' on me." He turned and went to the van, his chin high, not looking back. Jennifer fussed over his seat belt, apparently insisting that he use it, and then waved as she climbed into the driver's seat.

The bishop looked at his wife. She stood with her arm around Tiffani's shoulders, and both had tears running down their cheeks.

"Daddy, I'm so sorry," Tiffani wailed, throwing her arms around him. "I was being a selfish little beast, and I'm glad you didn't listen to me! I wasn't in tune at all, and you were."

He hugged her tightly. "We all have times when we're not in tune with the Spirit," he told her softly. "It's good when we can recognize the difference."

"It's just so neat, what he gave you. I can't believe it!"

He hugged his wife next.

"I can't, either," he said. "It's only thanks to the good Lord, I can tell you that, because when I went to sleep last night I didn't have the faintest inclination to come visit Junior again today. But the Lord knew what was in that box, and He brought it to Junior's remembrance."

"It's amazing," Trish said, wiping her eyes. "I'm glad we came back today for Junior's sake, too. Poor old fellow—it was hard for him to leave."

"We'll keep in touch with him," the bishop vowed. "It's the least we can do."

"What is the matter with you guys?" Jamie demanded. "Why's everybody crying, for Pete's sake?"

His mother reached out and drew him to her for a quick hug. "Everything's fine, Jamie. We're crying because we're happy, and thankful."

"Oh, like at testimony meeting, huh?"

"Pretty much. Daddy just got a whole lot of information about his grandpa and his family."

"And if he'd listened to me, and gone on home today, we wouldn't ever have gotten it," Tiffani explained. "The Holy Ghost told him to come back here, because Mr.—Junior—just remembered he had it."

"That's cool," Jamie opined. "I just don't get why you want to cry about it. I mean, Mom cries at a lot of stuff, but you don't, Dad, and Tiff mostly cries when she's mad, and Mal cries if she gets hurt, but I haven't cried since I was a little kid, so—"

"Oh, right," Tiffani said. "You cried when T-Rex got hurt, and when—"

"I did not!"

The bishop intervened. "The thing is, Jamie, the Spirit touches our minds with information and our hearts with feelings. It's the feelings that get to you and make tears come—even for grown men, sometimes. And intense happiness or gratitude can be one of those feelings."

Jamie looked unconvinced. "I don't think I ever want to be that happy," he said.

"You will," his parents spoke together, then looked at each other and chuckled. Jamie rolled his eyes in a manner befitting his elder sister and headed for the car.

The bishop got his camera and jogged across the highway.

"What're you doing, Daddy?" Mallory asked.

"I'm taking some pictures of Junior's house to send him," her father replied.

"Why?"

"Because Junior's moving away, and he'll want to remember this place. And so will we," Trish said softly.

They had a prayer of thanksgiving before they continued their journey.

CHAPTER SEVEN

"... O HOME BELOV'D, WHERE'ER I WANDER"

S o, hon—I'm sure you'll want to check out the Lee County courthouse while we're this close, won't you?" Trish asked, as her husband slid in behind the wheel and put away his camera.

"It's the best chance we'll have for a while," he responded. "How about it, troops?"

"Go ahead, Dad," Tiffani answered. "I think you should, now that you're hot on the trail of these people." To Tiffani's credit, the bishop noted, she didn't even heave a regretful sigh about the missed square dance.

They determined the route to Leesburg, the county seat, and headed in that direction. While they drove, Trish took the opportunity to examine more carefully the precious pages obtained from Junior Rhys.

"What're you finding, babe?" her husband asked, as she looked up from the pages and took a deep breath, then blew it out slowly.

"Whew! I'm finding that I can't read while riding in a car like

I used to do. Being pregnant may have something to do with that. But anyway, from what I could see, it looks like you've got at least a partial record of about four generations here. That's amazing."

"Yeah, it is! I just can't get over how that happened."

"I think it's called faith and prayer, sweetheart."

"The Lord really came through for us, didn't He? Beyond my wildest expectations." He was silent for a moment, then said, "You know, I have a testimony of the gospel on a lot of fronts—overall, of course, and of things like the value of tithing, and guidance in our callings or our families, and the need for a restoration through the Prophet Joseph—and now I can add a real witness of family history. I'm absolutely positive now that the Lord wants these records found and preserved—and used, of course—to provide temple ordinances. I don't mean that I ever doubted other people's testimonies of that fact, but now it's real to me in a way it never was before."

"Me, too," Trish agreed. "It's pretty humbling, isn't it?"

"It's both humbling and gloriously happifying!"

"Um, Dad? Is that a word?" asked Tiffani from the backseat.

"In my new vocabulary, it is!" he replied. "It means I'm excited and delighted and surprised and tickled pink."

"I can tell. Hey, Mom—can I please look at those pages?"

"Sure, Tiff—carefully, I don't need to say."

"Well, duh—it's not like I'm going to crumble them and throw them to the birds."

"I know. But they are kind of fragile."

Bishop Shepherd didn't care for "duh," either in word or tone, when the children spoke to their parents, but he let it go. "First thing I'm going to do is make copies and put them all in sheet protectors," he stated. "And mail a set to Junior, of course."

"With a little box of goodies," his wife added. "I'll bet there's nobody else to do something like that for him."

"You gonna put some snuff in for him?" Jamie queried, grinning.

"Not on your life, funny boy," his mother replied. "I'm thinking little boxes of candy and homemade cookies."

Y

Lee County also turned out to be a "burnt county," having suffered courthouse fires in 1857 and again in 1874.

"What is it with courthouses burning?" the bishop wondered aloud, and the clerk behind the desk nodded sympathetically.

"My friend who's a researcher says burning courthouses is the devil's hobby," she replied. "Personally, I think it has more to do with crooks destroying evidence and getting back at the judge and officers of the court. Though in some cases, lightning's to blame, especially in the older courthouses. Often the courthouse was the biggest building in town, with the tallest steeple, and I reckon maybe they didn't know about grounding them. It's too bad. Lots of records have been lost that way. We're lucky in that we still have most of our records from the 1874 blaze, but we sure lost a bunch of early ones in the first fire."

She directed the bishop to the deeds and marriage records and also suggested their fine collection of wills and probate records. Trish opted to study the probates, and the bishop headed for deeds and marriages, while Tiffani supervised the younger children outside in the shade of the trees surrounding the courthouse.

A couple of hours later, thanks to helpful clerks and the miracle of copy machines, they emerged clutching more booty— several deeds, four Rhys marriages, and a copy of the last will and testament of Robert Rhys Sr., who died before the 1857 fire, but whose will was brought forward for probate afterwards, and thus barely missed being destroyed. The woman who helped Trish with the probate records suggested a visit to the local library and a chat with a certain librarian there who had created a local and family history collection that, she opined, might be of help to them.

"We barely have time to make a quick visit before the library closes," Trish advised the children as she hurried them to the car. "These are our last few minutes of research time on this trip, and we don't want to waste a second."

They were grateful to find the librarian in question still at work, and she was delighted to show them items of interest. She was aware of a book of tombstone inscriptions, including some photographs of interesting stones, and she thought she recalled a picture of a Rhys marker in the collection. While she was look-ing for that, she pointed them toward a volume entitled *Lee County Heritage*, from which they were able to copy several ref-erences to the Rhys family and their origins. The grave marker, once located in the first book, was in obelisk shape, and turned out to have been erected in honor of one Llewellyn ap-Rhys, born 1787 in Wales, died 1849 in Georgia.

"What does this 'ap' mean?" inquired Trish, frowning at the photograph.

"I believe that's something like 'son of,' rather like 'Mc' or 'Mac' in Scottish and Irish names," the librarian replied. "In fact, I recall reading that sometimes it was retained in family names as a 'p,' which in this case would make the name 'P-R-H-Y-S,' or as we would say, 'Price,' or 'Preece.'"

"So do you think we might have relatives around who go by those names?" the bishop asked, and the lady nodded.

"It's quite possible, since your emigrant ancestor here, if that's who he is, used the 'ap.'"

"Well, that's really good to know! And where is this marker located?"

She wrote down for them the location of the marker and the cemetery that contained it, and then regretfully told them that the library was closing. Then she took pity on their disappointed expressions and gave them her card, saying that if they had questions or anything that she could look up for them in her spare time, she would be glad to do so.

"People are so nice," Trish mused as they headed back to the car. "Everyone's been such a help to us—even Leanore St. John. And Miss Susie, even though she didn't agree with our purpose in doing research."

"We've been well and truly blessed, and I'm grateful beyond measure," her husband agreed. "Now let's find a good room for the night!"

"And a pool, Dad," reminded Jamie.

"And some supper," added Tiffani. "My chicken sandwich is long gone."

"All the above," agreed their father.

"I already know, you don't have to break it to me gently, that we have to locate that tombstone thing this morning before we can leave for home," Tiffani stated the next morning.

"Surprise, Tiff," her father said, smiling at her affectionately. "In appreciation for your being such a good sport yesterday, I went out and found it this morning while you guys were still snoring. It didn't take long."

"I wondered where you went," Trish remarked. "I thought maybe you were getting some exercise before we have to sit in the car for hours."

"Well, that too," he admitted. "I jogged around the cemetery until I found and photographed the marker—and a few other interesting ones next to it—and then I jogged some more before I came back. Now I'm hungry as a bear."

It was an interesting phenomenon, the bishop reflected. The closer they got to Fairhaven, the more his thoughts and concerns turned to his home, his ward, and his store. Five days away had been a nice break, and his mind had been sufficiently occupied with their mission that he hadn't worried overmuch about things at home, but now he couldn't wait to get there. The traffic tie-ups around Birmingham annoyed him more than usual. It had been a pleasant respite, too, to drive around mostly country lanes and small-town streets for a few days.

"I'm first in the shower," Tiffani announced as they pulled into their driveway. She had been communing with her friends on her dad's cell phone, announcing her imminent arrival, and plans for the evening were set. "Claire says Billy twisted his ankle, so he didn't go to the square dance last night after all," she confided with a measure of satisfaction.

"Hope it doesn't keep him from work too long," her dad said mildly. "He's going to need his paycheck to contribute to all the fun times you and Claire have planned for him and Ricky."

"Oh, Dad—we're not high-maintenance dates," his daughter informed him. "Most of the time, we think of fun, cheap stuff to do—even free stuff."

He thought of the elaborate plan she had concocted to ask Billy Newton to Girls' Preference the previous school year. "So, all those fancy balloon invitations and acceptances, they're only occasional deals?"

"Of course. Once you start going out with somebody, you

don't have to go to all that trouble. You just—you know—make plans to hang out."

"Mmm. Interesting."

"Come on, Daddy, hurry and unlock the door! I want to see Samantha!" urged Mallory.

"You bet, honey—and I expect she wants to see you, too."

"Unless the lady next door got her," teased Jamie, and both his parents hushed him firmly. "Well, she's weird enough," he insisted.

Samantha wound around their legs, purring and making little throaty trills of welcome as they carried in their luggage. Mallory scooped her up and kissed her, assuring her pet that she'd missed her terribly and worried about her. The bishop sent Trish upstairs to lie down while he and the children cleaned out the car and started a load of laundry. Once the debris had been cleared, he sat down at his desk in the corner of the dining room and retrieved the messages that had been left there for him. His cell number had been printed in the ward directory, but many members of the ward still preferred to call him at home or work. It had been three days since he had checked his home phone messages, and there were several waiting for him. Two were from Ralph Jernigan, who didn't trust cell phones.

"Bishop," came his guarded tones on the first message, "got something to tell you. Feel you should know. Can't speak of it on these lines, of course, but if you'll contact me ASAP, we can get together. Thanks."

The bishop sighed and punched the erase button, then listened to the second one. "Bishop, Brother Wright says you're out of town. Sure hope you're taking all precautions. The world isn't safe to travel in as it once was, sorry to say. Please see me soon as possible when you return. I have—information." The bishop could practically hear the capital "I" on "information." What now? He wondered. He would have to see Ralph right away, if only to soothe the man's frayed nerves.

The third message was from Ida Lou Reams, the ward's tireless Relief Society president. "Hey there, Bishop, sorry to trouble you—can you hear me? I declare, I hate these answering things—half the time they hang up on me before I get my piece said! Anyhow, I wanted you to know that Sister Hildy has went into the hospital for some tests. They think maybe it's her gall bladder, she's been in quite some pain, but I don't know yet. I'm going back to see her tonight. Oh, and she's here in Fairhaven, not down to Birmingham. Um—this is Thursday, at about five-fifteen. Hope ya'll are all well. 'Bye."

Another one that would require immediate attention. He listened to the final message.

"Hey, Bishop? It's Buddy. Um—I reckon ya'll ain't back yet, and that's fine. But, um—I was wondering iffen there's any way I might could stay at your house for a few days? See, Daddy—he's got, um, comp'ny, and Mama, her and Jeter's goin' down to Biloxi for a little vacation, like, and you know they don't give me a key, and I'd sure appreciate it iffen I could stay with ya'll. I won't be no trouble. I can sleep on the floor good as anywheres, and of course I'll be at the store all day. Iffen it's okay, I'll just bike over on Friday night. Thanks."

It was Saturday afternoon. Where had Buddy stayed last night? He walked out onto his covered patio, and immediately spotted Buddy's backpack stashed behind a cushioned chaise lounge. That answered his question. He picked up the boy's pack and carried it into the house, then dialed the store. Mary Lynn was off on Saturdays, and Art Hackney, his produce manager, answered the phone.

"Hey, Art, we still in business?" he queried.

"Holdin' the fort, Jim, but just barely," Art replied with a chuckle. "Ya'll back, are you? How was the trip?"

"It was great. Had some fun, and found out a lot about my grandpa. Hey, is Buddy working, today?"

"Sure is. Best worker we got. Want to talk to him?"

"Please. Thanks, Art. I'll be in bright and early on Monday."

Buddy came to the phone, and the bishop assured him of his welcome, apologizing for not being home the night before.

"Oh, that ain't no problem, Bishop. I ate and used the bathroom here at the store, and just slept on your back patio. It was fine, 'ceptin' for that lady who lives by you. I reckon she thought I was goin' to break in, or somethin'. She kept goin' out in her back yard and peekin' at me over the fence."

"Over that high fence? What in the world—she must've been on a ladder!"

"Reckon she was. She just stood up there and frowned at me. Finally, I was afraid she was goin' to call the police, so I says, 'It's all right, ma'am. I belong to Bishop Shepherd's church and work at his store, and I'm just waitin' for 'im to get home.' She give me a real mean look then, but I didn't see her no more."

"My goodness. I'm certainly glad she didn't call the police!"

"Boy-howdy, me too! I really didn't have no place to go to, and they mighta run me in for trespassin', or loitering, or somethin'."

The bishop felt his anger rising again at Buddy's selfish parents. It always simmered just below a boil, anyway, and bubbled over whenever they neglected their son this way.

"You know, you can always call Brother Wright or Brother Patrenko, or just about anybody in the ward. What about the Rexfords? They'd love to have you stay with them. Or the

Birdwhistles. Don't ever feel, Buddy, that you have no place to go. Not while you belong to this church!"

"Reckon I coulda done that, all right. I didn't think. I guess I'm way too used to bargin' in on your family. I'm sorry, Bishop."

"Son, there's nothing to be sorry about. You're welcome here anytime, I didn't mean that. I just don't want you to be left in the lurch if we're not home, like yesterday. Of course you were perfectly welcome to be here, and I'm sorry about Mrs. Busybody next door. I'm afraid she's a thorn in the flesh to all of us."

"Well, yessir, I can see how she might be. So, well, if you're sure, I'll come there after work."

"We'll be watching for you. We need to tell you all about our trip."

He went upstairs and followed Tiffani in the shower rotation, then put on clean clothes and updated Trish on Buddy and the other messages.

"I'm going to run over to the hospital and check on Hilda," he told her. "Then if I have time, maybe I'll make a quick dash out to Ralph's and see what's bothering him."

"Okay, honey. I think I'll just make sandwiches for supper, so don't feel you have to be on time for anything."

"You take it easy, babe. You were a real trooper on the trip. I know it wasn't easy, being pregnant and all."

"I enjoyed every minute," she assured him. "It was only when it got a little long between bathroom breaks that I worried." She giggled. "I even used Junior's outhouse. Now there was an experience!"

He grinned. "Not one that Mal was willing to share, I gather."

"Not likely. But my bladder wasn't quite as fastidious as hers at that point."

Y

He located Hilda Bainbridge's room at the hospital and tip-toed in. She was alone and appeared to be resting comfortably. The only thing that didn't seem right was a yellowish cast to her skin. He tiptoed out again and questioned one of the nurses on the floor.

"Well, yes, she's a little jaundiced," the nurse agreed. "We're keeping an eye on that. Are you family?"

"No—I'm her bishop—her clergyman."

"I see. Well, Doctor Asbell is her physician, and I suggest you talk to him about Mrs. Bainbridge. He can tell you more about her condition than I can."

He nodded and went back into Hilda's room, where he sat for a few minutes and wrote a brief card to be read to her, to go with a pleasant-scented lotion he had picked up at the small gift shop downstairs. Trish had suggested it, since Hilda couldn't see well enough to enjoy a colorful bouquet but could appreciate the fragrance and feel of the lotion. He sat beside her for a while, praying silently for her comfort and well-being, and for the Lord's will to be done concerning her, then left her still sleeping soundly—no doubt sedated.

Ralph Jernigan's dogs went through their usual security-check gyrations before his truck was allowed inside what the bishop thought of as Ralph's "compound," but then, as usual, the dog called "Corporal" came wagging his tail and sidling up to the visitor for a greeting.

"He sure is partial to you, Bishop," Ralph said, holding open the door to his home for the guest to enter. "Shows he's smart, I figure. Stand down, Corporal." The bishop felt unaccountably flattered; he had often been almost spooked by the feral intelligence in Corporal's eyes. He wouldn't have wanted the dog to consider him an enemy.

"You're back. That's good. Any trouble?" Ralph asked.

The bishop sat down on a sofa that was a little high, resting as it did on boxes of canned goods. "No trouble at all. We had a wonderful trip, Ralph, doing some family history research."

Ralph nodded. "Good work, that. Hope to have time for it someday. Got my messages, did you?"

"Sure did, my friend. What's troubling you?"

Ralph leaned forward, as if the very furniture were listening. "There's trouble afoot," he whispered.

The bishop lowered his voice, too—it was almost an automatic reaction. "What kind of trouble?"

"Not sure exactly what form it'll take, but it's to come down sometime this summer. And it won't be pleasant. The enemy's gathering."

As usual, when talking to Ralph, the bishop felt confused. It was often difficult to establish just what Ralph's vague predictions or premonitions, whatever they could be called, were about.

"Who's the enemy?" he asked, keeping his face straight with less trouble than he once had in such a situation. These matters, he knew, were of utmost import to Ralph, who had suffered from paranoia since the Arkansas kidnapping of his only child, Jodie Lee, several years earlier. Ralph frowned and shook his head.

"Hard to identify, exactly," he said. "Wife and I've been monitoring them for a couple of weeks now. Hints on the Internet, on talk radio, Christian radio, and on TV."

"Um—are they enemies of the nation, Ralph, like terrorists? Or organized crime, or—"

Ralph shook his head again. "Enemies of the Lord, Bishop. And they're coming here."

"Now, just exactly what do you mean? What've you heard?"

"Oh, bits and pieces. You have to put it all together, like a puzzle. I just wanted to give you a heads-up, so you can prepare and strengthen the people."

"All right. Well, if you get anything specific, will you let me know?" the bishop asked.

"I'll do it, Bishop. You have my word."

"Thank you, Ralph. How's Linda?"

"Doing well, thanks. Taking a rest, right now. She took the night shift last night, with the shortwave radio."

"I see." He didn't, not really, but it usually worked better to play along with Ralph in his world of intrigue and conspiracy. "Just remember, Ralph—love and faith cast out fears. We all need to pray and trust the Lord with our concerns. He knows all."

Ralph nodded. "He inspired me to trust you with this information."

The bishop patted Ralph's shoulder. "I'll do my best, Ralph," he promised.

"All I can ask," the man responded.

CHAPTER EIGHT

" . . . ZION EVERYWHERE IS GROWING"

Bishop Shepherd drove away from the Jernigan compound with his usual mixed feelings of compassion, affection, and confusion. He knew from past experience that it was fruitless to try to pin Ralph down to specifics or sources for his fears and warnings—that only upset the man further and frustrated both of them. Perhaps he would have a chance at church on Sunday to ask Linda privately what was really troubling her husband. She partook of his paranoia, but to a lesser degree, and she was more articulate than Ralph.

He decided to drop by the Arnaud family home and pay a quick visit to little Currie, he of the broken arm. Turning onto Bessemer Street, he spotted a familiar sight that made him smile. Elder Rand Rivenbark was being pushed in his wheelchair along the sidewalk at a pretty fair clip by his present companion, Elder John Moynihan, who had post-mission track and field aspirations and ran whenever he could. The bishop slowed and drove alongside the pair until Elder Rivenbark noticed him and waved, grinning. Since he was holding both missionaries' backpacks on his lap, and gripping the armrest of his chair with his free hand, the bishop was afraid the gesture would send something tumbling. He envisioned the chair hitting an uneven section of sidewalk, of which there were many due to the roots of historic trees in this part of town, sending Elder Rivenbark and the packs sailing to a hard landing.

"I thought speeding was against mission rules," he called out, and Elder Moynihan slowed and turned his companion's chair down a sloping driveway to approach the Bishop's now-stopped truck. The tall, lithe missionary laughed.

"We're careful, Bishop," he assured him. "There's this one smooth stretch of new sidewalk along here, so we air it out a little. Don't worry, I haven't dumped him, yet—he's the best comp I've ever had!"

"Well, you be careful, both of you. How's the work going?"

"It's going great, Bishop," Elder Rivenbark said. His cheeks were rosy, and he looked as happy and healthy as the Bishop had ever seen him. "We taught three discussions today, and we've got another meeting tonight."

"Who're you seeing? Just in case I know any of them."

Elder Moynihan replied. "We've got the Finell family—a young couple with one baby—and a young lady named Caroline Marsh—she's a nurse—and an older man named Charles Stagley. Oh, and tonight, it's our first meeting with Mrs. Edith Simmons and her daughter, Chelsea."

The bishop thought for a moment. "This Charles Stagley—how old an older man would he be?" he asked. He had gone to school with a Chuck Stagley, but surely someone his age wouldn't qualify for the title "older man," would he?

The missionaries looked at each other. Elder Rivenbark shrugged. "Maybe mid-forties?" he suggested, and the bishop smiled. He supposed when you were in your early twenties, someone more than twice your age would qualify as "older."

"I think I may know him," he said. "A little shorter than I am, reddish hair thinning in back?"

"That's him! Can you help us with him, Bishop?" asked Elder Moynihan.

"Well, I don't know—what kind of help do you need?"

"Oh, just fellowshipping and all. And he needs to stop smoking and drinking coffee. I think he's lonely, too. He said he has never married."

The bishop was surprised. He had lost track of Chuck years ago and had only glimpsed him around town a time or two since then, but he recalled that Chuck had been going steady with a shy, pretty girl named Beverly something, and he'd been sure they would get married. It was sad to think of Chuck missing out on the kind of companionship and family life he had shared with Trish for the last twenty years.

"Well, I'll sure do whatever I can," he agreed. "Give him my best, will you?"

"We'll be happy to," Elder Rivenbark said, and his companion nodded eagerly. It was always good if the investigator knew someone who was a member of the Church—especially if that member was active and faithful and set a good example. As bishop, he knew he'd certainly better fit those criteria—although sometimes he doubted his adequacy in many aspects of Christian living—especially when it came to his dealings with his neighbors, the Lowells. He winced and tossed that unhappy thought to the back of his mind as he bade the Elders "Goodbye and Godspeed—but not too speedy."

Y

Little Currie Arnaud, age six, proudly showed the bishop his bright green cast.

"Just like the Hulk," he bragged.

"Wow, are you going to be that strong?" asked the bishop.

"Yep," answered Currie.

"Yes, sir," corrected his mother, Camelia, softly.

"Yes sir," Currie repeated, smiling and butting his curly head against his mother's hip.

"So how'd you break that arm, Currie?"

"Fell off of a dumb ol' bike," Currie responded.

"He thought he could still ride his sister's bike, even though she just got her training wheels off," Camelia explained. "But I reckon it just felt different to him."

"Stupid bike," Currie agreed. "Ain't ridin' that one no more."

"I'm not riding that one *anymore,*" his mother prompted.

"Me, neither," Currie agreed, and looked puzzled when the adults laughed.

Y

"Look at this, Jimmy," Trish called when he entered the back door. She was sitting at the kitchen table looking through the week's accumulated mail. She held out a photograph to him.

It was of his sister-in-law Meredith, her husband Dirk, and their baby son, Dirk James, or D.J., as they called him. Merrie had, to the bishop's everlasting surprise, insisted on giving the baby his name for its middle one, hinting that little D.J. might never have come into being if she hadn't followed her brother-in-law's counsel and laid her feelings on the line to her super-busy husband. The bishop studied the picture. All three looked exceptionally happy; he didn't think in the few times he'd met

Dirk that he'd ever seen him looking that pleased with life—not even at his wedding. He nodded in satisfaction.

"That is so cool," he said softly. "Isn't it, babe?"

"Way cool," she agreed, using the children's vernacular. "I'm so happy for Merrie. Glad that she has D.J., and that Dirk's more attentive. I'm glad he got a wake-up call. Thanks for seeing to that."

"Me!" He hadn't supposed Trish had known about his advice to Merrie—and Merrie had asked him not to say anything. "So she told you about it, huh?" he added sheepishly.

Trish gave him a knowing smile. "Nope. But I can add two and two, and Mom's good at dropping hints that she doesn't even realize. So did you call Dirk, or did you persuade Merrie to talk to him? I know she was miserable."

"She talked to him. I just told her to be honest with him and to tell him she was lonely, and it was time to start a family, and that money and material stuff just wouldn't cut it. She needed him."

"Well, I'm also glad she finally saw the light about you and was willing to talk to you about Dirk. Honestly, she was such a high-and-mighty little toad when she was younger! I apologize for her."

He bent and gave her a kiss. "No need for that, babe. Your sister already apologized all I need. And I'm happy for her, too."

After their simple supper of sandwiches and fruit, and after he had checked with Dan McMillan about the next day's schedule for appointments and with both his counselors to be sure he was up to speed on everything he should be, he stole a little time for himself to peruse the treasured documents he had collected on their trip. He spread them out on the dining table, guiltily grateful that Trish had been too tired to set out the china and silver for Sunday dinner as she often did before going to bed. He had kissed her goodnight and had had prayer with her, Jamie, Mallory, and Buddy, and then had volunteered to wait up for Tiffani's return from her date with Billy.

He set out a couple of blank pedigree charts and a stack of family group sheets, sharpened some pencils because he didn't trust himself to record things in ink just yet, and lost himself in plotting out the relationships and dates in the Bible record, will, and deeds. When Tiffani let herself in the front door, he looked at the clock, amazed that it was time for her to be home. His eyes felt gummy and his shoulders were a little stiff, but he had hardly been aware of time passing.

"I know, I know, I'm five minutes late," Tiffani began. "See, what happened was, Ricky was driving, and he had to stop and get gas, only it turned out that he had left his gas money home on top of his chest of drawers, and none of the rest of us had enough between us to even buy a gallon, so Ricky had to call his brother to bring him his money, and that took about half an hour, and then we had to take Claire home first, because her dad is *so* strict about time, and—"

"What—and I'm not?" her father asked, frowning in mock displeasure. "*I* want to have the reputation as the strictest dad! What is this—Bob Patrenko getting ahead of me? Unthinkable."

"Yeah, well—sorry, Dad, but you're in second place on this one. Anyway, sorry I'm late."

"Actually, Tiff," he confessed, "I was looking at the clock because I was surprised it was already time for you to be home. I've been having so much fun with all this family history stuff that the time got away from me."

"Oh—good. You know what they say—time flies when you think you're having fun."

"So it does. And I really *was* having fun. So how was your evening? Did time fly for you, tonight?"

"Sure. We had a great time. Oh, and we ran into the MacDonalds at the show. Mr.—er—Big Mac said to tell you hi, and that he'd be calling you soon. Something he wants to run past you, he said."

"Oh, okay. Fine. How's Billy's ankle?"

"Wrapped up, and still pretty sore, but doing some better, he said. At least it's not broken."

"That's good, although I hear some sprains can take a long time to heal. Well, night-night, Princess. Guess I'd better turn in, too."

She paused by the table to give him a quick hug and to glance over his group sheets.

"Wow! You got all that?"

"Yep! Isn't that amazing? We had a fruitful trip, don't you think? I say we were blessed."

"I guess! That's cool. Well, 'night, Dad."

"'Night, Tiff. Oh . . ." He lowered his voice. "I should warn you—Buddy's sleeping in the family room."

Her eyes widened. "Again?" she demanded in a whisper. "We might as well adopt him!"

Her dad shook his head. "There are times," he confided, heading toward the stairs with her, flicking off lights as they went. "There are times when I almost wish we could."

"Well, what's the deal? His sleazy mother out of town again, and won't leave him a key?"

"Exactly. Although I shouldn't allow you to call her sleazy."

"I can think of another word that begins with the same letters—"

"Tiff . . ." he warned.

"Okay." She sighed. "But, really, what is it with her? It's not like Buddy's the type to invite the whole school over to party and wreck the house while she's gone! You'd think she'd be worried about her son—where he is, and who she's imposing on to keep him! And what about his worthless dad?"

"Well, I understand that Gerald has company this weekend."

"M-hmm. Likely the same kind Buddy's mom has. Dad, how can people live that way? How can they do that to their kids—or kid, in this case?"

Her father shook his head. "It doesn't compute to me either, honey." They paused at the top of the stairs, still speaking in whispers.

"Well, I think they're the ones who ought to have family services called out to investigate 'em. I mean, if they took little Andi Padgett away from her mom, surely Buddy deserves as much attention!"

"I know. But you know Buddy—he doesn't complain. He just deals. And he probably wouldn't want to be taken away from either of his folks, even though they neglect him shamefully, and set a rotten example for him."

"Well, I feel sorry for him, I really do—but on the other hand, I get kinda tired of him popping up here anytime at all. I mean, people ask me if we're related! It's sort of—I don't know—creepy."

"I'm sorry, Tiff. I am planning to talk to both his parents about the key thing. There's just no excuse for that to continue. Meanwhile, try to be patient, okay?"

"I'll try."

"That'll do, I reckon. Sleep well. Don't forget your teeth and your prayers."

"Dad! This is me, Tiffani—not Mallory."

Y

"Bishop? May I see you for just a tiny second?" inquired Sister Conrad, hovering in the open doorway he maintained whenever he could during the Sunday School hour, just for such drop-in visits. A bishop, he felt, should be accessible. He had hoped to catch the eye of Linda Jernigan, but the couple had not put in an appearance this Sabbath.

"Of course," he said warmly, rising to greet his visitor.

Tina Conrad was a large woman with unusually slender legs and feet, and the bishop suspected her of being naturally rather vain about those dainty portions of her anatomy, since she always wore elegant, strappy high heels that showed them off to good advantage. She reminded him of a plump robin. She and her husband, Wallace, had moved into the ward the previous March, and while they seemed to be good, solid members, he had to admit that there was something about Tina that bothered him. He pushed that something aside as he stood to shake hands and invited her to sit down.

"How's everything, Sister Conrad?" he asked pleasantly. "What can I do for you?"

"It's just a little thing, and I wouldn't bring it up, except it keeps troubling me. It's my daughter-in-law. They've been married in the temple, but she just doesn't seem to care for my son's underclothing properly. His garments, you know. I've always maintained that all underclothing, whether Gentile or Mormon, should be folded in such a way that the—um—the front, you know—doesn't show when you open a drawer or a suitcase. But she said she'd never heard of such a thing—and she's from a good LDS home, too—and I just wonder if you don't stand beside me on that?" She cocked her head to one side and awaited his answer, again reminding him of a watchful bird.

Bishop Shepherd was not about to take sides in a mother-in-law, daughter-in-law dispute, and certainly not one over the correct folding of underwear, about which he had no clue. He had a sudden impulse to laugh—to just let go and laugh until tears came. But he could not. Sister Conrad was obviously serious. He tried to picture his own underclothing as Trish folded it into his drawer. Did the "front" show? And how could it possibly matter?

"Well, now," he said judiciously, "I'm just wondering how you became aware of how your son's underwear is folded. Did he complain?"

"Oh, no. He's so besotted with that girl that she could do things any old way and he wouldn't say a word."

Good for him! cheered the bishop silently.

"So then, how'd you discover the problem?" he pressed.

"I first noticed it when they were visiting in our home and she did some laundry before they left, but I thought surely she would do better at home. So when we were at their house, I just happened to peek into the bedroom, and a drawer had sort of been left open, and I saw that she hadn't been careful about it, at all."

"Um, I see. Well, it's true that the garment is a symbol of the sacred covenants we make with the Lord in the temple and should be treated with respect, but on the other hand, I think it's pretty natural for most women to have their own preferences and standards in matters of housekeeping, and unless your daughter-in-law's doing something so awful that it endangers the physical, mental, or spiritual well-being of your son, why, I don't think I'd be too concerned. It sounds like she makes him happy, and that's something to be grateful for."

"So am I to understand, Bishop Shepherd, that you refuse to back me in this?"

Oh, dear. This was not going well. Apparently, it was he who was on trial here, as much as the errant daughter-in-law. He bowed his head and thought for a moment.

"You know," he said, "someone once gave me some really helpful advice on bringing up children, and I find it applies to other situations as well. It was simply, 'Pick your battles.' I took that to mean that some things just aren't worth fussing over, especially if doing so would damage a meaningful relationship. You've obviously already brought the matter to your daughter-in-law's attention, and she knows how you feel about it, so I'd say you've done your part. Who knows? Maybe one day, if you keep good feelings between you, she'll come around and see it your way."

Tina Conrad shifted in her chair and frowned. "I've been careful to maintain very high standards in my home," she stated.

"I'm sure you have," murmured the bishop.

"I just hate to see those standards lost to the next generation. What will my grandchildren know about propriety?"

"When your grandchildren come to your house, by all means show them how you fold underwear. Let them help you. Maybe they'll pick up on it. By the way, what does your daughter-in-law do that pleases you?"

Tina had to think long and hard on that question. Finally she said, "She's patient with the children—to a fault. They'll be spoiled rotten if she doesn't watch out. But I do have to admire that patience."

"That's great. What else does she do that you think is positive?"

"Oh, she makes a nice chocolate layer cake. And she helps my son with the yard, though I wonder if that's proper work for a woman."

The bishop ignored the comment about the division of labor and said, heartily, "Excellent! Will you do something for me? Next time you see her, will you be sure and compliment her either on the yard or on her patience with the kids? And will you ask her either to make that chocolate cake for some special occasion, or to share the recipe with you? And don't even bring up the subject of underclothing. Just as an experiment. Will you do that?"

"But I'm not concerned about her cake or her yard! I'm worried about her sense of decency and right. I could teach her these things, if only she'd let me—"

The bishop leaned across his desk and looked Tina Conrad in the eye.

"I know you've heard this saying before, Sister Conrad, and I want you to apply it here: 'She won't care how much you know, until she knows how much you care.' Or how about this one— 'You catch more flies with honey than with vinegar.' Next time you're with her, just think 'cake and compliments, cake and compliments,' over and over, and see if that doesn't help."

"Well, you're just full of pithy sayings today, Bishop Shepherd, but I prefer to rely on the scriptures, and they talk about the righteous being clothed with purity, and having clean hands and a pure heart, and letting virtue garnish our thoughts unceasingly. Those are the sayings I live by."

"Those are excellent. But the scriptures also admonish us to live together in love, and to forgive all men, and to add to temperance, patience—and to patience, godliness. I counsel you to be patient with your daughter-in-law, Sister Conrad, and to love her the best you can."

He stood up, indicating that their visit was over, whether she thought so or not, and held out his hand. She shook it, but she looked disgruntled as she took her leave. He closed the office door behind her and leaned against it. He no longer had a desire to laugh. He shook his head, then bowed it.

"Help me, dear Lord," he pleaded. "Solomon, I'm not—nor Job."

CHAPTER NINE

" . . . Mocked on every hand"

I've heard a change is as good as a rest, and I reckon I believe it, now," Bishop Shepherd remarked to his wife as they strolled hand-in-hand through their shaded neighborhood on Sunday evening. It had been a long, hot late June day, but now that the sun was dropping behind the houses and trees of Fairhaven at last, a little breeze found its way along the streets to bring a suggestion of change.

"You're referring to our trip, I suppose?" Trish asked.

"M-hmm. It was funny—when I looked over the congregation in sacrament meeting, I felt like I'd been away a long time, even though I realized I hadn't missed a Sunday."

"In some ways, it does feel like we were gone more than five and a half days," she agreed. "Maybe it's because we learned so much and met interesting people. Speaking of those people, I wrote thank-you notes to Miss Susie, Leanore St. John, and May Hinton. And I made chocolate-chip cookies for Junior, with no nuts. I wasn't sure about his chewing capacity."

The bishop grinned. "He chews some things just fine."

His wife socked his arm lightly. "Snuff isn't crunchy and hard—and besides, you don't chew that, do you? Don't you just sort of stick it inside your lower lip and suck on it?" She made a face at the thought.

"I sure don't. Do you?"

"You're naughty. Anyway, I'm going to fix up his box first thing in the morning, including of course his copies of the Bible record. Plus, I thought I'd send him a new pair of PJs, since he'll be living around other folks and might need more than an undershirt."

"Thanks for doing that, babe. You're a real sweetie."

"Well, so is he, in his own way. Jimmy, I'm still so amazed by how we came to find him and how you were led back there for a second visit. I was writing it up in my journal a little while ago, and the awe just washed over me all over again. It's very humbling."

He squeezed her hand. "It *was* a sweet experience," he said. "All the sweeter for sharing it with you and the kids."

"It wasn't lost on Tiffi, and I'm glad of that."

"Me, too. Now I'm excited to try the census records again, under R-H-Y-S."

"So am I—we'll have to get right on that. Soon as you have a little time, of course."

"Ah, yes—time. That rare commodity."

"What do you have to do for the rest of the evening?"

"Um—write a couple of letters, and figure out some tough home-teaching changes the elders quorum president requested. I don't know—maybe there'll be an hour or two to get on the computer, if I'm efficient—and if no one calls."

She smiled knowingly at him. "Fat chance," she said mildly.

"I know. Plus, I'd like to spend a little time with the kids—

but after all that togetherness of the last week, maybe they need a break."

"Let's play it by ear."

"Hey, babe—how well do you know Sister Conrad?"

"Tina? Not very well, really. She's been a little outspoken in Relief Society, and some of her remarks have seemed a little—oh, I don't know—maybe just a little over-the-top or super-zealous or something. But I really don't know her well enough to judge."

"Uh-huh. Okay. Um—let me ask you something—when you fold our family's underwear, does it matter to you whether the—er—front shows?"

Trish frowned. "The front?"

"You know—the crotch part. I mean, is there some unwritten rule somewhere that nice people fold their undies so that part is hidden?"

She stopped and stared at him. "What in the world? Does this have something to do with Tina Conrad? Oh—of course it does."

"She's a little concerned that her daughter-in-law isn't caring for her son's garments properly."

"I see. Sort of. Well, let me think. I'm sure I probably fold all our clothing the way my mom taught me." She sketched a few movements in the air. "I think that part probably doesn't show, the way I fold it, but it's not deliberate. We'll look, when we get home." She shook her head in confusion and chuckled. "What a thing to worry about!"

"Now, see, that was my first reaction—but then I began to second-guess myself."

"I remember one time she was talking about how she makes every little thing in her day a matter of prayer," Trish said. "I mean, like, which outfit she should wear, whether to serve potatoes or rice, what to name her new puppy, and which store she should shop in. I felt guilty at first for not living quite that close to the Spirit, and then I decided her approach was a bit extreme. I mean, I do believe we'd weary the Lord with such detail and that He expects us to be able to make some decisions on our own! There is that scripture about having our hearts drawn out in prayer continually, but I'm not sure that means praying about every tiny decision in our day. Don't you think?"

He put his arm around her shoulders and they continued their walk.

"I do think," he agreed. "And I'm grateful you're a reasonable woman."

They stopped in to say hello to their dear old neighbor, Hestelle Pierce, to see how the summer heat was treating her.

"Oh, y'all are back from your trip," she said, opening her lace-curtained front door to them. "I'm so glad you're home safe. The way traffic is nowadays, I don't hardly dare get out and drive anywheres!"

"Well, we mostly drove on back roads," the bishop told her. "Farm areas, most of the time, down in southwestern Georgia."

"Sounds fine to me. Even Fairhaven's getting a bit trafficky for my nerves."

"Now, Miss Hestelle, anytime you want to go somewhere that you don't feel like driving to, you call me," Trish told her. "I'd be glad to drive you."

"Y'all are so sweet," she told them. "Come in. Sit down, and I'll run make us a pitcher of punch. I've got cherry or grape."

"Oh, we're fine, Miz Hestelle," the bishop said, holding his wife's elbow and steering her into the house. "We just stopped in to see how you're faring."

Hestelle Pierce always took this question seriously. "Well," she said, seating herself in her favorite chair, "to tell you the truth, I haven't been quite as perky as I'd like to be. This heat just saps my strength, and seems like it takes me twice't as long to get anything done as it used to. I suppose that's my age, although I wonder if there might be something else coming on. I keep thinking I might be diabetic, but every time I ask doctor, he says my blood sugar's normal. I'm not so sure, though. Doctors don't know every little thing, do they? And then I get these funny little zingy feelings in my scalp, like some electric little bug is crawling in my hair, but when I go to touch it, there's never anything there! Then you know, my sister has eczema real bad, and I b'lieve I've seen some little red, rough patches starting on my elbows, too. You can't really cure that, you know. You can only control it."

"Is that right?" murmured the bishop. "Well, you're looking in the pink of health to me, Miz Hestelle, so I sure hope you can ward off any troubles that might come your way."

She looked doubtful. "Well, land—I hope so too, but we just never know, do we? And how are you coming with your little addition, Mrs. Shepherd?"

Trish smiled. "So far, so good, thank you. We're doing fine."

"That's a blessing. Now, I just want to ask y'all a question, see what you think. That girl of the Lowells, down on the corner—well, reckon she ain't exactly a girl, still, is she? Anyway, do you figure she's all right? All there, I mean?" She tapped her forehead significantly.

"We really don't know her very well," Trish explained. "We've barely met her a time or two, but her mother keeps her pretty close to home."

"She brung her over here one time when she was out deliverin' her little papers, which I must say I never read, after the first one that was so nasty about you folks, and not at all right according to what I've known about you over the years! They go right in the trash when she hands 'em to me, I can tell you! But of course I take one, to be polite and all. Anyway, the girl came with her, but she seemed scared to say boo!"

"Mrs. Lowell's definitely in control," the bishop said wryly. "I get the impression Marguerite would like to be friendly, but she's not allowed." He shrugged. "She may have some limitations, but I honestly don't know if she was born with them, or if they're a result of being brought up by her mother."

"Um—Miss Hestelle," Trish said. "I wonder if we might ask you a favor? Next time Mrs. Lowell gives you one of her circulars, would you mind setting it aside for us to look at? She doesn't favor us with a copy, and we're curious. I am, anyway," she added, with a glance toward her husband, who looked perplexed.

"I'll be glad to do that for y'all," Hestelle agreed, fanning her wavy white hair with a folded newspaper. "I declare, the humidity comes right inside, don't it? I hope we get us a little rain, soon, to break the heat."

"There is a breeze coming up," the bishop told her. "Maybe you'll get your wish."

"Dad, Mr. MacDonald called," Tiffani told him as he and Trish let themselves in the kitchen door. "He's coming over in a few minutes. I told him you were just out for a walk."

"Oh, okay. Thanks, honey." He sent an apologetic glance toward his wife. "Maybe he won't stay long. Maybe we can still get to the census."

She nodded and headed to the kitchen to put together their dessert. The bishop sat down at his desk to get a start on his chores while he could. He wrote a letter to Elder Pratt Birdwhistle, presently in the MTC at Provo, Utah, preparing for

his mission to Peru. Just before he could sign the letter, the door-
bell rang, and he went to welcome his boyhood friend, the
Reverend Peter "Big Mac" MacDonald.

"Mac! Hey, buddy—how's everything?"

"Things are mighty fine at our house, my friend, and peace
to yours."

"Thank you. Come sit down in the living room. I think Trish
will have some dessert for us in a minute."

"Oh, I had cake a while ago, and I don't know that double
dessert is something I should attempt, though the flesh is willing." He chuckled, then sobered. "Jim, I stopped by to show you
something that I find a little puzzling and disturbing. It came to
the church office a few days ago, and I don't know quite what
to make of it." He passed an envelope to the bishop, who
removed the letter inside and leaned near a lamp to read it.

"Dear Brethren and Sisters of the Christian Faith," he read.

"More and more these are perilous times for the true faith of
our Lord and Savior, and for those who adhere to the teachings
of the Holy Bible. There are those among us, masquerading as
Christians, who would add to and pervert the right way of God.
They send out their young men and women, nicely groomed and
dressed, often educated and well-spoken, to lure the naive
and innocent among us to their ruin—indeed, to consign their
souls to everlasting torment and damnation! As you may have
surmised, we refer to the Mormons, who seek to rob your
Christian congregations of their fairest and best, to build up their
unholy empire throughout the world. They even go so far as to
say openly that believing Christians make the best Mormon converts! As you may know, they promulgate the spurious doctrine
of continuing revelation from God in our modern day, and offer
copies of the Book of Mormon to replace the Holy Bible in our
study and worship.

"This devil-inspired and man-made cult is surely worthy of our scorn and ridicule, and just to show one example of their hideous twisting of the truth, they teach that Satan and Jesus are brothers! Well, friends, the Jesus I worship, and the Jesus you know and worship, is no brother to the devil! Perish the thought.

"In spite of the many books, articles, tapes, and films that have been produced to fight against this unholy organization, they continue to grow and gather converts. Now we are announcing a new program, coming soon to your area, which will effectively show the Mormons up for the wicked, deceitful, and deceived perverts that they are! A rally tour is being organized by the Tri-State Christian Fellowship in which a well-organized group of vocal believers in Christ will travel from state-to-state this summer, holding rallies aimed at exposing Mormonism's ugly, white underbelly for what it is! Watch for further bulletins about when they will be coming to a spot near you, so that you can gather up your flock to go and hear the truth about this pandemic of poison that is spreading among us!

"Your brethren in truth,

"The Tri-State Christian Fellowship"

The bishop turned the envelope over to see if there was a dated postmark. He could make out June, and he thought it came from California.

"Well!" he said. "How about that?"

"It troubles me, Jim. You and I have known each other practically all our lives, and we've had many an honest debate about religion and theology—and you know I don't agree with everything you folks teach—but I know you to be a genuine Christian. I'd stake my life on it. And I know you're sincere in your beliefs. I mean, I don't agree with everything my Catholic friends believe, either, but I can't label them non-Christian and condemn them to hell!"

"And 'non-Christian' is about the kindest thing they called us, here," the bishop said, tapping the letter against his knee.

"What I really don't understand is, why does your church attract such hatred?"

"Mac, from my point of view, the simplest and most basic answer that I can come up with is because the Church is true. Satan has to inspire people to fight against the truth, lest it roll forth like that stone mentioned in the Bible, made without hands, which goes on until it fills the whole earth—which it'll do, anyway. That's my honest belief. We teach truth, and that disturbs and annoys the powers of darkness, so that they have to fight against us. But . . ." He held up one hand, and smiled. "I realize that won't sound good in your ears, since you don't believe all we teach to be truth, so I'll just say that in a large part, ignorance and prejudice can be used to turn people against us, and to make them feel righteous and vindicated in their rejection."

"Well, I certainly don't feel edified or inspired when I read that drivel," Mac said, nodding toward the offensive document. "I detest that confrontational, in-your-face kind of approach to religious dialogue. In fact, they obviously don't want dialogue of any kind. They want to out-shout the opposition. They have 'vocal believers,' isn't that what it says? That means shouters, not singers, you can bet your boots on it."

The bishop shrugged. "It might be a group similar to the folks who gather outside of Temple Square in Salt Lake twice a year, when we hold our conferences, and do their best to insult our members as they go and come. As if that would influence anybody to want to join them! But you know, Mac—or actually, probably you don't know—we have prophecies that foretell greater persecution of our people in the latter days than even the pioneer Saints went through. So it's not like we're surprised by this sort of thing—though of course we sure don't enjoy it."

"Well, I will definitely counsel my congregation to refrain from attending or encouraging any such rallies that may be organized around here. It doesn't at all seem to fit the criterion we so often ask ourselves, of 'what would Jesus do?'"

"Oh, they'll compare themselves to Jesus cleansing the temple of the moneychangers, and say they're just experiencing righteous indignation," the bishop said. "They claim they worship a different Jesus than the one we preach, and that ours is an interloper—a false Christ."

"Right, I've heard that one. So what is the truth about this business of Jesus and Satan being brothers? I think I know, but set me square on it, okay?"

"Remember all the talks we used to have about the possibility of a premortal life—not just for Jesus and the angels, but for all of us? Well, this harks back to that belief. We believe that Jesus was the firstborn of all the spirit children of our Heavenly Father, and that Lucifer was not far down the line—a son of the morning, the Bible calls him. He was influential, and had great potential, but he chose to use it to defy and rebel against the Father, and to try to gain power and glory for himself, by pushing a plan of forced obedience for all of us, denying us our agency. Jesus, on the other hand, volunteered to implement the Father's plan, and was chosen to be our Savior. Lucifer came out in open rebellion, and a third of our spirit brothers and sisters followed after him. They were disowned, you might say, and cast out of heaven."

Mac nodded thoughtfully. "Like the third of the stars that fell with the dragon, mentioned in the book of Revelation," he commented.

"Exactly. But you see why, unless people have a knowledge

of our belief in a premortal state, they can't understand the concept of Jesus and Satan ever having been brothers. Many of them say the same God who created Jesus couldn't possibly create someone so inherently evil."

"But according to your belief, Lucifer was a rebellious child, not a deliberately created entity of evil. He made himself Satan—right?"

"That's how I see it."

"It's sad to think that God Himself would lose a third of His children to evil."

The bishop nodded. "Our scriptures say the heavens wept over the loss."

"So where are those third now? Cast out into the earth, doesn't the Bible say?"

"Yep. Right here on earth, working diligently to tempt us all and lead us astray."

"So—C. S. Lewis wasn't so far off, after all," Mac said with a chuckle.

"How's that?" the bishop asked.

"Oh, a little book called *The Screwtape Letters,* which purports to be letters from a devil to his nephew, offering advice on how to tempt and distract mortals from the Christian path. It's both amusing and sobering—and very pointed."

"Yeah, I've heard of that. I'd like to read it sometime."

"I have it. I'll drop it by when I think of it. Well, Jim, I just thought you deserved to know what's going on behind your back, so to speak, among these rabble-rousers who call themselves Christians. I personally don't think they're great examples of the faith, but there are those around here who would fall for their rhetoric."

The bishop thought about his next-door neighbors. "I'm sure

there are. Oh, hey, Trish, I just told Mac you had some dessert for us!"

"'Deed I do. Hi, Mac, how are you?" Trish greeted, as Mac stood and smiled at her.

"You're blooming as ever, Trish," he told her. "I told Jim I really shouldn't have another dessert tonight, but that looks delicious . . ."

"This is light," she promised him. "It's just a strawberry parfait—mostly non-fat ingredients."

He accepted a serving and, as Trish exited, sat down with a sigh. "I sure hate to be the bearer of ill tidings, Jim, but I thought you'd want to know what's out there."

"I do appreciate the heads-up," the bishop said, and even as he spoke, he heard his words echo those of Ralph Jernigan. "So!" he muttered. "This must be what Ralph's onto."

"Excuse me?" said Mac, and the bishop gave him a brief rundown on the Jernigan story.

"Well, bless his heart," Mac said feelingly. "What a noble soul, to carry on in spite of all his fears and sorrows. And it sounds like this time, he's picked up on something real."

"I'm afraid it does. So, I guess my next challenge will be preparing my ward for whatever comes."

"And I'll try to do the same with my congregation," Mac promised.

"Thanks, Mac. You're a good friend."

CHAPTER TEN

" . . . OUR SHELTER FROM THE STORMY BLAST"

The bishop took the disturbing circular Peter MacDonald had brought and stuffed it into a pigeonhole on his roll-top desk in the corner of the dining room. He debated for a few minutes whether to show it to Trish, then put off that decision and tried to concentrate on his other letter, an answer to Elder Rivenbark's mission president about how that missionary was faring. He was happy to be able to give a positive and straightforward report that the young man seemed well and happy and productive, that he had apparently adjusted to the at-first onerous medical requirement that he live at home for the remainder of his missionary service and that he take a rest period in the middle of each day. As the bishop had predicted, Elder Rivenbark's companions had no complaints about meeting him at his parents' house for their early-morning study periods, especially since Sister Rivenbark was an excellent cook and kept them nourished and cheered with her cinnamon rolls and buttermilk biscuits.

He turned his attention next to the needed changes in home

teaching assignments proposed by Don Quaverly, the elders quorum president, but found his attention wandering back to the offensive notice. He had seen numerous "Anti-Mormon" tracts and books over the years, and occasionally some of the local members would be disturbed or dissuaded by them. Most of their arguments he could fairly easily refute, seeing the obvious errors in either understanding or interpretation that the authors had committed. Some, he felt, came from honest folks who simply disagreed with one or more facets of the Latter-day Saint faith, while others were so obviously and deliberately misleading and misrepresentative that the reader could feel the ill-will that oozed from between the lines.

The letter pigeonholed in his desk fell primarily into the latter category. That people of this ilk were planning an actual tour to attack the Church wherever they could get a crowd together was a disturbing thought. Most of the members of varied faiths in Fairhaven seemed content to live and let live, saving their most active competition for the Interfaith Summer Softball League. He would be sorry to see that kind of tolerance changed by outside interference. Was Stake President Walker aware of this situation? He would talk to him.

He stood suddenly, feeling the need to do something positive and useful and pleasant.

"Trish!" he called, "Come on, babe, man the computer! It's time we came to our census."

An hour and a half later, they rose triumphantly from the computer in their family room with three census-years' worth of Rhys data—1910, 1900, and 1880.

"Man, I wish the 1890 census hadn't been destroyed," the bishop said, looking over the information they had obtained.

"I purely hate knowing there once was useful information about these people that doesn't exist anymore. It's like those marriage records with only a partial index left. It's so frustrating!"

"I know," soothed Trish. "But you've got tons of stuff now that we had no idea of, even a week ago."

"That's true. The glass is way more than half-full, isn't it? I should be grateful. And I am." He glanced at the clock. "Hey, gang—it's time we all headed for bed and let Buddy get some sleep in here. He's got to go to work in the morning!"

"Oh, I'm okay, Bishop," Buddy said, his cheeks reddening. "I'm cool."

The bishop grinned. "I know, friend. I'm using you for an excuse to get to bed, myself. It's been a long day."

The next day, after speaking to his stake president, Bishop Shepherd faxed him a copy of the letter. Later that morning, President Walker called him back.

"You know, Bishop, I don't believe we need to be unduly concerned about this," President Walker advised. "It doesn't state any exact wheres or whens, and besides, as I'm sure you realize, the general policy of the Church is to allow all folks their constitutional freedom of speech in such matters, and just go on our own way, preaching and teaching what we know to be true without mounting any counterattacks. However, I would suggest that if you learn more specifics about this proposed tour—or rally—that you might advise your ward members to stay away, and not to engage with these people. Some of them might just be looking for a fight, and we'd surely like to disappoint them in that desire."

The bishop thanked him and realized the wisdom of his advice. A "turn-the-other-cheek" attitude would seem to be the

Savior's way—and therefore it should be theirs. Still, he wanted to monitor the situation, and he knew he could depend on Ralph Jernigan and Peter MacDonald to help him do that. He decided not to share the information with his family just yet, particularly wanting to avoid burdening Trish with any unnecessary worry during her pregnancy.

Y

"Bishop?" inquired Buddy's voice behind him in the canned fruit and juice aisle. He turned to see the boy nod toward the front of the store, where Elders Moynihan and Rivenbark proudly ushered in Jim's old classmate Charles Stagley.

"Well, for heck's sake! How in the world are you, Chuck?" he greeted, going forward and thrusting out his hand.

The man smiled widely and nodded. "I'm tolerable, Jim. It's good to see you. Took over your dad's business, did you?"

"Sure did. My goodness, it's been years, man! Come on, gentlemen, let's go visit in my office, where we can all sit down and relax."

He led the way to his office in the front corner of the building, gave Mary Lynn an early lunch break, and pulled over a stool to sit on as he offered his own chair to Chuck Stagley and Mary Lynn's to Elder Moynihan. Elder Rivenbark, being in his wheelchair, was provided for.

"Care for a cold drink?" the bishop asked. "On the house, of course."

He raided a cooler for four bottled lemonades.

"Well, this is a pleasant surprise," he stated, uncertain as to just what the missionaries expected of him.

"We were telling Brother Stagley that you remembered him, but he wasn't sure you really did, so we thought we'd pop in for a visit. He doesn't live far from here," Elder Moynihan explained.

"Are you kidding me? After all our baseball games and Saturday mornings out at the racetrack? Of course I remember him! I haven't seen you around for a long time, though, Chuck—are you recently back in town from somewhere else?"

Chuck nodded. "Been living down in Dothan," he explained. "Had my mom down there in a care facility close by. But after she passed on, I decided I'd better come back up and see what could be done about her house. It's been vacant the last couple of years and needs a lot of repair. Most of the work I reckon I can handle, but it'll take time and money. Her insurance was just enough to cover her needs, so there's nothing of that left over. I'm just exploring options, I reckon you could say."

"I see. And how'd these two young ruffians get hold of you?"

Chuck grinned. "Well, a guy gets desperate for company, Jim. He takes what he can get."

"Aw, come on, now," Elder Moynihan objected, grinning broadly.

"You know you love us," added Elder Rivenbark. "We're your best friends."

"You may be, at that," the man admitted. "The truth is, these guys found me when I was feelin' pretty low, thinking about my mom, wondering about the hereafter and all, and they ferreted that outa me, and then set about tellin' me their ideas on the subject."

"How'd their ideas sound to you?"

"They made sense, you know? Reckon I'd like it to be the way they say. Don't know if it is, but they paint a pretty picture."

"They're telling you the truth, my friend, I can vouch for that. The more I learn and the longer I live, the more I know this church teaches the true, restored gospel of Jesus Christ, and that's something I never fail to find both comforting and exciting."

"I can see it would be. Well, these dudes have got me convinced to come to your church this Sunday, so reckon I'll give it a try. Been a while since I been to any church. I've tried a few different ones, but they don't seem to fit me somehow."

The bishop reached over and patted his old friend's knee. "Maybe this one'll be tailor-made. I sure hope so."

The man ran a hand over his balding head. "Gotta say I hope so, too. Say, you don't happen to know of any jobs open around here, do you, Jim? I'm lookin' for work."

"Not off-hand, but I'll keep my eyes open. What's your phone number?"

"I don't have a phone hooked up, yet. I'll write down my address for you, though."

The bishop pushed a small notepad toward him and then folded the address into his shirt pocket.

"What kind of work do you want?" he asked.

"Anything I can get—handyman, house painter, truck driver, car parts salesman—whatever's needed, I'll give it a try. I don't really have me a skilled trade, nor no college, but I'm a hard worker, and honest."

"Well, those are the best qualities I know for any job. I'll let you know if I turn up anything. Ya'll have a good day, now," he added as they prepared to depart.

Mary Lynn was leaning against the end of the dairy cooler, eating a container of salad from their new deli.

"Sorry to put you out, Mary Lynn," her employer apologized.

"No problem," she replied. "Reckon I was ready for an early lunch."

"Ma'am," Chuck acknowledged with a nod as he stepped past her, then stood aside to allow Elder Rivenbark to maneuver his chair into the aisle. "Salad looks good," he remarked to her with a smile. "I'll have to try that sometime."

"You should," Mary Lynn replied, then ducked her head so that her long brown hair obscured most of her face. Then she quickly retreated into the office she shared with her employer and closed the door behind her.

"Thanks," Elder Moynihan mouthed in the bishop's direction, as he and his companion waved to Buddy, then turned to follow Chuck out of the store.

The bishop patted his arm. "Anytime," he whispered.

By the time he left work, the slight promise of change carried on the breeze of the previous evening was fulfilled in a rainstorm that turned the afternoon to early evening with the blackness of its clouds and the lightning that knocked out power just as he turned into his drive. Trish was lighting an oil lamp as he entered the kitchen, brushing off rain. He greeted her with a kiss.

"Hey, no fair!" Jamie complained from the computer corner. "I was doing real good, and then bam! No power."

"Too bad, champ," his dad said. "Maybe it'll be on, soon. Where are the girls?"

"I'm over here," Tiffani called from the sofa in the gray gloom of the family room. "I was reading, but like Jamie said—bam!"

"And Mallory's doing something secret in her room for family home evening," Trish explained.

"I'd better go up and make sure she's not scared," the bishop said. "Some storm, huh?"

"I heard on the news it's a band of thundershowers that was flung up our way from that tropical storm in the Gulf," Trish replied. "There are apparently several other bands following it, so we may be in for a rainy week."

"Oh, great." Jamie moaned. "I've got soccer practice, and me and Mal are s'posed to start our swim lessons this week!"

"Well, maybe you can just swim at soccer practice," teased his mother, listening to the enthusiastic gurgle of the water pouring out of the drain spout onto the grass by the patio. "At least we didn't have to deal with this kind of weather last week, on our trip."

Tiffani yawned and wandered into the kitchen. "And at least we have a gas range, so we still get dinner. Can I help, Mom?"

"Well, since you can't read right this minute, how about breaking up some lettuce for taco salad? It's in the left crisper drawer, and please grab the cheese while you're in the fridge, and do it fast, so things will stay cold. There's no telling how long the power will be off."

It was off for the rest of the evening and into the night, so the family went to bed with their windows opened just a little to catch any coolness the rain had brought without too much danger of its blowing in and soaking the carpet. The evening had been a refreshingly quiet one. They had played games by lamplight and talked about how oil lamps and candles had been the only means of lighting people's homes during the lifetimes of many of the people whose records they had found on their trip. Jamie and Mallory found it difficult to imagine daily life without television and computers, let alone phones, cell phones, electricity, running water, indoor bathrooms, airplanes, and cars.

"Lots of things have been invented or improved in just the last few years," Trish explained. "When I was young, computers were just huge mainframe machines that some colleges and businesses had. People certainly didn't have them in their homes, or play games on them."

"I can outdo that," the bishop challenged. "When I was a

little boy, we had party lines on our phones here in Fairhaven. Anybody know what that is?"

Tiffani giggled. "Only party lines I've ever heard of are the ones we talk about in American Government class. It's what the Democrats and Republicans give out as their opinion on things."

"Right on, Tiff. But the kind I remember meant that your phone line wasn't yours alone. We had three parties on our line, and we heard the phone ring for the other two families as well as our own. Our ring was two short rings, another family had one long ring, and the other had one short followed by a long. And if we picked up the phone while someone in one of those homes was using the line, we could hear their conversation. Your Aunt Paula was really naughty, and if Grandma wasn't noticing, she would lift up the receiver a few seconds after hearing the one long ring, especially, and listen in to what was being said."

Jamie grinned at the idea of his staid, grown-up Aunt Paula being young and naughty. "Why'd she listen to that ring, instead of the other one?" he asked.

"Because she knew it belonged to a sweet little old lady who hadn't had much education and said funny things. I remember one time Paula just doubled over laughing so hard she had to hang up. The lady was telling her friend that she'd been having the sniffles, and she'd gone to the doctor to see why she kept catching colds. But he told her she didn't have a cold, she just had the algebras."

"What?" demanded Mallory, wrinkling her nose. "I don't get it."

"She meant allergies," Tiffani explained. "She just got the word wrong, and said 'algebras' instead. Right, Dad?"

"Exactly. And I guess she was always saying things like that. Grandma finally caught Paula at it, though, and she was grounded from using the phone for a long time."

"That'd be kind of fun," Tiffani said. "Not being grounded, but listening in. You could learn a lot of interesting things about people that way."

"Yeah, what if we had a party line with the Lowells!" Jamie said. "We could hear all the stuff they say about us."

"I don't think I'd want to know," Trish said wryly. "I haven't seen any of them since we got back—but I can't believe that woman climbed up a ladder to spy on poor little Buddy out on the patio!"

"I wish she'd of fell off," Jamie said. "Ka-boom! Would've served her right."

"Well, now, James," the bishop began, "I think that was sort of a strange thing for her to do, too, but maybe—just maybe— she knew we were gone and she was making sure Buddy wasn't a burglar."

"Dad, you always cut people so much slack," Tiffani complained. "It's like you can't believe anybody's just plain mean."

The bishop thought about the letter tucked away in his desk. He knew full well there was real hostility in the world and that some of it was directed against him and his loved ones merely because of who they were and what they believed to be true. He just hated to acknowledge that it had moved in next door to him. He smiled in Tiffani's direction but said nothing.

"I think she was looking to see if Samantha was out, so's she could take her again," stated Mallory. "Where is Samantha, anyway? Mommy, she's not out in the dark, is she?"

"She's right down here, wrapped around my ankle," her dad told her. "She's waiting for me to move my foot so she can grab it and bite."

Mallory giggled. "Those are just love bites," she advised her father.

Y

Later, snuggled close to Trish, listening to the drumming of the rain on the roof of their home and waiting for sleep to come, Bishop Jim Shepherd hoped that all his ward members were as safe and sheltered as he. He hoped Twyla Osborne, Buddy's mother, had come home on time and welcomed him in—and if not, that her ex-husband, Gerald, had rid himself of his "company" and allowed his son to sleep at his house. He hoped that Hilda Bainbridge was doing better in the hospital. He didn't like that yellowish cast to her skin. He hoped the rivers and creeks in the area wouldn't be so swollen by the rain that they would overflow their banks and flood homes or destroy crops. He hoped the uneasy feeling that kept him from relaxing and drifting into slumber was just that—a feeling and nothing more.

Trish stirred and yawned. "Jimmy? Are you awake?" she murmured.

"M-hmm."

"Are you worried about something?"

"You know me too well."

"Is that what you're worried about?"

He smiled in the dark, and leaned up and kissed her hair. "Nope."

"What's bothering you?"

"I dunno. Can't tell. One of those—what d'you call 'em—free-floating anxieties, or something."

"Have you prayed?"

"M-hmm."

"Well, then—if there's something to be worried about, likely it'll turn up soon enough. Try to rest so you'll be ready for whatever."

"I'll try. Sorry if I disturbed you, babe."

"You didn't. The rain keeps waking me up, and the baby's really active, too. Would you just put your arms around me and hold me? Maybe that'll comfort both of us."

It did.

CHAPTER ELEVEN

"... EARTH HAS NO SORROW THAT HEAV'N CANNOT HEAL"

With morning light, the storm had blown over, power had been restored and so had Bishop Shepherd's normal good cheer and optimism. He ate breakfast with his family and headed off to the store. When his cell phone rang, he pulled over to the side of the street to fish it out of his pants pocket and answer.

"Bishop? Is that you?" came Ida Lou Reams's voice, shaky with emotion.

"It's me, Ida Lou," he acknowledged. "What's going on?"

"Well, I've lost me one of the finest friends I ever had, is all! I'll miss her like a sister, and in fact she is my sister. We've lost our Hildy, Bishop."

"Have we! I was worried about her, and I knew her color wasn't good, but I sure had hoped she'd pull through. When did this happen?"

"Just this mornin' as it was gettin' light, I reckon. I got the call a little bit ago, and I flew over here to the hospital hopin' it wadn't so, but it was."

"I'm so sorry, Ida Lou. I know you'll truly miss her. I've seen how close you two ladies have become, since Roscoe died. Hilda's really depended on you, and you never let her down. You've been the truest kind of friend, and you can take some comfort in that."

"I don't know about that, Bishop. I feel like I shoulda been here. Shoulda been with her, you know? So's she didn't have to die alone." Ida Lou began to cry, and he turned the wheel of his truck to head toward the hospital.

"I'm coming right over, Ida Lou. You'll be there a little longer, won't you?"

"Yessir. Hildy made me her—um—personal representative, I reckon you call it. I got to sign some papers. I'm in the office on the second floor." She gave a little hiccup of a sob. "I hate to disturb your mornin', but I'd be real grateful to see you."

"I'm on the way. I'll just be a minute."

He called Trish to tell her the news, then notified Mary Lynn that he would be a little late to work. He found Ida Lou in the second floor office and let her cry against his shoulder for a bit.

"I tell you what, Bishop, I never knowed when I took this president job that I'd get so attached to all the sisters—'specially this one."

"Well, Hilda's a wonderful woman. I'll never forget how calm and faithful she was when Roscoe passed. She grieved, of course, but she felt joy, too—you remember that?"

Ida Lou sniffed. "Yessir, I sure do. I thought she was the strongest little thing I ever seen."

"Mrs. Reams?" asked a young nurse with rosy cheeks. "I'm sorry to interrupt, but could you please sign this? It's the release form, to allow the mortuary folks take Mrs. Bainbridge's body."

"All right," Ida Lou said, and signed the form. "You helped take care of her, didn't you, hon? Wadn't she the sweetest thing?"

"She sure was," the nurse agreed, patting Ida Lou's arm. "It really surprised me when she died this morning. I thought she'd have a long fight with liver and kidney failure ahead of her." She smiled wistfully. "I'm sorry to see her go, but I'm glad she didn't have to go through all that. I should've known, too, the way she was acting during the night, but I just brushed it off."

"How was she acting? Was she hurtin'?" asked Ida Lou.

"Oh, no—nothing like that. I'd have done something to help her in that case. No, I just went in to check on her, because we were on generator power due to the storm, and I wanted to be sure everything was working okay—and there she was, awake and laughing and talking. I said to her, just teasing, 'Mrs. Bainbridge, have you got visitors here in the middle of the night? It's not visiting hours, you know.' And she said, 'Oh, it's just Ross and Carolyn. They've come to take me home with them.' I said, 'Now, Mrs. Bainbridge, you know you can't go home till the doctor says so.' And she just giggled like a little girl and said, 'Reckon I can if Ross and Carolyn take me.'"

The nurse shook her head solemnly. "I thought she'd been dreaming, but I should've known better. I've seen it happen often enough—just before folks pass on. They'll be talking to somebody or smiling or waving or looking around the room, all startled, like they're surprised to see people there. At first it used to freak me out, but now it gives me a lot of comfort, to think we're met by loved ones when we go. Some folks in my field don't believe in an afterlife, but I'll tell you what—they haven't worked where I have! So I just wonder, do y'all happen to know if she knew somebody named Ross and Carolyn?"

Ida Lou was crying quietly into a handkerchief, but she nodded. "She did," the bishop told the rosy-cheeked nurse. "They're her husband and daughter—both deceased."

The girl's eyes twinkled. "Well, then—they took her home,

then—right out from under our noses. And I can't help being happy for her."

"Me, too," the bishop agreed. "We'll all miss her, though, at our church."

"I'll bet you will. Which church is that?" the nurse inquired.

The bishop told her, and a curious mix of expressions crossed her face.

"Really! Do y'all happen to know two missionaries from that church? One uses a wheelchair, and the other's a blond fellow—"

"That'd be Elders Moynihan and Rivenbark," the bishop replied with a smile. Everything fell into place suddenly. He noted the name on the plastic tag she wore on her uniform. It read, "Caroline Marsh, R.N.," and he seemed to recall the elders mentioning they were teaching a nurse by that name. "They're both fine young men. I'm especially well-acquainted with Elder Rivenbark, since he's from this area. Say, Miss Marsh—if you happen to be available when Hilda's funeral is held, why don't you come? I know that'd please her."

"I do try to do that, if I'm not working," she agreed. "Or at least the viewing or visitation." She handed the signed paper to a young man who appeared in the doorway, then turned back with a small frown. "Do y'all believe the deceased actually know who's at their funeral?"

The bishop gave a small shrug. "I wouldn't be at all surprised," he told her.

She nodded. "Neither would I. Seems fair."

"I think Hilda might be around just to comfort her good friend here," he added, patting Ida Lou's shoulder. "This lady's been like an angel to her since Roscoe died."

Caroline smiled. "I know she has—at least lately, I mean, because I've seen her up here a lot. Hilda was blessed to have such a good friend."

Ida Lou shook her head vehemently. "The blessin' was mine," she stated firmly.

Y

It was decided to hold Hilda Bainbridge's funeral on Saturday, so that more people would have the chance to attend. Sometime earlier, she had suggested to Ida Lou that a simple graveside service would suffice, since she had no remaining family, but Ida Lou reportedly had informed her in no uncertain terms that she had a loving family of several hundred people who would want to see her off into eternity. And so it turned out to be—the chapel was full to capacity on Saturday morning, so that they had to open the accordion-fold curtains and set up extra chairs in the cultural hall. Not only members came, but numerous neighbors and old friends of Roscoe and Hilda, and people who had been friends of their daughter, Carolyn.

Ida Lou read the simple obituary that Trish helped her prepare from Hilda's own story as recorded in her book of remembrance, with a few additions from her closest friends. Sam Wright spoke of his long association with Hilda and Roscoe and told of the qualities he had observed in the patient and cheerful Hilda, even in her afflictions of widowhood, the loss of her only daughter, and the debilitation and near-blindness of recent years. Then the bishop invited any of the congregation who wished to pay tribute to Hilda to come forward and take a couple of minutes each. One by one, people approached the pulpit, some with confidence, others with fear and trembling at speaking in public, but each to tell of some way in which Hilda had touched his or her life.

"She taught me to sew."

"She mothered me after my own mother died when I was eleven."

"She was my visiting teacher for eight years, and she never missed a visit. She taught me the gospel by word and by example."

"After my wife passed on, she and Roscoe used to bring over a dessert once a month, and always a cake on my birthday, and they'd sit and eat it with me, and talk and laugh about old times."

"She was the best Primary teacher I ever had. I was an insecure, bratty little kid who tried to disrupt things and get attention for myself, and she'd have me sit on her lap while she taught. I felt so safe there I got to where I'd act up just to get to sit with her. I know she figured that out, but she still held me. She would've been a wonderful grandma."

Just as the bishop was ready to close this portion of the service and give his own remarks, he saw Caroline Marsh coming forward, and sat back. Caroline, her face radiant and eyes shining, shared with the attendees the same story she had related to him and Ida Lou the morning of Hilda's passing. Handkerchiefs appeared, and sniffles were heard throughout the congregation. He regarded Caroline; he was impressed with her open manner, her fresh young beauty, and the sweetness of her spirit. He hoped she would respond positively to the missionaries' message. He suspected there was a good chance of it. She was quality.

"Brothers, sisters, and friends," he began when it was his turn to speak, "is there a doubt in anyone's mind today that this dear lady, Hilda Bainbridge, has gone forward to meet the God who gave her life with a refined and polished spirit? That she has gone in the choice company of her beloved Roscoe and their daughter, Carolyn? That she has, in her quiet and cheerful way, touched for good the hundreds of lives that crossed her path? That, indeed, she has kept her second estate, and now will have glory added upon her head, forever and ever? There's no doubt in my mind as to these things. Sister Hilda, we will miss you, but we bid you to enter eternity with the joy and anticipation of one who has known and loved the Lord Jesus Christ and served Him all your days. May God bless you forever."

He continued his remarks with a few scriptures and thoughts on the nature of life and death and the reality of the Atonement and the Resurrection, mostly for the benefit of Caroline Marsh and other non-members present, so that they would have an understanding of Hilda's beliefs on the subject. He knew she would want her services to be as much a missionary opportunity for people as a tribute to her.

"Fine funeral sermon there, Jim," greeted Chuck Stagley as people headed for their cars in the brilliant sunlight of the parking lot. "Reckon I liked it better than any I've heard."

"Well, thanks, Chuck. I didn't realize you were here."

"Oh, those two missionaries of yours couldn't let me miss a chance like this to see how the Mormons do things," Chuck replied with a grin. "Gotta say, that was likely the happiest funeral I ever been to. I liked how it was so personal, too, and not just reciting things and sad organ music. You made it all feel so natural."

"Glad you feel that way. Death's just a natural part of the whole picture, I figure—although the separation it brings can be mighty painful. Hilda's passing is a little easier than most, of course, because those closest to her are already on the other side."

"Reckon that's true. Hey, you know the part the little nurse told—about the husband and daughter being there to take the lady home? That kinda rung a bell with me and made me recall something my mom said shortly before she passed. She looked over in the corner of the room and said, 'Well, there's Vera—don't she look good!' See, Vera was her sister—been dead for twenty or more years. It kinda stuck with me. I didn't know whether Vera was there for real, or whether Mama was just seein' things, being so sick and all. Now I think it mighta been the first."

"It could've been, all right. Listen, Chuck, I'd better head off to the cemetery. My family's waiting in the car. But have you had any luck finding work?"

The man shook his balding head. "Nary a nibble. Got any ideas?"

"Well, if you don't mind a little temporary work, I could use some help around the store this summer, with employees going on vacations and such."

"Jim, I'd be grateful for one day's work, at this point."

"Well, come on by on Monday morning, and we'll get you started. With the provision, of course, that if you find something better, you'll take it."

"Hey, man—thank you so much. More than you know."

"It'll help us both out. See you soon."

At sacrament meeting on Sunday, Bishop Shepherd spotted something in the congregation that made him do a double take. There, on a back row, sitting stiffly beside his wife and three children, was none other than Sergeant Forelaw. Elaine, his wife, kept smiling as she glanced around at people. She was obviously thrilled and probably a little nervous too, to have Sergeant accompany the family to church. To the best of the bishop's knowledge, it was a first for them. As their home teacher, he was privy to the knowledge that Sergeant had been secretly reading the scriptures in recent weeks, his wife having spotted copies of them in his work truck, but he hadn't known the man was anywhere near taking this step.

Quickly he reviewed the sacrament meeting program, hoping it was one that would be representative of the gospel in action in people's lives. There were two youth speakers, Billy Newton and Rosalyn Rivenbark. Excellent. Then a musical number by Claire Patrenko on the piano. No problem there. Then a talk by Elder Don Smedley, recently returned from Brazil, speaking on assignment with Brother Reid Dorset of the stake high council. He exhaled. It should be a good program. Brother Dorset did have a tendency to run on a little long, but his talks were always well-organized and spiritually mature.

Things went well—everyone performed at a high level, and the Spirit was present in the meeting. After the benediction, the bishop dodged people and practically leap-frogged over pews to get to the back of the chapel just as the Forelaw family was preparing to exit.

"Hey, there, Sergeant—nice to see you," he said, shaking the man's hand and trying to keep any surprise out of his voice. He wanted it to seem like a casual greeting—no big deal—instead of the very big deal he felt it to be. "Elaine—how're you? And Katie? Hey, Carter, want to shake hands? And little Arnie. Say, I'm looking forward to coming out to visit on the last Wednesday of the month, if that still works for y'all? Great. See you then."

He moved on, to shake hands warmly with other people, including the missionaries and their guests—Chuck Stagley and Ed and Megan Finell with their baby, Fiona. It was the first time he'd met the Finells, and he took a moment to establish where they lived and the fact that Ed worked in the accounting office of Birmingham–Southern College. They seemed a sharp and likable young couple, and he hoped they would accept the gospel.

"Bishop, I have a bone to pick with you."

Trying not to cringe visibly, he turned to face Sister Tina Conrad bearing down on him.

"Sister Conrad, how are you?" he asked.

"I'm well enough, but we need to talk about a condition in the Relief Society that needs correcting."

"Oh—have you brought it up with Ida Lou?"

"She's the problem."

"Really? That's unusual—she's generally part of the solution. Listen, Sister Conrad—I have a couple of interviews I need to see to, right now. Could you possibly make an appointment with Brother Dan McMillan for Tuesday night? We'd have a little more time then to chat." He reached an arm to draw Thomas Rexford toward him. "Ready for our little visit, Thomas?" he asked, turning his head to wink at the boy so that Sister Conrad couldn't see. "Let's head for my office. I won't keep you long. I know you need to get to Sunday School."

T-Rex looked confused. "Did I forget an appointment?" he asked, as the bishop propelled him along the hall. "I reckon my head ain't quite as good as it used to be, but—"

"No, son—you just saved me from another interview that I want to put off for a while. Come on in and let's catch up on things. How're you feeling?"

"Real good, Bishop. I only get dizzy when I turn or change levels real fast—and the doctors say that'll go away after a while." He gave a shamefaced grin. "Coach is still mad, though. He ain't speakin' to me. I know I broke trainin' rules, but heck— the season was over, and I'd just got new stuff for my bike, and I wanted to get out and ride the thing! You know what? I reckon he's gonna want me to keep his trainin' rules even after I graduate!"

"Well, Thomas, you are one of his prize players. He sees your potential, and he doesn't want you to blow your chances by doing dangerous things. Have the doctors said whether you'll be released to play football this fall?"

"Not yet. I should be in summer football camp right now, though, and I don't know whether Coach'll let me play iffen I don't jump through all the hoops."

The bishop nodded. He didn't know, either. Coach was tough and stubborn, there was no doubt. He ran a tight ship with his Fairhaven Mariners, and not even the famed and beloved T-Rex could break rules with impunity—especially since such actions had broken his head and nearly cost the boy his life the previous winter.

"I'm so proud of you, Thomas, for the progress you're making in the Aaronic Priesthood. It does my heart good every time I hear you give the prayers on the sacrament."

"Aw, thanks, Bishop. That was purely freaky at first, but I'm gettin' a little bit used to it."

"You're doing fine. How's the social life?"

Thomas shrugged his considerable shoulders. They weren't quite as beefy as they had once been, before his accident and period of forced inactivity, but they were still impressive. "I don't know—okay, I reckon. I hatn't been dating much. I mean, I ain't been working, and I finally got the picture, you know, of my folks' situation. It's not like I can hit 'em up for money to take a girl out, when I already cost 'em thousands they didn't have, with my accident and surgery and all."

"I'm glad you have that attitude. And I'm glad your dad's working again. That helps, doesn't it?"

"Yessir, I'll say it does. And thanks for helpin' him find that job."

The bishop shook his head. "It wasn't me. He found it himself. It was posted on the list that came around from the stake employment specialist. He just recognized that it was something he could do and applied. I'm grateful he got it."

"Me, too. And he helped Brother Dolan find work, too."

"Yep. That's what it's all about, Thomas—helping each other. That's a large part of what the priesthood is for. You ever see a priesthood-holder with his hands on his own head, giving himself a blessing?"

Thomas looked startled, then grinned. "No sir, reckon I ain't seen that."

"And you never will. We're called to bless each other, and help each other, any way we can. And thank you, right now, for helping me to put off seeing a sister I wasn't quite ready to see."

Thomas looked wise. "It was that Conrad lady, wadn't it? Saw her comin' for you. She's kinda—um—different, ain't she? She poked her head into our Sunday School class one day just as we was gettin' started and told us that if we tilted our chairs back in class, or laughed loud enough that the person right next to us could hear us, that we were breaking the solemn commandments of the Lord and we'd be severely punished. I mean, those was her very words, Bishop—I ain't fergot 'em. Is that true?"

"Um—not exactly. There are times to be solemn and times to be respectful and pay attention, and times to play and enjoy ourselves, and some of us, when we're young, get those times confused. But, no—I don't suppose anybody'll be severely punished for tilting their chair back—unless they fall and damage their head, which I surely wouldn't advise you to do! But let's cut Sister Conrad some slack. I think she's pretty hard on herself and everybody around her, from all I can tell. We'll just try to help her." He grinned. "In fact, I promise to gather up my courage and try to help her Tuesday night." He patted Thomas's back and saw him out.

"You're a good guy, Bishop," the boy told him with a mischievous grin. "I won't tell nobody how you're shirking your duty."

CHAPTER TWELVE

" . . . EVERY HUMAN TIE MAY PERISH"

Tuesday night came all too soon for Bishop James Shepherd. He had several interviews scheduled, most of which he felt good about, but there were two that, for differing reasons, he approached with a bit of uncertainty and dread. He interviewed Claire Patrenko, which was a pleasure, and found himself grateful that his daughter Tiffani was blessed with such a fine young woman for her best friend—bright, sensible, faithful, and fun. He knew how important it was for young people to have quality friends.

He was more and more grateful for his own boyhood chum, Peter MacDonald—for the good times they had shared, going camping, fishing, playing ball, and working on their vehicles— and for the many heart-to-heart discussions that had occupied their leisure hours together, on everything from girls to sports to religion. "Mac," though he wasn't a member of the Church, had provided a stabilizing influence on him, the bishop acknowledged, serving as a nonjudgmental sounding board and a reminder that life held more than racing trucks on Saturday mornings.

The Reverend Peter MacDonald had gone on to acquire far more formal education than his friend, which had caused the bishop to study harder in the scriptures and in doctrinal works than he might otherwise have done, in sheer anticipation of future discussions with the budding minister. In fact, Mac was such a fine example of Christian thought and practice that the bishop had a difficult time understanding how he couldn't see the veracity and worth of the restored gospel. They agreed on so many things—even things that many other Christians disagreed with in regard to the Church—yet Mac couldn't seem to accept the idea of the need for a living prophet to guide the Lord's Church in modern times.

Mac felt that the combined body of believers, worldwide, whatever their differences in theology or practice, constituted the church of Christ and that the Lord blessed and inspired them all according to their need and faith. He was a true ecumenical, and while the bishop was grateful for this, in that it allowed Mac to respect his friend's LDS beliefs, it also seemed to blind him to the scriptural mandate for "one Lord, one faith, and one baptism." Still—what a friend to have had, all these years, and how much growth he had experienced because of that friendship!

A brief break in his schedule after the interview with Claire allowed him time to sample the platter of Southwestern delicacies supplied by Sister Ramona Cisneros, who had signed up to bring dinner for the bishopric this particular Tuesday—according to the pattern the Relief Society had adopted when the new bishopric had been organized with several of its members from far-flung sections within the ward boundary who wouldn't have time to go home for supper and make it back to the church on time for their meeting and their duties. The bishop scooped up a serving from a layered dish of refried beans, sour cream, chopped tomatoes and chiles, green onion and sliced black olives, and dug into it with a corn chip.

"How's Ida Lou holdin' up, Bishop?" asked Sam Wright. "Know it's been a blow to her to lose Hildy like that. Felt bad when I saw her come in to sacrament meeting all on her lonesome, Sunday."

"Well, she's grieving, there's no doubt about it," the bishop agreed. "But she's got her hands and heart full with other women, too, and that helps a lot. I know she visits Sister Mobley quite often, and some of the younger women rely on her like a mom, to help out with everything from recipes to sewing to tending sick babies. Then she still takes a group to the temple once a week. She'll really miss Hilda on those days."

"Oh, Bishop, I forgot to mention that Sister Padgett wants to visit with you," Dan McMillan said. "There wasn't time tonight, so I told her Sunday, after you get done with the settings-apart. Is that okay?"

"Sure, Dan. Thanks."

"How's she doin', anyway?" inquired Sam. "Think there's any hope of them two gettin' back together?"

The bishop shook his head. "I'd sure like to see it happen, if—and only if—Jack can make enough progress with his problems that Melody can know she's safe with him. Jack's really trying, and I worry about how he'll take it if she can't bring herself to give him another chance. On the other hand, I won't blame her if she can't, either. She put up with an awful lot that no wife should have to put up with."

"She's gotta think about that little girl, too," Robert Patrenko put in. "A child shouldn't have to see her mother taking any kind of abuse."

"Well, there just can't be any hint of abuse, if they do try to get back together," the bishop declared. "I know for a fact that Melody's so skittish that she'd take Andi and never come near Jack again, if he so much as looked at her wrong. The man's going to have to walk on eggshells."

"If not on water," Sam added wryly. "It's hard to wipe that kinda thing out of a woman's memory."

The bishop nodded. "Brethren, let's remember to keep praying for them, both personally and in our bishopric meetings. Sometimes when situations drag on and on, it's too easy to forget how vital it is to keep doing that."

"So, Sister Conrad, what I hear you saying is that because the visiting teachers are allowed to wear pants when they go to visit, you feel that their spirituality is being compromised?"

Tina Conrad lifted her chin high. "Certainly it is! It's disgraceful. When those two young women came to my house the first time, I very nearly asked them to leave. And one of them actually wore blue jeans! I don't believe in women wearing trousers of any kind. The Bible is adamant about that, and I don't understand, if this is the true Church, why we countenance such behavior. You'll certainly never see me in men's clothing."

"Ah-hah. Well. Um, naturally you have the right to dress as you see fit, to be modest and appropriate. To be honest, I don't know what the official Relief Society policy is on dress standards for visiting teaching, or even if there is one. I'll have to look into that. Did you check with Sister Reams?"

"I did, and I couldn't believe she took it so lightly. She practically laughed at me! She said I ought to be grateful my teachers even come! I'm not accustomed to having my standards ridiculed by someone who, of all people in the ward, should be maintaining the dignity of womanhood and teaching the younger women how to dress and act appropriately when they represent the Lord. In fact, it's my feeling that Ida Lou Reams should be replaced in her position, immediately."

The bishop took a deep breath and leaned across his desk to establish eye contact with his visitor. "That," he stated softly but forcefully, "is not going to happen."

Tina Conrad sat up straight, pursed her lips, and narrowed her eyes. He was almost sure he felt a burning sensation just above his nose, where her gaze was drilling into his skull. He sat back in his chair, and was the first to break the stare.

"Ida Lou Reams is a fine woman, and a wonderful Relief Society president," he said. "I'm certain as I'm sitting here that she wouldn't ridicule your feeling on the subject of dress standards. I promise I will consult with her on this subject, and we will get back to you on it. And please, Sister, in the meantime, try to understand that while we may not be perfect in this ward, we are sincerely trying to do our best. If you have visiting teachers who make the effort to visit you and befriend you, please try to overlook their faults in favor of their good intentions! Once again, the example you set may be as important to them as any message they bring may be to you."

"Oh, I put them on notice. I don't think they'll come into my house in jeans or pants again. If they do, I'll simply refuse to see them. I can't countenance such blatant worldliness."

The bishop passed his hand wearily over his face. "Thank you for coming in, Sister Conrad," he said. "You've certainly— um—raised my consciousness on matters of propriety."

"That was my intent," she told him. "What you do about it is up to you—but I'll be watching."

Y

"Welcome, Scott," the bishop said to Dr. Scott Lanier as that gentleman shook hands and sank into the chair recently occupied by Tina Conrad. "How are things going for you?"

The bishop didn't think things were going all that well; Scott Lanier seemed to have aged and to have dropped a good twenty pounds in recent weeks. The doctor struggled to speak, and to keep tears at bay.

"I'm—um—excuse me." He cleared his throat and seemed to draw a deep breath. "I hate to say this, Bishop—but I'm leaving Marybeth."

"Scott, I'm so sorry to hear that. What brought you to this decision?"

"Things have become intolerable. I don't even know how to respond when she talks to me the way she does—so scornfully, with such contempt for all I believe in and hold dear. I—she—I don't even know who she is, anymore."

The bishop couldn't imagine what it would be like. He tried to imagine how he would feel if Trish changed like that, spoke to him with contempt. He failed.

"Is it just about the gospel and the Church that she speaks that way? Or is it personal, as well—about you?"

"Both." He hung his head. "I tried to take it patiently, for a long time. To pretend that our marriage was still sound, even though she'd lost her faith. But things went from bad to worse in a hurry, Bishop, and now she—she continually taunts me, insults my intellect, belittles my belief, and even—you know— ridicules my manhood. And you were right, when you warned me about that Winston fellow. She's taken up with him—spends all her time with him. She probably even brings him into our home, when I'm at the office. I've seen . . . signs."

"I'm so, so sorry," was all the bishop could bring himself to say. "I'd hoped that wasn't the case, but—"

"I know. For a long time, I hoped things would change, that she'd come to herself, but that hasn't happened. So I just wanted to tell you what I'm doing, so you won't be taken by surprise. I've got to leave—I can't stand to live there any longer. There's only so much a man can endure."

"I understand. Where will you live?"

He shrugged. "I've lined up a small apartment over on Bessemer Street. If my practice weren't here, I'd move somewhere far away. Maybe I'll do that, anyway, one day. It's hard to see patients, and to wonder if they know—if they've seen—I mean, this is a fairly small town, and a lot of people know who Marybeth is. And, apparently, she hasn't made any effort to be discreet about things."

"It doesn't seem fair that you should have to be the one to leave your home," the bishop said.

Doctor Lanier shrugged. "That doesn't matter. I built it for Marybeth, and she chose most of the furnishings. None of that matters to me, in my present situation. I'll just take my clothes and books and a few personal belongings. She can have the rest."

"How's your son taking all this?"

"He feels terrible. He's as baffled by the change in Marybeth as I am. But he's busy with his life and his young family. I think that helps."

"Do you have an attorney, Scott?"

Scott shook his head. "I haven't talked to anybody. Bishop, I don't care. She can take it all. It doesn't matter."

"I think you need to retain somebody good," the bishop advised. "Right now you're understandably depressed over this whole miserable situation, but I firmly believe that will pass, although you certainly might want to see a doctor in that regard, as well. Marybeth's tried to deprive you of your marriage and your happiness and dignity and even your faith—and now your home. She's apparently become ruthless. It's not in your best interest—or hers, for that matter—to allow her to continue in that path without any checks or balances at all."

Scott shrugged. "If she wants my coat, I'm willing to give her my cloak, also."

"That's great, if you're doing it out of love and kindness and obedience to the Savior. But I don't think the Lord would want you to act out of hopelessness and despair, and just throw up your hands and say, 'Whatever—destroy me. I'm not worth anything, anyway.'"

Scott frowned. "But that's how I honestly feel, Bishop. Like the rug's been pulled out from under me. What's left in life? What do I have to look forward to?"

"So much, though I know it's hard to see it now. You're a gifted doctor. A wonderful person. A faithful, obedient servant of the Lord and your fellow man. A dad and a grandfather. A solid citizen with absolutely nothing to be ashamed of. Marybeth's the one who should feel ashamed!"

"Then why doesn't it work that way? She's flaunting herself, and I can hardly hold my head up and meet anyone's eyes."

"That's how she wants you to feel, but you don't have to go along with everything she wants, not financially, emotionally, or spiritually. Right now you're in the depths of this, but you can fight your way up to the surface with the help of the Lord and whatever professional help you may need, as well. Just keep breathing, my friend. Keep putting one foot in front of the other, and let the Lord carry your burdens for a while. He's fully capable of doing that and even eager to do it for you. Remember he bore our sorrows as well as our sins. Just turn those sorrows over to him, Scott. He invites us to lay our burdens at his feet."

Scott shook his head. "I don't think I know how to do that."

The bishop stood up. "Come on, Brother—let's kneel together."

When he arrived home later that evening, the bishop stood outside on his patio for a few minutes, breathing the fragrance of Trish's flowers and looking at his family gathered in the lamplit room beyond the long windows. Trish was doing something with a pair of scissors, Tiffani and Jamie were playing a board game, and Mallory sat near Trish's feet, moving two Barbie dolls through a drama of her own making. His heart swelled with love for each of them and with gratitude to his Heavenly Father for allowing him to share their lives. He sighed with compassion for all who were without such blessings—for Scott Lanier, whose wife had unaccountably changed so drastically, and for Muzzie Winston, whose husband had left her and their three children to gravitate to Marybeth's new persona. He thought of Buddy Osborne, a fine son by any standards, neglected or ignored by both his selfish parents. He felt for the Padgetts, once newly in love but now deprived of each other's company by Jack's unbridled temper and need to control his wife and daughter. Then he thought of the joyful reunion of the Bainbridge family that must have occurred when Ross and Carolyn came to "take home" their precious wife and mother. Now, that—that was how it should be, he thought—a happy reunion in the end, no matter what earthly sorrows had intervened for a while.

"Let it be that way for us, dear Lord," he whispered. "Please help our family so live that we can be sealed by the Holy Spirit of Promise and be together someday in the heavenly worlds."

Y

It was something he had meant to do for some time, but had put off for fear of making things worse. Wednesday evening was his time for home teaching and for visiting ward members, and Twyla Osborne was, technically at least, a ward member. He took Sam Wright with him, because Sam had known Twyla since she was a little girl and might possibly have some leverage with her. They drove to the mobile home park where Twyla lived with Buddy and her boyfriend, Jeter, and after a brief prayer for guidance, approached the door. Jeter's little sporty red car was not there, for which the bishop sent up another prayer of thanks. It was a muggy, warm evening and the place was closed up, the air conditioner running.

"Buddy ain't here," Twyla said when she opened the door to emit a blast of chilled air. The bishop knew that; he had made certain that Buddy was with the Young Men of the ward, doing a service activity.

"That's fine, Twyla, it's you I'd like to talk to, this evening. You know Brother Sam Wright, I believe."

"Hey there, young lady," Sam said in a friendly tone. "How you been? It's been a while sinc't I seen you. How's your mama?"

As if propelled backward by Sam's friendly barrage, Twyla backed up and held the door for them.

"Mama's doin' okay," she replied. "Got arthritis pretty bad, but otherwise she's all right. Now, what do y'all want with me? It ain't like I go to church no more."

"We actually came to talk with you about Buddy," the bishop said.

"Mm. Y'all go ahead and sit down. Good of you to give him summer work at your store, Mr. Shepherd," she added reluctantly.

"Oh, Buddy's a good worker. In fact, he's a great kid, all around."

"He sure is," put in Sam. "Responsible, talented, teachable, polite—you done a real good job with him, Twyla."

"Well, it ain't easy, bein' a single mom," she said defensively, as if they had criticized her mothering. She reached for a cigarette and her lighter.

"Wouldn't be easy, all right," the bishop agreed. "Y'all doing all right financially? Is there anything we can do to help?"

She gave him a look that was half suspicion and half anger.

"I know you don't come to church these days," he explained, "but you're still a member of the ward, and we like to look after our folks."

"Huh! Then where was you when me and Gerald first broke up and I was stuck with a sickly little baby and couldn't hold a job? Just where was all the lookin' after folks, then?"

"I don't know. I'm sorry if the Church failed you then—I wasn't in leadership and didn't know anything about it. But I'm bishop now, and Sam here's one of my counselors, and if there's anything we can do to help you, we'd be glad to try."

"I don't need nothin' from nobody. I bought me this place on my own, and it's almost paid for, and so's my car, though it ain't new. I keep food on the table and clothes on our backs, and I dare anyone to say otherwise—especially his no-good daddy!"

"No one says otherwise, Twyla. We haven't talked to Gerald, and certainly Buddy doesn't complain about anything."

"Then how come you're here, wantin' to talk about Buddy?"

"Well, he's such a good, responsible kid. Sometimes when you're out of town, and it's not convenient for him to stay with Gerald, he comes to our place for a night or two, and we sure enjoy having him there. My little boy really looks up to him, and

Buddy's good to play with him, almost like they were the same age. But it's a little awkward for Buddy."

Twyla pointed a finger at him. "Mr. Shepherd, I don't never go out of town 'ceptin' when it's Gerald's weekend to have Buddy!"

"I understand. But there've been times when Gerald's had company staying over, or he hasn't been feeling well, and Buddy gets kind of caught in the middle, if you know what I mean . . ."

"Oh, I know exactly what you mean—when Gerald's got a woman there, or he's fallin' down drunk! That lousy, shiftless, no-good excuse for . . . Buddy hatn't never told me about that!"

The bishop shrugged. "Well, he wouldn't, would he? He never wants to cause anybody any trouble—not you, nor Gerald either. But we were thinking that maybe now he's mature enough to have his own house key to your place here. I mean, it's not like he's the type to mess things up or call in a bunch of friends to party or something like that."

"That's right," Sam added. "He'd prob'ly do no more mischief than watching a little TV and making himself a snack. He's just a good boy. What do you think, Twyla?"

"I'll tell you what I think. If Buddy has a key to this place, then Gerald has a key to this place, and I'm not havin' that! I wouldn't put it beyond him to come over here scroungin' after money or anything he could sell to get money for his beer and whatever else he does."

"Do you really think Gerald would take advantage of you, that way?" the bishop asked.

She shrugged one thin shoulder and blew smoke high into the air. "He did when we was married," she replied. "I couldn't keep a dime for groceries or diapers, let alone anything else to try to make a home. He drank up or gambled away ever' last penny I earned, him and his fine old poker friends."

"Hmm," said Sam Wright, gazing in perplexity at the carpet. "Tell you what, Twyla. What if someone else—a responsible third party, you might say—kept the key for Buddy, and he had strict instructions to pick it up from them as needed and return it right away? Maybe a neighbor you trust around here, or—"

"He could leave it at my place, for that matter," the bishop offered. "We could have a special place for it, and give it to him whenever you're gone—and Gerald will never know."

Twyla frowned, and crushed her cigarette in a metal tray. "I don't know," she said. "I'll think on it. I didn't know about Buddy campin' on you folks, puttin' you out like that. But I've gotta be real careful, or I'll lose ever'thing I've worked for. I mean, I don't even give Jeter a key, and I don't put one under the welcome mat, neither."

"That's all we ask," Sam said gently. "Just think about it."

"And please, please know that whenever Buddy shows up, he isn't putting us out in the least. We love him like a son," the bishop added. "But he's kind of embarrassed about it, so we thought we'd just speak to you privately, without his knowing."

"He don't know nothin' about this? He didn't put you up to askin'?"

"Not at all. That's why we came when we knew he was busy."

"All right, then," Twyla said, standing abruptly. "You've said your piece, and I'll think on it."

They took their leave, and Sam Wright heaved a deep sigh.

"She used to be such a pretty little brown-haired girl, shy and sweet. And her and her mama was at church ever' time the doors opened. I don't know what changed things for 'em, but sometime durin' Twyla's teenage years, they backed off and quit comin'. Wish't I knew why."

"Somebody must know more about it," said the bishop. "Maybe we can find out."

CHAPTER THIRTEEN

" . . . SACRED AS YOUR OWN
GOOD NAME"

Trish was addressing envelopes to several of their neighbors in an effort to aid the Cancer Drive. She paused, pen in hand, gazing at the list she had been provided.

"I don't know whether I dare send one of these to the Lowells, Jim," she said, her forehead wrinkling. "I mean, the deal is that people return their donation envelopes to me, and I compile it all and send it off to the charity. Maxine would probably think I'd abscond with the funds! But if I don't send her one, and she somehow discovers she was left out, she'll probably write headquarters and lodge a complaint against me. What'll I do?"

The bishop considered the problem, but at the same time he was enjoying the sight of his beloved wife—cheeks rosy and dark hair shining. Of late, one or two lighter hairs had appeared along her temples. "I'll think of them as highlights," she had said, frowning into the bathroom mirror. "When did they come, anyway? They sneaked up on me."

"They do that," he had agreed, aware that his own scalp was

sprouting more ash than ash blond in recent months. Now he addressed himself to the present problem.

"I seem to remember it was our decision to be as friendly and normal as circumstances will allow, so that Mrs. Lowell has as little as possible to use as ammo against us. So I'd say send her one, same as everybody."

"But I'm supposed to write a little personal note at the bottom. What can I possibly say?"

"What've you put on the others?"

"Just something like, 'Thanks so much for any help you can give this good cause.'"

"What's wrong with that for Lowells?"

"Nothing, I s'pose. But I'm sure she'll find something!"

He shrugged. "Seems to me the worst she can do is say no. And who knows, maybe she'll even donate a buck or two. At least you're offering her the chance to help."

Trish made an uncertain face. "Okay. But I'm spending a stamp to send it next door. I'm not going over there."

He grinned. "Fine with me. She'll probably do the same if she replies."

"I can hope." She continued writing and sealing her notes.

"Hey, babe?" he asked after a moment of silence.

"M-hmm?"

"Do you wear slacks when you go visiting teaching?"

She regarded him steadily. "Tina Conrad, again?"

He nodded.

"Well, the answer is usually yes. Most of the sisters I know, do—although some of the older ladies like Ida Lou, or Nita Mobley, stick to dresses. I think it's just a generational preference, though, not a matter of manners and morals."

"Okay. Thanks."

"She's really giving you a hard time, isn't she?"

He sighed. "You have no idea."

Y

"How's Chuck working out, Art?" the proprietor of Shepherd's Quality Food Mart asked quietly of his produce man, Arthur Hackney.

"Oh, fine, Jim—but did we really need somebody to cover for us during vacations? We've always just covered for each other before, and I thought it worked out okay."

"Well, to tell you the truth, it's more like a favor to an old schoolmate. He's fallen on hard times right now and needed something right away, so I figured the budget could stretch to cover one more very basic wage for a while. Appreciate your not mentioning I told you that—to him or any of the others, though."

"Sure, I hear you. Besides, it's kinda fun to watch Mary Lynn these days, idn' it?"

"Mary Lynn? Why? What's she doing?"

"Oh, my gosh, man—hatn't you seen the sparkin' that's goin' on?"

Jim shook his head slowly. "You mean Mary Lynn and—Chuck?"

"The same! Them two's headed for romance, if not the altar, sure as shootin'!"

They were? Where had he been?

"How do you know, Art? I mean, what've you seen?"

"Oh, just how she blushes whenever he says hey, and how they've taken to eatin' lunch together, and how he looks for her first thing ever' day when he comes in. You watch, you'll see."

He did watch, and he did see. Mary Lynn suddenly seemed to have several new blouses in bright summery colors, and to his amazement, she came in on Friday with her long mane of brown hair pulled back into a thick braid, tied with a pink ribbon to match her shirt. In her ears, which he was sure he'd never glimpsed before, were tiny pink butterfly earrings. The transformation was astonishing.

"Good morning, Mary Lynn," he said. "You look especially nice, today."

Her head ducked in its customary manner, but there was no loose, flowing curtain of hair to hide the bloom on her cheeks.

"Thanks," she all but whispered, as she settled at her desk and began flipping through a stack of invoices.

"I like your hair like that," he went on. "It's very becoming. It looks cooler, too, for such hot weather. I can't believe it's almost July."

"Me neither," she replied. "June just flew by."

"I'm told time flies when you're having fun. Or as Tiffani puts it, when you *think* you're having fun!"

"Reckon if you think you're havin' fun, you must be." She flicked a glance up at him. "Mr. Jim Shepherd, what're you grinnin' about? Cain't a girl change her hairstyle once in a while, if it makes her happy?"

"Miss Mary Lynn Connors, I approve of whatever—or whoever—is making you happy." He sat down and swivelled his old leather office chair around to face her. "It's whoever, isn't it? It's Chuck, right?"

She tried to keep from smiling, and couldn't. "Jim, don't tease me! I ain't never had a boyfriend before. I don't hardly know how to act. All these years, I been scornin' any man that looked twice at me—not that so many did—on account of I could see right through 'em. And now this'un comes along and he's so nice, such a gentleman, but still fun to be with—I don't hardly know how to credit it."

"Wow! That's exciting. And as far as I know, Chuck's the real thing. I mean, I haven't been around him for a long time, but he was always a good kid, back in school. Kinda shy, only had the one girlfriend, that I recall. I don't know what happened there, but apparently he's never married."

"Her name was Beverly. She died," Mary Lynn said softly. "She had sugar diabetes real bad, and one time she went into a coma and never woke up. Chuck said he didn't have the heart to date anybody else for a long, long time. Then he just got out of the habit and was workin' hard to keep his mom in a rest home close to him, down in Dothan. He paid all her costs, bein' the only child and all. He didn't want to sell her house, 'cause she kept hopin' she could come back to it. But she never did."

"And now he's back, and trying to fix it up. I guess he's quite a handyman."

"I seen what he's doin' with the back porch, and it looks real good. It was plumb fallin' down. And he's scrubbed the place clean as a new-bathed baby! I don't reckon any woman could get it cleaner. I know he ain't got much right now, but I do feel the man's got potential."

"I see that in him, too. Well—good luck, my esteemed office assistant! I hope everything works out for the best, for both of you."

"He ast me to go to church with him, come Sunday," she said shyly.

"Really! You mean—to my church?"

"Uh-huh. It's okay, ain't it?"

"Oh, well, it's more than okay. It's great! That'll be wonderful."

"I wadn't sure. I mean, it wadn't like you'd ever invited me."

He stood there openmouthed, convicted in his heart of that sad truth.

"You are so right," he said slowly, "and I am so, so sorry!"

She shrugged. "It's okay. I mean, you've talked to me about it, and explained things when I ast you, but I always wondered why you didn't just say, 'Come and worship with us sometime, Mary Lynn.' 'Cause I would've done."

He nodded. "I have no idea why I never invited you. I reckon I just thought you enjoyed going up home every weekend and going to church there with your family."

"Sure—and that's what I've done, for years—it's all I know. And Pastor McCracken's a sweet old man. But lately—I don't know if this makes any sense at all—lately, I've been yearnin' for somethin' with a little more to it, if you know what I mean."

"I believe I do. And I truly hope you find what you're looking for with us."

"Well, thank you, Jim. So do I."

Y

In the sullen heat of early evening, Bishop Shepherd was mowing his back lawn, grateful to Trish for having planted the entire front yard with perennials and wildflowers, creating a riot of color behind the ornamental wrought-iron fence and leaving him free of having to mow that area. In the yard to the west of theirs, he saw Hestelle Pierce tiptoeing toward him, waving a piece of paper in one hand and beckoning to him with the other. He cut the motor and went to meet her.

"Mr. Shepherd," she said in a stage whisper, peering beyond him to be sure she wasn't spotted, "I don't want Miz Lowell to know I'm givin' you this, but I do feel y'all deserve to know what-all she's spreadin' around about you."

"Well, thanks, Miz Hestelle, for not believing everything you hear or read about us and our church. We appreciate that, and you're a fine neighbor."

"Oh, I take up for y'all all the time over to Gadsden Street Baptist. Ever' now and then, somebody'll say how y'all ain't Christians, and I tell 'em to look inside their own hearts before they start in on judgin' others, because my neighbors is Mormon, and the finest Christian folks I know."

"We're not anywhere near perfect, but we do try to be good Christians," he said.

"Well, sometimes folks start in to tell me all their reasons why you ain't, but I always say Christian is as Christian does, and that's good enough for me. Now, don't y'all take this too much to heart, all right?" She indicated the paper. "Just consider the source, is what I think."

She waved and made her way back to her house. The bishop wiped his sweaty face on the sleeve of his tee shirt and headed for the shade of the patio, where he perched on the end of a chaise lounge and examined the circular prepared by Maxine Lowell.

"Dear Neighbor," it read, "Time and time again we have warned you about the menace in our midst. In spite of our best efforts, however, people in our community are still being duped and tricked by the phony, fake imitation of Christianity that uses friendly faces and smooth words to lure away members of the real body of Christ into a deceitful mockery of the truth. We speak, of course, of the Mormons. There are some of these deceivers right here in our own neighborhood! They appear to be good family people, good citizens, and they even use some of the language of Christianity to appear to be one of us, but they are not to be trusted, and we must not offer them the hand of Christian fellowship!

"They send out nice-looking young wolves in sheep's cloth-ing (good wool suits) from Salt Lake City, Utah, to try to steal our lambs away to their horrific temple ceremonies, where they themselves speak of 'binding' and 'sealing'—words that ought to alert us to the real purpose of this cult—to bind innocent people to Satan, the father of lies and deceit! Do not be deceived! Keep your children from association with them. Cut off their access to your minds and hearts. Do not attempt to argue or discuss with them, as they are trained in techniques to trip you up. Let's all remain safe from their grasp!"

It was signed, "A concerned neighbor."

The bishop scooted back so that he was reclining on the chaise, closed his eyes and offered a silent prayer.

"You okay, Jim? It's so hot out here, I brought you a drink to restore your electrolytes, or whatever. What's this?"

Trish lifted the paper from his chest and handed him a chilled sports drink. "Oh! Did Miss Hestelle give you this? It's one of Maxine Lowell's little efforts, isn't it?"

She sat down on a nearby chair and read through it, frowning. He watched for her reaction.

"Ugh, that's sickening," she said. "I wonder how many of these she hands out? And how many people read them and take them seriously?"

"You know, I just feel our neighbors have more sense than to do that, don't you?"

Trish raised her eyebrows. "Not necessarily. I haven't said anything, because I didn't want to worry you with what might be nothing, but I have noticed things lately that make me think she's getting through to some people. People I like, too."

"Who, and what?" he asked.

"Well, for example, when Pam Michaelson brought over her cancer fund donation, she just handed it to me and said, 'Here you go,' with never a smile or a 'how're you doing' or anything. That's not like Pam. We've been friendly. Worked together in PTA last year. And then, the last few times Mallory's asked to play with Joanie Carter, Mrs. Carter's had some reason every time as to why Joanie couldn't play right then. One time Mallory saw Joanie right after I called, playing with the little Sumsion kids, and said, 'I thought your Mom said you couldn't play.' And Joanie said, 'I just couldn't play with *you*.' Mal came home crying."

"Maybe—just maybe—it isn't this at all. Maybe Pam Michaelson was tired or out of sorts. Maybe Mrs. Carter objects to the way Joanie and Mallory get along together, or something."

Trish gave him a small, tired smile. "The kids are right. You do cut everybody way too much slack. But then—it's one of the things I love about you. What can we do, Jim? It isn't fair that Maxine Lowell can just waltz in here and destroy our reputation and affect friendships we've had for years!"

"No, it certainly is not fair. But I still think the best defense is a good offense, and that we need to continue to be ourselves, and to be as friendly to our neighbors as we've always been. I mean, this house was my grandfather's, and then my dad's, and now it's mine, and I'm not about to be driven out by the likes— and the lies—of Mrs. Lowell."

"That's really what she's after, don't you think? To run us out of the neighborhood—and preferably, out of town?"

"I expect so."

"And how can I act like I haven't even noticed Mrs. Carter snubbing Mal, or Pam being cool to me? I'd look like a clueless idiot!"

"Well, I reckon if it comes to really obvious snubbing, we could go to the person and ask if we've offended them in some way, and apologize if we have. Just—you know—to see how they react."

"I hate this, Jim. We've always been so happy here. I mean, we've got Catholics on this street, and Baptists, and Methodists, and the Briersons are Jehovah's Witnesses. And we've always all gotten along just fine!"

"Yep, but now we've got a rabble-rouser, who's determined to be a spoiler. We've got to find a way to out-think her, to beat her at her own game."

They were silent for a few minutes.

"Maybe I have an idea," the bishop said. "I don't know if it could help, but what if we gave a neighborhood barbecue on the Fourth of July?"

"Hmph. And what if nobody came? Wouldn't that be a triumph, next door!"

"Well, what if we invited a mixture of people—neighbors, ward members, other friends—surely somebody would come. Hey—what if we invited the MacDonalds? Mac's becoming known as the new preacher in town, and he's really friendly to everybody."

Trish sighed. "I don't know, Jim. It sounds exhausting to put on a big party right now, with me pregnant. I don't know that I'm up to it."

"No, no—you're not to do any cooking at all. I'll bring meat from the store and salads from the deli. And I'll man the grill. All you need to do is supervise Tiffani's putting together the ice cream recipe, and Jamie can tend the freezers. The kids and I can set everything up out here, and all you'll need to do is mingle with the guests, fanning your blushing face and charming the socks off everybody."

"Right. Just call me Miss Scarlet."

"Invite Muzzie to come. She'll help you with anything, you know that."

Trish pondered. "We still have all that patriotic bunting we used at the ward party that time. There's tons of it. We could put that up along the front porch, and the patio—and would we dare—along that monstrosity of a fence?"

"Sure, why not? It's light stuff, right? Can't we just fasten it with thumbtacks?"

"Right. But Jim—what if she kicks up a fuss again, about people parking on the street, or something?"

"Then she'll just have to kick. If she makes herself look outrageous enough, maybe people will take a second look at her and wonder about her motivation."

"If we invite people from the neighborhood and from the ward, won't they just naturally separate into two groups—that is, if they come at all?"

"They will, but we can think up some kind of mixer, can't we? Some game or something to make them talk to each other?"

They could and did. They decided to put a sticker on each guest's back with the name of an important American, past or present, and have everyone mingle and ask different people "yes or no" questions about their assigned person, with the exception of questions such as, "Am I Abraham Lincoln?" After a while, they would all take turns telling their real name, as well as whose name they thought was on their back and why.

"Well," Trish said at last, "I s'pose Maxine Lowell isn't the only one who can make up flyers to hand out to the neighbors. If we're going to do this, we'd better get the invitations out tonight. Come help me," she instructed and headed for the computer.

"We're not inviting those people, are we?" demanded Jamie, nodding toward the east.

"It's all done," his dad informed him. "I already took an invitation over and handed it to Marguerite. She seemed thrilled."

"They won't come. You know that," Tiffani declared.

"Probably not," the bishop agreed. "But they can't complain they weren't included."

"I'm locking Samantha in my room for the whole time," Mallory announced.

"She'll hate that," said Trish. "You know how she loves to be in the middle of everything and greet people. But—maybe it's best."

"Well, not everybody likes cats," their father said. "Even when they're smart and beautiful like Samantha," he added, holding up both hands to ward off Mallory's protest. "And we do want her to be safe. Now you kids get the rest of these flyers delivered, and Mom and I will call and invite the others."

The bishop was as good as his word. He groomed the yard, set up tables and the barbecue, and tacked up the loops of bunting around the house and fence—just below the top of the fence, so that the Lowells wouldn't see it unless they came to the party. He put up small white twinkling lights in the trees, placed the two ice-cream freezers on the patio, and brought home plenty of ice, soda, burgers, chicken breasts, and salads from the deli.

"Mom—what if none of the neighbors come?" worried Tiffani, as the hour approached for the barbecue to begin.

"Then we'll just enjoy ourselves with our friends from the ward and elsewhere."

"I don't get exactly why we're doing this," Tiffani pursued. "It's not like coming to a party is going to make people think we're real Christians, if they don't already."

"I know," her mother said. "It's just an effort to reach out to our neighbors and to show them we're the same people we've always been, and not what Mrs. Lowell says we are. I know the

Briersons aren't coming, because Mrs. Brierson called and explained that they don't believe in celebrating holidays."

"Why not?"

"They feel like it's putting other concerns above God."

"Oh. What about the Michaelsons?"

"I haven't heard, one way or the other. I know Hestelle will come, of course, and I'm pretty sure the Rogers will, and the Oppenheimers said they would. I rather doubt the Carters will, and I know the Sumsions are out of town. We'll just have to see about the others."

"And who's coming from the ward?"

"Let's see. We've got the Patrenkos and the Wrights and the McDaniels, and Brother Lanier, and Melody and Andi, and the Smedleys, the Rexfords and the Warshaws. And other folks, including the MacDonalds, and Muzzie and her kids, and Art and Carol Hackney, and Mary Lynn and Dad's friend from school who's investigating the Church. I also invited Donna and Raegene and Ralph Morrison from the store, and the Reams and the Winslows from church, but they all had other plans."

"Billy's coming," Tiffani added, with a small, satisfied smile. "He was s'posed to go to his grandma's, but he got out of it."

"Well, nice for you! I think we'll have a fun evening, with whoever shows up."

"Good thing we've got a big backyard."

"Yes, and people can spill over to the inside, if they prefer. Thanks for helping me clean, Tiff. And for making the ice cream."

"Oh, that's okay. I didn't want you to be too tired to enjoy the party."

Miracle of miracles, Trish wasn't too tired, but the bishop nearly was. However, as people began to arrive, and as he fired up the grill and turned on the patriotic music they had chosen, his spirits revived. The mixer game brought a lot of interaction and much laughter, and he was pleased to see the Michaelsons and Rogers talking with the Patrenkos and the Warshaws. Mary Lynn and Chuck sat close together in a corner of the yard, under the shade of a mimosa tree, and seemed to have no end of things to talk about. Hestelle found that she and Sister Wright were from the same hometown, and the two chatted happily about people they both knew there.

The MacDonalds, social beings that they were, made themselves acquainted with everyone present, and their children mingled happily with the Shepherd children and their friends, although the bishop thought he saw young Petey MacDonald looking Billy Newton over with a critical eye. Petey, he suspected, still had a bit of a crush on Tiffani, as she had once had on him. The bishop sighed. It was, it seemed, too often the sad lot of youth to suffer unrequited love. He also saw, however, that Petey hung on every word spoken by the school hero, Thomas (T-Rex) Rexford.

It was interesting, he thought, and perhaps natural, that Muzzie and Melody would drift together, each being alone due to the misbehavior of errant husbands. Scott Lanier seemed lost until the Warshaws reached out and engaged him in conversation with their group, retelling the story of how they came to be Americans. That was good, the bishop reflected. He hoped they would tell their story over and over, to everyone they met this evening. It was an inspiring one. He also hoped that Scott and Muzzie wouldn't meet and compare notes. He didn't think that either of them knew that Muzzie's ex-husband was presently keeping company with Scott's wife.

The Lowells, of course, didn't attend—but the bishop did happen to see, at one point, Marguerite's curious face appear over the top of the high fence, and smiled at her. He also heard her mother's furious summons, and Marguerite hastily disappeared.

Just at sunset, several boys in the yard adjacent to the Shepherds on the south set off some bottle rockets and other fireworks, and the bishop, who had not allowed his children to have so much as a sparkler in order to avoid trouble with the Lowells, winced. And indeed he should have, for it was only a matter of minutes until a uniformed officer appeared, asking for the host of the party. The bishop tried to steer him around the corner of the house, to avoid upsetting Trish or his guests, but Big Mac spotted the policeman and came forward to see what he could do to help.

"We've had a complaint about excessive noise and fireworks and parking violations here, sir," explained the officer. "Right now I don't hear any unnecessary noise from your party, and everyone seems to have parked just fine—no driveways are blocked—but what about fireworks? You do know about our new city ordinance against the private use of fireworks, don't you? Every year they cause injury and fires, and they've been declared illegal."

"I'm aware of the ordinance, and we have no fireworks at our party, officer. Not even a sparkler."

"And could that be because you already used them all up?"

"No, sir. We have not used any at all, nor do we intend to."

The Reverend Peter MacDonald spoke up. "There were some bottle rockets and such set off in a neighboring yard," he said. "Maybe whoever reported them mistook this yard for the offending one because of the barbecue going on."

"So which yard did they come from?"

"From somewhere back there, to the south," Mac reported.

Just at that point, the unsuspecting boys set off another round of firecrackers, shouting with glee at the noise.

The police officer raised his eyebrows, then nodded to the bishop and his friend. "You folks have a good time," he said to them. "Sorry to bother you. Happy Fourth."

"You, too, officer," the bishop responded.

"So who reported you for all these supposed offences?" asked Mac, grinning. "I thought all your good neighbors were here at the party."

The bishop grinned back. "All the good ones are," he replied, and then motioned toward the high fence on the east. "The lady on this side is of the same opinion as those who wrote the letter you brought me. In fact, she produces flyers of the same persuasion every week or so and distributes them around the neighborhood."

"Wow. So she'll be disappointed if you're not tossed in jail."

"She's disappointed that we haven't packed up and moved out yet, in spite of her best efforts. I don't know, Mac—we're running out of cheeks to turn."

"I hear you, brother. Well, I guess, 'Pray for them that despitefully use you and persecute you.'"

"That's about all we can do," the bishop agreed.

CHAPTER FOURTEEN

" . . . IN A NOBLE CAUSE CONTENDING"

Before the party broke up so that all who so desired could go to watch the fireworks that were being professionally set off (by the fire department) at the Fairhaven City Park, the Reverend Peter MacDonald stepped forward and held up both hands for people to settle down and give him their attention.

"Uh-oh, here comes the preacher's voice," warned his son Petey, sotto voce, causing the young people around him to giggle. The bishop, standing nearby, smiled as well. He too knew that deep and commanding voice.

"Friends, isn't it a great thing to be an American?" boomed Mac. There was a smattering of applause. "Isn't it wonderful to live in a country where we have the right to peaceably assemble? To gather for occasions like this in peace and fellowship and good will? To gather for other peaceful purposes with no one putting us in prison for suspected treason? Isn't it wonderful to be an American, free to worship how, where, and when we please, unmolested?"

It seemed to the bishop that Mac's voice was deeper and louder than he had ever heard it, and he noticed that it was directed eastward.

"Isn't it a blessing from God that we have freedom of speech and can speak our minds? That we can vote and elect our own representatives? That we can travel from one part of the country to another without governmental permission? That we can live peaceably with our neighbors, be they of whatever race, religion, or ethnic background? I, for one, am grateful for these great blessings, and—"

Hestelle Pierce's gasp alerted the bishop to the presence of Maxine Lowell, who had stepped around the corner of her fence and made her way into the backyard, her arms stiff by her sides, her whole being bristling with indignation.

"I, for one," she said loudly, "resent having to listen to all your fine Mormon speechifying and your music and your loud talking and the fireworks you no doubt provoked those boys into setting off, which is against the law of this country you're so proud of! I, for one—"

"What Mormon speechifying would that be, Madam?" inquired Mac, his voice as deep as ever.

"You!" she screeched. "You're the one. I don't want to have to hear your false notions and your ranting and raving about America. You have no business even living in this country! All Mormons should be deported, and leave this country to those who worship the true God!"

"Madam, you are mistaken. I happen to be the Reverend Peter MacDonald, pastor of the Fairhaven Friendship Christian Church," Mac boomed. "And who might you be?"

"I—you lie! You're a Mormon, or a Mormon-lover—all of you! You're deceived, you're entrapped by the lies of these people. I know you're having this party just to get back at me, but I'm not backing down. I'm going to continue fighting for Jesus. But none of you should even boast about being Americans, because you have no right to call yourselves that! America's a Christian nation."

Bob Patrenko stood. "Ma'am, I fought in Vietnam, and my father died in World War Two. I am a Mormon, and I believe I also have a right to call myself an American, which I'm proud to do."

Brother Warshaw stepped forward. "And I can tell you that my wife and I have come to this country from Germany and Poland, where they killed our families because we were Jews. I have studied the history of this country, I have been tested on it, and I have made oaths to uphold and defend the Constitution and to be a good citizen. I believe I know what it means to be an American! I also happen to have learned to love and worship the Lord Jesus Christ, as a so-called Mormon."

Jackie Rogers was right behind him. "Well, I'm not a Mormon. I'm an active Methodist, but I'm insulted on behalf of these folks, who've always been the finest kind of neighbors and very active, involved citizens of this town and this country. I might not agree with all that they believe, but I do believe they worship the Lord Jesus according to their own lights, and I know they're good Americans and not deserving of the kind of abuse you've been heaping on them with your mean-spirited little letters. Don't bring any more of those to my house!"

"Yeah," chimed in Mick Michaelson. "Maybe we ought to ask what kind of American *you* are, since you apparently don't support freedom of religion for some groups!"

"Hear, hear!" several people called out.

Maxine Lowell looked confused but still furious. She sought out the bishop. "You did this to me, to humiliate me," she accused. "You invited all these people here to trick me!"

"We invited you, too," the bishop said mildly. "We invited the whole street, plus other friends, just to celebrate the Fourth of July. Since you're here, why don't you come on and have some food and get acquainted with these folks? Maybe you'd like them if you got to know them."

"Never!" Maxine cried, and turned on her heel to march back to her own house.

Mac spoke up again. "Isn't freedom of speech wonderful?" he boomed, with a twinkle in his eye. "And freedom to assemble? And isn't it great of Jim Shepherd and his family to throw this delightful party for all of us? I say he's a jolly good fellow!"

"My dad's unbelievably corny," Petey said, covering his eyes, and Tiffani answered sympathetically, "I know. So's mine."

The bishop chuckled. It was apparently requisite for teenagers to be embarrassed by their parents.

Mac began singing the "jolly good fellow" song, and the whole group chimed in, clapping at the end. The bishop stole a glance at his wife, who still sat staring at the space vacated by Maxine Lowell. Finally, she shook herself and rose to smile and bid their guests goodbye and thank them for coming.

"Who *is* that woman?" Billy Newton asked Tiffani, as the group of young people headed out to watch the fireworks.

"That's Mrs. Lowell, our Mormon-hating neighbor," Tiff replied. "Dad calls her our 'thorn in the flesh.'"

The Patrenkos and Wrights stayed behind to help the Shepherds clear up and put away the tables and chairs.

"That ice cream was yummy," Sally Patrenko commented. "I don't think I've ever tasted blueberry ice cream before. And the fresh strawberry was great, too."

"Just an effort to be patriotic with our colors," Trish

answered with a smile. "Thanks so much for coming, folks, and for helping out."

"Honey, it's our pleasure," Mamie Wright told her. "Don't know when I've had more fun at a party. Even your neighbor was entertaining!"

"Can you imagine behaving like that—calling the police, then coming over here spouting off like she did?" asked Sally. "Is she all right, Trish—mentally, I mean? She was practically foaming!"

Trish shrugged. "She seems obsessed with ridding the neighborhood of Mormons—and since we're the only ones on this street, we get to be the targets of her wrath. It's a challenge, I can tell you that. This is the second time she's called the police on us. The first time was when I hosted the visiting teachers last year. She complained about the parking then, too, although like tonight, nobody was blocking anything. Then she stole Mallory's cat and took it to the animal shelter."

"And she calls herself a Christian?" asked Mamie.

Trish sighed. "Sometimes I get the feeling she thinks she's the only Christian around. Sorry, I shouldn't say that—it sounds mean. But it wears on you, after a while! I think she's just ignorant of the truth and unwilling to listen. I'm sure she feels justified in her attacks. She thinks she's defending the Savior."

"Well, I'm sure sorry you folks are having to go through that," Mamie said, patting Trish's shoulder. "Y'all don't deserve it."

"Thanks, Mamie. But maybe we need it. You know—for growth, and patience, and all that."

Mamie laughed. "Whoo-ee! Sure hope I'm patient enough that I don't get stuck with a neighbor like that!"

ϒ

"So, what do you say—was it a success?" the bishop asked, as he stretched out beside Trish in their cool, dimly lit bedroom later that night, after all the booms and blasts had quieted.

"I think so, for the most part. I was mortified when Maxine Lowell showed up, but I thought Mac handled her superbly, and I was amazed when Bob and John—and even Jackie Rogers and Mick Michaelson—stood up to her like that. Good for them!"

The bishop smiled. "I think Mac knew she was listening and was trying to flush her out," he said with a chuckle.

"Well, it worked."

"Only thing is, I'm sure nothing that happened did anything to make her feel any better about us."

"As far as we know. She just might have been impressed that we're friends with Mac."

"I don't know—she called him a liar, and told him he was deceived."

"Of course," Trish mused, "at that point, she had to stand her ground. But after she thinks about it, maybe it'll help just a little. Or not."

"At least she knows we have friends who'll stand up for us, and for the Church."

"True. And thanks, Jimmy, for all you did to make the party happen. Sorry I couldn't do more, this time."

"Oh, I'm real good at bringing home salads and flipping burgers," he said. "And you're very welcome."

"Jim?" Trish asked sleepily, after a few minutes. "Do you think there are very many people who see us the way Mrs. Lowell does?"

"Ask me that tomorrow," her husband replied. "I'll have a better answer, then."

"Look, Jim, what we got in the mail," Trish greeted the next day when he ran in for a bite of lunch—leftover salads and grilled chicken. "It's priceless."

He accepted the envelope and took out the contents. In a scrawl that could only belong to Junior Rhys, the letter read, "Dear cuzins, I am so proud of all the prezents you sent me and I sure can use the pujamys and thank you for the copys. I showd them to the nurse here I was so proud to get them and dear lady yer cookies are top-knotch, and thanks for them and all the goodys. I feel like a rich man I truly do. God bless and I hop to see you agin som day. Junior."

He looked up and smiled at his wife. "It *is* priceless," he agreed. "Junior is priceless."

The bishop was helping check on a busy Saturday morning when Ralph and Linda Jernigan came into the store, chose a few items, and got into his line. Ralph leaned over the counter to whisper, "See you outside for a minute, Bishop? Got some specifics."

"Sure thing," the bishop said, bagging their purchases and putting a 'closed' sign on his register. He carried the sack out to their car.

"If you want to get in the car, Bishop, I think it's clean," Ralph suggested, and the bishop knew he wasn't referring to the physical state of the car's tidiness. He slipped into the backseat and set the sack of groceries on the floor. Ralph started the car and turned up the air conditioning before twisting around in his seat the best he could.

"Got some specifics, like you requested," Ralph said, in a low voice, which the bishop leaned forward to hear. "Seems we've got some troublemakers coming from out of state, planning a rally against the Church out at the County Fairpark on the third of August, seven P.M. Not nice people, Bishop. Looked into their group, and they've done some mischief here and there—vandalism, mostly, although there've been a couple of suspicious church fires when they've been in an area."

"What do they call themselves?" the bishop asked.

"Seen two names," Ralph replied, keeping his voice low. "'Tri-State Christian Fellowship' and the 'A.M. Sunshine Task Force for Jesus.' Don't know what 'A.M.' stands for, but I'd guess 'Anti-Mormon.' Doubt it means morning."

The bishop nodded. "I expect you're right. I've heard of the first group. They've been sending letters around to local churches, announcing what they call a 'rally tour.' I reckon they're holding these meetings in several places, to try to disturb the missionary work and draw people away from the Church. But I'd never heard of the 'A.M.' bunch, and I hadn't known any specific time or place. Good work, Ralph—and Linda. Thank you both."

Ralph nodded curtly. "Forewarned is forearmed," he said.

"We don't like the sound of this, Bishop," Linda put in. "It seems well-organized and pretty vicious."

"It does, doesn't it?" He patted Ralph's shoulder. "I appreciate the heads-up. We'll work on it."

Trish was relaxing on the family room sofa Saturday night after the children had gone to bed, reading an article in the *Ensign* magazine. Her husband came and lifted her feet into his lap as he sat down, massaging them gently.

"Mm. Feels good. I promise they're clean—I already showered. So, Jimmy—when are you going to answer my question?"

"Which question would that be, babe?"

"You know—the one you hedged on the other night, when I asked if you thought a lot of people see us the way Maxine does."

"Ah. That one. Well, yes and no. Of course I have no way of knowing how many people share her views, but I do know she's not alone, and I think we're going to be seeing more and more of that attitude right away, here. In fact, there's a lot going on in that department right now."

Trish was not one to be put off. "Why do you say that?" she asked.

"There are letters being sent around to local churches that have the same nasty, accusatory tone, and the same twisting of doctrine."

"You don't mean Maxine's sending them!"

"I'm afraid this is much bigger than Maxine," he said reluctantly, and went on to tell her about the letter Mac had brought him—and then, of course, had to produce it and let her read it for herself, as her magazine slipped to the floor. He also told her about the Jernigans' sleuthing.

She frowned. "You know," she said, "I have no problem with people disagreeing with our beliefs. After all, I disagree with many of theirs. It's natural. What I cannot understand is this . . . this vicious negativity, and the personal nature of their attacks on our character, as if we were totally in league with the devil and out there deliberately trying to lead people to spiritual destruction! It's absurd, and it's wrong, and it's shameful."

He nodded. "All the above. But you know what? That kind of behavior actually says a whole lot more about them than it does about us."

"I hate that it even comes down to an 'us and them' mentality."

He sighed. "Me, too. As a church, we've always gotten along well with our neighbors here in Fairhaven. We've played in the Interfaith sports tournaments, we've helped with charitable functions, we've let the Seventh-day Adventists use our building when theirs was out of commission. Mrs. Simmons, who used to teach history at the high school—you remember her? For many years, she used to ask the missionaries to come and teach her class for a day when they were learning about the western trek and the pioneers—and she was Catholic! Nobody objected. And when the tornado hit out by Hanceville, folks were glad enough to get our help. We've always enjoyed a position of respect in the community, and I'd sure hate to see that spoiled."

"So, we've got what—about a month, to prepare for this onslaught? What're we going to do?"

"We're discussing it in bishopric meeting tomorrow morning, and then we'll need to say something to the ward. I've asked President Walker, and his take on it is that we should just keep on teaching and preaching our beliefs and not try to fight back or argue with these guys. Some of them, as he pointed out, are probably just looking for a good fight—and we want them to be sorely disappointed in that."

"Religious bullies, that's all they are. You don't think they'll try to hassle the members, do you, or vandalize our building?"

"I sure hope not. But I think I'll alert the police, just in case." He chuckled. "Our great big, three-man police force. Maybe I'll mention it to the sheriff, too, since these guys have apparently obtained a permit to use a county facility. Wonder how they wangled that."

"Probably lied about the purpose of the meeting. They

accuse us of lying and deceiving, but I suspect it's a technique they know pretty well."

"Looks that way, although I imagine they'd deny it, even to themselves. Well, I hated to tell you about it at all, Trish, because I know this kind of thing upsets you."

"It does, but not as much as you might think. Only when it gets up close and personal, such as when Maxine pulls one of her stunts. I mean, I have a testimony of the gospel and the Church—and I know the prophecies about persecution getting bad in the latter days. So in a way, I sort of expect this kind of stuff to happen, don't you? Even so, it makes me want to stand up and yell back—but apparently that's not the answer."

"Even if we did, and countered all their arguments with truer and better ones, d'you reckon any of them would really listen and see the light, so to speak?"

She smiled sadly. "Probably not. To begin with, they must be pretty entrenched in their ways to come after us like this. But, you know what? Isn't it all a bit ridiculous, when you think about it? I mean, turn it around—can you imagine a national 'rally tour' of Mormons against some other faith, especially some other Christian church? It's laughable. We just don't behave that way."

He shrugged. "Apparently we're successful enough with our one-on-one missionary program that they feel the need to come out against us in full battle array. Maybe we should feel complimented!"

Trish stretched and chuckled. "Now, there's a thought. Maybe we should just say, 'Thanks for calling attention to us! Lines to learn the truth from our missionaries form on the right.'"

He laughed with her. "There you go. Even negative advertising is better than none, right? Who knows what effect it'll all have? Hopefully, these dudes will be disgusting and transparent enough that everybody'll be able to see through 'em. By the way, on a totally different note—did I tell you that Chuck's bringing Mary Lynn to church tomorrow?"

"Oh, that's great. They were so cute the other night. I've never seen Mary Lynn looking so good."

"Trish, I feel so bad that I never got around to inviting her to come. All these years she's worked for me, and I never even suggested it. How dense can I be? Some missionary I am! I'm trying hard to repent of that."

"Well, maybe now's the right time for her—especially with Chuck in the picture and taking the missionary discussions. Who knows? Maybe she'll want to do the same."

He shook his head. "Or maybe she could've already been enjoying the blessings of the gospel for years, now, if I'd have just opened my mouth."

"Don't beat up on yourself, Jimmy. You've been a good example to her and a good friend and honest employer. Example counts, too, you know."

"I know. She said something like that. But I still feel like I let her down."

"Well, then just try to think if there's anyone else you know who might like to be invited to church, so it doesn't happen again."

He nodded. "Good thought. I'll work on that."

CHAPTER FIFTEEN

" . . . WHEN THORNS ARE STREWN ALONG MY PATH"

The bishop watched with pleasure as Chuck Stagley escorted Mary Lynn Connors into a pew at sacrament meeting. Elders Moynihan and Rivenbark came in with a woman he had never seen before and a girl of about twelve. Must be the mother and daughter they had mentioned working with—was it Simmons? He was glad to see Ralph and Linda Jernigan there, and Brother and Sister Conrad. At least Tina Conrad hadn't apostatized yet because of her bishop's many shortcomings! Just as the meeting started, the Birdwhistle family filed in and headed for the front row, theirs by default and tradition. Even with Pratt off on his mission, they still filled the center pew. He watched as Brother Ernie Birdwhistle deftly inserted his bulk between the twins, Lehi and Limhi, while his wife put the two youngest on each side of her. With the distance they had to drive from their log home up in the hills, he thought they were remarkably valiant to get there at all—yet they rarely missed a Sunday. The youngest son, little Kimball, caught the bishop's attention and waved, and the bishop sent him a wink in return.

The Rexfords—parents and son—took a seat near the overflow area. Since recovering from his near-fatal accident, young Thomas, or T-Rex, had seemed considerably more amenable to staying for the whole three-hour block of meetings. He still teased, still exercised his mischievous sense of humor, but his bishop recognized that the young man's brush with eternity had given him a new maturity and sense of purpose in his life.

Lisa Lou Pope made her entrance, dressed in a very grown-up pair of high-heeled sandals with a short denim skirt and a shirt that was very nearly too low, too tight, and too high in the midriff. He caught a look of disapproval from Sister Castleberry, whose self-appointed task was to keep the young girls of the ward at arms' length from the missionaries.

Lisa Lou smiled and waggled her fingers at T-Rex and then at Billy Newton and Ricky Smedley, who were seated at the sacrament table. Billy looked down and pretended not to notice, and Ricky gave an embarrassed little nod before he glanced away. The bishop sighed. He worried about Lisa Lou, who seemed alternately naive and worldly. Billy Newton had actually been her missionary contact and had been baptized the year before, partly due to her encouragement. Then Lisa Lou's fickle attention had turned elsewhere, and the bishop felt it fortunate that Billy's attraction to the gospel had remained constant. In fact, Billy had moved on, spiritually and socially, and now seemed light-years ahead of the young woman who had introduced him to the Church.

As the meeting progressed, his attention roved over the congregation as it often did, and he prayerfully tried to ascertain anyone who might need his particular aid or counsel. On this Sabbath day, he also prayed that the message he had to deliver to his ward would be understood in the spirit he intended it to be. These people had grown so dear to him in the time he had served as their bishop—even those who caused him grief also often brought him joy. In that, as in so many ways, being a bishop was like being a parent of a very large, diverse family with children ranging in age from newborn to their nineties!

During the second youth speaker, he saw LaThea and Harville Winslow slip into the back of the chapel, then make their way toward a side pew near the front. LaThea triumphantly carried her new grandson, and the child's parents, VerDan and his wife, Beth, for whom the ward had rallied to provide a hasty wedding the previous autumn, trailed after them, looking a little sheepish. LaThea made quite a fuss with the baby, bouncing him on her lap and then holding him against her shoulder so that everyone behind her could admire the little face. The bishop had all he could do not to chuckle when the baby, predictably after all that bouncing, spit up all down the shoulder of his proud grandmother's silk blouse.

After an intermediate hymn, "How Firm a Foundation," in which he had asked the director to be sure that all seven verses were sung—perhaps making it more of a marathon than a rest, but he wanted the encouraging strength of those verses to sink in—the bishop stood to address the congregation.

He began by speaking in general terms of the persecutions the faithful had always suffered, from the Old Testament prophets to the Savior and his apostles and the early Saints, on down to the Prophet Joseph Smith and the pioneer Saints of the present dispensation.

"Trials of this sort seem always to accompany the true gospel," he explained to them. "Some folks say that if this were the true faith, we would be spared such problems—but think about it, brothers and sisters—does Satan want most to disturb and destroy those religions that unwittingly include false doc-trines among their teachings, or does he want to disturb and destroy the one church that carries forth the fullness of the restored gospel of Christ and its accompanying priesthood seal-ing power? So, in fact, if we find ourselves being persecuted, could that not be a sign that we're on the right track? If history is any example, it must be, for as the Lord himself said, 'Blessed are ye, when men shall revile you, and persecute you, and shall say all manner of evil against you falsely, for my sake. Rejoice, and be exceeding glad, for great is your reward in heaven: for so persecuted they the prophets which were before you.'

"At this point, you may be thinking, 'But, Bishop, what are you talking about? This is a time of great peace and progress and respect for the Church. Our missionaries are having success, and our members are growing in the faith and excelling and being honored in many different fields, and we've learned to get along well with our neighbors. Why are you talking to us about persecution?'

"Well, my dear brothers and sisters, it has recently come to my attention, with the help of some good friends, that a round of persecution may be on our very doorstep. Before I tell you what it is, I want each of you to think in your own hearts how you would respond to hurtful lies and accusations because there will no doubt be some. Will you fight back, and give as good—or as bad—as you get? Will you insist on an eye for an eye and a tooth for a tooth, and sink to the level of those who heap persecutions on you?

"Or will you take the high road and behave in the manner the Lord prescribes, when He says, 'Love your enemies, bless them that curse you, do good to them that hate you, and pray for them that despitefully use you and persecute you; that ye may be the children of your Father which is in heaven, for he maketh his sun to rise on the evil and on the good, and sendeth rain on the just and on the unjust.'

"Now, I'm sure I have your attention, and I'm sure you're wondering what in the world I have to tell you. The situation is that we're soon to have some visitors in our area, some folks from a couple of out-of-state organizations of so-called anti-Mormon persuasion. You've probably heard of the street preachers who demonstrate outside of Temple Square during general conference in Salt Lake City. They've generally been loud and rude and accusatory, in an attempt to provoke a response from those attending conference. The enemies of the Church misrepresent LDS doctrine, as well as tell outright falsehoods and resort to name-calling to try to make us look foolish and deceived and even willfully wicked.

"It appears that it's people of this type who are touring the country this summer on what they call a 'rally tour,' planning to hold anti-Mormon rallies in various areas and trying to disrupt missionary work and turn members and investigators away from the truth. They've sent letters to local churches, encouraging attendance at this rally, which will be held at the County Fairpark on the third of August. I'm indebted to our good brother Ralph Jernigan and his wife, Linda, and to my long-time friend the Reverend Peter MacDonald of the Friendship Christian Church for a heads-up on this matter. Without them, I'd be totally in the dark about this whole thing."

He noticed Ralph's embarrassed little smile before he modestly looked down, and he also noted the somewhat surprised glances exchanged by several ward members.

"Now, my dear friends," he continued, "the question is, 'How should we respond? How can we respond in a way that will honor our Lord and Savior?' I've talked this over with President Walker and with my counselors, and we all agree and strongly counsel that everybody should stay away from the rally. Many of these folks are quite combative in nature, and may just be spoiling for a fight. We don't want to give them one!

"Certainly we have strong young men who could meet them on those terms, and we have able scriptorians who could go head-to-head with them on doctrinal matters, but would either one do any good? You may think, 'Yes! It'd show them we're not wimps, that we're not just going to take this kind of attack lying down.' But would they be convinced? No. Are they interested in seeking out any truth we have to offer? I'm afraid not. They simply want to start trouble, especially for our missionaries.

"President Walker has talked with the mission president and all of the bishops in the stake, and this is what he proposes: Each ward will have a special fireside—ours, of course, will be here in our building on that evening, August third. We will invite members and interested nonmembers and friends to meet with us, and we will pray and speak and bear testimony and sing the songs of Zion and try to generate such a Spirit that the work of the Lord will go forward with renewed vigor in this area! Since the next day is fast Sunday anyway, we ask those who can, to fast the evening meal and the Sunday morning meal, and break your fast after our regular Sunday meetings.

"My friend Peter MacDonald is going to counsel his congregation to stay away from the rally as well, and he's contacting other clergymen in the area and encouraging them to do the same. Still, we know there are a number of our fellow citizens who will attend the rally and who will be disposed to agree with the organizers. What should we do about them? Simply what the Lord said—pray for them. Do good to them. Is this always easy? I can tell you from personal experience that it is not. But it's the right thing."

He continued for a few more minutes, enjoying the most

undivided attention he had ever had from a congregation, including that of his own two, wide-eyed older children—and then the meeting closed with the hymn "God Speed the Right."

After the prayer, people whispered to one another as they gathered their families, lesson manuals, and scriptures and prepared to head to their auxiliary meetings. The usual buzz was subdued, however, and the bishop knew the people were shocked, absorbing the news he had given them. He knew the feeling; the letter Mac had brought had shocked him, also. He made his way to the foyer, where he greeted Chuck and Mary Lynn, explaining that this was not the usual tenor of their meetings and inviting them to return the next Sunday.

As was his habit during the Sunday School hour, he made himself available in his office—half hoping and half dreading that Sister Tina Conrad would stop in and take him to task again. This time, however, he was at least somewhat prepared for her. He had conferred with Ida Lou Reams, and together they had consulted the Relief Society guidelines, finding only a general statement of encouragement to sisters to dress appropriately for their meetings and when attending the temple. There had been not one word regarding the wearing of pants or skirts for visiting teaching. By the end of the hour, when Sister Conrad had not appeared, he began to breathe a little easier, hoping that perhaps she, too, had consulted the same source.

He did, however, receive a visit from VerDan and Bethany Winslow, whom he welcomed heartily and whose little son he admired with the enthusiasm a first baby commands.

After the door to the office was closed and the couple was seated, VerDan said, "Bishop, I want to thank you. Thanks for being honest with me and for not condemning me when you found out what was really going on. That has meant a lot to me because I was doing some pretty heavy condemning of myself. I know I acted like some kind of idiot playboy, but that wasn't really how I was feeling. I was just scared stupid and couldn't see my way out of a paper bag. I'm so glad you didn't let me go on a mission."

"Well, you know how it is—you just can't argue with the Spirit, and the Spirit was telling me pretty emphatically that there were reasons why we shouldn't send you out. As a bishop, I'm grateful for that help because sometimes we want so badly to believe what the person across the desk is telling us, that it'd be hard to know which way to turn without the Spirit's discernment."

"I'm glad you had that help, too," Bethany put in. "I want you to know that Danny and I are working hard to repent and make things right. We want to be sealed in the temple, soon as we're worthy."

The bishop nodded and smiled at her. She had a mature serenity about her that he knew was a steadying and calming influence on her young husband, and he was glad for it.

"Your mom's sure proud of this little guy," he remarked to VerDan, who ran a hand over his face and shook his head.

"Bishop, I shouldn't probably say this, 'cause I love my mom, but sometimes she embarrasses the heck out of me!"

The bishop smiled. "I know. But I just figured out recently that embarrassing their kids is part of a parent's job description. I embarrass mine regularly."

VerDan shook his head. "Not like my mom, I bet," he said.

"Dad," Jamie said, later that afternoon just as the bishop was relaxing for the first time all day, stretched out in his favorite family room recliner with the cat Samantha sleeping on his chest. "Dad, there's a—like a van, or something, in our driveway. I don't know who it is."

"Mmm. Maybe they're just turning around."

"Huh-uh. They're gettin' out."

"Okay," his father said wearily, sitting up and dumping the reluctant Samantha, who stalked away with ears laid back in annoyance. "Here we go. Let's see who's here."

He peeked out the living room window. A heavy-set man stood stretching and looking around the neighborhood, while a woman and two small children climbed out of the other side. The old Volkswagen van was battered and scratched, and it appeared that steam was rising from the undercarriage.

"Who are they?" asked Jamie. "Do you know 'em, Dad?"

"I don't think so," the bishop replied. "Let's go find out."

"Uh—you go find out," Jamie said, in a voice that said he had already made an initial assessment and found the visitors less than welcome.

"Aw, come on, James. Who knows—maybe they're relatives! Maybe Junior told them about us."

"Yeah, right. Like I said—you go find out."

The man had started toward the house while the woman stood beside the van and seemed occupied with something in the front seat. The two little ones followed their presumed father. One looked to be about four, and the other was just barely walking. They were clad only in underpants or diaper and dirty tee shirts.

The bishop walked out onto his front porch. "Hello, there," he greeted.

"Well, hey!" the man returned. "You the Mormon bishop around here?"

"That I am. Bishop Jim Shepherd. And you are . . . ?"

"We're the Lubells—Hank and Candy Lee. We're headin' down to Floridy for a vacation trip and thought we'd stop here in Fairview overnight. We went and found the church house, but there was just one fella there, and he was leavin', but he told us your name, so we looked up in the phone book and found your place. It's real nice," he added, looking around.

"Thank you. The town is Fairhaven, by the way, not Fairview. And church meetings are over for today, so what can I do for you folks?"

The man squinted in the sunlight and scratched the back of his head. "Oh, we just wondered if we might could camp in the church parkin' lot overnight—though we'd hoped to catch the place still open, so's we could use the facilities, you know? We're just a tad short of cash and cain't really afford us a mo-tel. We're sorta doin' this trip on a shoestring, if you know what I mean."

"Where are y'all from, Mr. Lubell?"

"Um—northern Missouri. Little-bitty old town, you wouldn't even recognize the name or nothin'. But we feel a mite safer, on the road, if we can stay close by a Mormon church or some good members, you know?"

"So you're members of the Church?"

"Oh, yeah, yeah—didn't I say? I'm sorry. We sure are."

The woman finished what she was doing, lifted a small infant into her arms, and came forward. Evidently she had been changing its diaper, as she carried a soiled one in her hand.

"Hey," she greeted. "Y'all got a trash can where I can throw this? They make the car so smelly."

"Let me take that for you," the bishop offered, and took the heavy and indeed odiferous object back to the can behind his garage.

"This here's my wife," the man said, as the bishop returned to the front porch.

"Sister Lubell," the bishop acknowledged, shaking her hand. "Brother Lubell," he added, grasping the man's pudgy fingers. "And your three little ones. What are their names?"

"Oh, that'n's our Sue, there," the mother said, indicating the oldest, who was tramping barefoot through Trish's wildflowers. "The boy's Eldon, and this here's Layla, but we just call her 'Squirt.'"

"I see. Um—maybe Sue might better not try to walk in the flowers," the bishop suggested. "Some of them have rough stems and even stickers."

"Oh, our Sue's gotta learn stuff like that for herself," remarked her mother. "It don't do no good to tell her."

The bishop, spurred by thoughts of Trish waking up from her nap and seeing the child's assault on her floral tapestry, went into action and swung the little girl up into his arms, brushing off her feet with one hand as she pulled back and gazed at him indignantly.

"Those flowers are pretty, but they have sharp little stickers that can hurt your feet," he told her firmly and handed her to her father.

Little Eldon, a small blond elf of a boy, sat down between his mother's flip-flop-shod feet and began to whimper.

"What'sa matter with Eldon?" demanded his father.

"Reckon he's hungry, but I ain't got nothin' to give him," Sister Lubell said. She swayed from side to side, rocking the baby. Eldon clutched her ankle and swayed with her, his face screwed up into a silent howl that the bishop was afraid would soon become all too audible. Sue wriggled out of her father's arms and headed back toward the flowers.

"Tell you what," the bishop said. "Why don't you folks come

on around back where it's shady, and I'll get you a snack and something cold to drink."

He didn't wait for an answer, but scooped Sue up again and carried her around to the patio, where he set her down on the grass. "Now, this feels good on your feet, doesn't it?" he said by way of encouragement. "You can play on the swings over there, if you want."

The Lubells had followed him, as he knew they would. The father swung Eldon along with one hand, and the boy still hiccuped with little sobs that the bishop was afraid might yet break forth into a howl.

"Just make yourselves comfortable, and I'll see what I can scare up," he told them, and went into the kitchen.

"So who are they?" asked Jamie, with interest. "Are they relatives?"

"No, no. Just some church members traveling through from Missouri, and kind of down on their luck."

"What does that mean?" Mallory asked, padding into the room.

"It means they're poor," Jamie told her. "They don't have any money. Right, Dad?"

"Well, something like that. They're hungry. I'm going to make a little snack for them. Jamie, would you get the lemonade out of the fridge? And the mayonnaise? I hope they like cheese and tomato sandwiches."

"I do," said Mallory. "I want one, too. How many kids do they got?"

"Have," corrected her dad absently, as he sliced tomatoes on a plate. "They *have* three—a little girl named Sue, a boy named Eldon, and a tiny baby named—uh—Squirt. I forget her real name."

Mallory went to peer at them through the family room windows. "Does Sue want to play with me?" she asked.

"She's younger than you, but you can go see," her father advised. "Just play around back, though, and don't let her get into your mom's flowers."

He carried a plate of sandwiches and the pitcher of lemonade out to the patio, while Jamie followed with a package of cookies and some paper cups and napkins. These Jamie deposited on the table and hurried back into the house after a quick perusal of the guests.

"Would the children rather have milk?" the bishop asked. "We've got plenty."

"Reckon Eldon would," his mother replied. "And Sue don't eat tomaters. I'll just pull 'em off of her sandwich." This she did, and popped the vegetables hungrily into her own mouth. She patted the cheese slice with a napkin to remove any vestige of tomato juice, and called her daughter to eat. The child grabbed the sandwich eagerly and took it with her as she ran back to the swings. She grabbed the chain of the swing Mallory was using and shook it, obviously wanting that one for herself. Mallory obligingly moved to the other swing, but Sue repeated her performance, so that Mallory jumped out, put her hands on her hips and said, "Well, okay, then—if you don't want me to play with you, I'll go back inside!"

Sue's face puckered, and she threw the uneaten part of her sandwich at Mallory, then aimed a kick at her shins. Mallory jumped back, then turned and ran toward her father, who lifted her onto his lap.

"Dad, she's not nice," she said tearfully. "She doesn't like me."

"Oh, Sue's a scrapper, all right," the girl's father affirmed, taking a huge bite of sandwich and motioning to Mallory with the rest. "You got to look out, around our Sue."

Sue jogged around the table, stuck her tongue out at Mallory as she passed, and grabbed two cookies from the package.

Candy Lee Lubell passed bites of cheese to Eldon, who sat again between her feet. "You happen to have any baby formula?" she inquired of their host. "Or canned milk?"

"No formula on hand," he replied. "We have a baby on the way, but not for a few more months. We might have some canned milk. I'll go see."

"Well, if you do, mix it half and half with warm water and put just a little sugar or syrup in. I'll go get Squirt's bottle from the car." She stood up and started for the car. Eldon clung to her ankle so that she had to shake him off, and he rolled over on his side, sobbing again.

The bishop moved back to the kitchen, searching the pantry for canned milk. Thankfully, he found a can and followed the mother's instructions, bemused at the way she had commandeered his help and given him his marching orders. He supposed a mother in such circumstance would feel justified in reaching for help from any source available. Her husband didn't seem to be of much assistance. How could the man bring his young family on such a journey, without sufficient resources to feed and shelter them along the way? What kind of man builds a tower or plans a Florida vacation without sitting down first to count the cost?

Tiffani came into the room while he was measuring and mixing.

"Dad? Who's here? I had to park out front."

"Hi, Tiff. Sorry about that. It's some traveling folks from Missouri."

"They're sitting down on their luck," put in Mallory, still sniffling from her encounter with Sue. "And their little girl's not nice."

"But why are they *here?*" Tiffani asked. "And what're you making?"

"Would you believe baby formula?"

She shook her head. "Weirdness. Where's Mom?"

"Still napping, I think. I'm trying to handle this without bothering her, but I don't know how long I can hold out."

Tiffani laughed. "So how come they landed here? Are they LDS?"

"Apparently so. They want permission to camp out in the church parking lot overnight. Or so they say. I think they're hoping they can camp here, instead, since we have bathrooms."

"You've gotta be kidding. We don't even know them!"

Her father shook his head. "I don't know about that. I'm already beginning to feel like I know them very well."

Y

Once fed, Eldon and the baby fell asleep—Eldon in the bishop's arms, as he couldn't stand to see the little fellow sleeping on the hot, hard patio, and his father didn't seem inclined to take him. Sue occupied herself by leaning her tummy over the seat of the lowest swing and walking around in circles to make the chain twist as tightly as possible so that when she released it, she pulled her knees up and twirled back to normal. The bishop hoped she wouldn't fall. He didn't want a lawsuit. Mallory had retreated back inside the house, her hosting efforts rebuffed.

"So do y'all belong to a ward or branch, back in Missouri?" he asked pleasantly.

The woman looked at her husband. "To tell you the truth, we ain't been to church real recent. It's hard, what with the babies and all."

"I can imagine," he responded. "Are you folks converts?"

"Yessir, that's what we are," Brother Lubell responded. "Only belonged to the Church for a coupla years. We just moved to Missouri, though. Joined in Arkansas."

"Well, that's wonderful. The Church is really growing. Where in Arkansas were you baptized?"

"A little tiny church just outside of Fort Smith," the husband said.

"So, did you get to be baptized in a font, or did you have to use a swimming pool or river or such?"

"Umm—it was in a font, in the church house."

"Oh, good. What was it that attracted you folks to the Church?"

"I liked the women's meeting," volunteered Sister Lubell.
"What's it called?"

"Relief Society?"

"That's it. I thought that was neat."

"And how about you, Brother?"

"Well, the thing that always impressed me the most about the Mormons was how they—or we, I should say—look out for each other. Never let one another go hungry, for example. Kind of like you done here, today."

"M-hmm, the welfare program is a great thing, isn't it? Have all your children been baptized?"

The mother nodded. "Well, older two have been. Not the baby yet, 'cause like I say, we ain't been too regular at Church for a while."

"Ah-hah. Then I wonder if you've heard about the changes the Church has made in recent months? For example, Sister Lubell, you'll be glad to hear that the priesthood has been extended to worthy women."

"Oh, really? That's great. I'm glad to hear it."

Her husband shifted his weight in the lawn chair and

recrossed his legs. "Only a matter of time, I reckon, till that come about," he remarked. "What with women's rights and all."

"Exactly," the bishop agreed, straight-faced. "Then the latest thing is, converts are allowed to choose their mode of baptism. It can be by immersion, pouring, or sprinkling. What do you think of that?"

"S'pose it makes sense, don't it?" the man opined. "Not ever'body wants to get all wet."

"I'm sure that's true. So, I take it you folks find yourselves in a bit of a predicament, do you, moneywise?"

Hank Lubell scratched his head. "Well, you know—travelin' cross-country's pretty dang expensive. Some places, you even gotta pay for air to put in your tires."

"That's how it is, all right. How's your van running?"

"'Bout on its last legs. It overheats real easy, specially in summer weather. We run a lot at night."

I just bet you do, the bishop thought. "Tell you what," he began, frowning as he tried to come to grips with what should be done. "Why don't y'all plan to camp out here at my place tonight? You can come in and bathe, and I guarantee it's good sleeping out here on the patio at night. Feel free to use the cushions, either on the lounges or on the floor, wherever you're comfortable. I assume you have a carrier or bed for baby, there."

"We got a carrier," the mother agreed.

"Then first thing in the morning, we'll go down to my grocery store and get you outfitted with enough food and ice to take you down the road a ways. And diapers and formula," he added, nodding toward the sleeping infant.

The two parents exchanged glances in which the bishop read both triumph and relief.

"We thank you, sir—knew a good bishop would come through for us," Hank said.

The bishop nodded. "I'm sure you felt real confident in that," he agreed.

CHAPTER SIXTEEN

" . . . To calm our doubts, to chase our fears"

J ames Dean Shepherd, you have got to be kidding me!" his wife unwittingly echoed their daughter, in a voice that warned him that she meant it. "People like that are absolute freeloaders and thieves! You can't encourage that kind of behavior—they'll keep it up all across the country!"

"I know, and I'm going to try to do something about that part," he soothed. "But the thing is, Trish, I kept thinking about that passage in the fourth chapter of Mosiah, where it tells us to impart of our substance to the poor and not turn away the beggar, even if we think he brought his problems on himself—remember that?"

"Sure, but . . ."

"And then I looked at those three pathetic little kids, and I knew I couldn't just turn them away."

She sighed. "You're right, you can't. But what about using the fast offerings given by faithful members to help dishonest nonmembers? It doesn't seem right to use Church funds that way."

"No, and I wasn't planning to, although if I had to choose, I reckon I'd rather err on the side of kindness than on letter-of-the-law strictness. But I thought I'd just do a little personal giving, if it's okay with you. A little money, and some food and ice from the store. What do you think, babe?"

She shook her head, but smiled. "I think 'you're a better man than I am, Gunga Din.' You're generous to a fault, and I'm glad of it. But I've got to admit, I'm also glad you didn't invite them to use the guest room. I don't think I'd be able to sleep. I wouldn't feel secure with them in the house."

"It's a clear, beautiful summer night, and they'll be fine out back. Way more comfortable than in their old van. They seemed okay with it."

"So—what's your plan to keep them from continuing their hopscotching from ward to ward?"

"I'll just get out my Church directory and make calls to a few stake presidents, who can spread the word to their bishops as they choose. These folks aren't hard to spot—they haven't done their homework very well at all."

Trish shook her head. "It's a good thing I wasn't out there when you ran your little test on them. I'd have cracked up and ruined the whole thing!"

He grinned. "It was hard not to—but I reckon I was caught somewhere between outrage and humor at that point, which is probably what saved me. They still don't know they're busted."

"Are you planning to tell them?"

"I don't know. I'll play it by ear."

"I reckon y'all's neighbors didn't know what to make of a slew of people sleepin' in your backyard," Mr. Lubell said the next morning, as Trish served his family a hot breakfast.

"Oh? Neighbors on which side?" the bishop asked.

"Right over yonder, where that big fence is at. Coupla women kept peekin' over the fence when we was tryin' to settle the young'uns down for the night. It weren't late, but maybe we was makin' a mite too much noise. Our Sue's kinda loud when she don't want to go to bed."

"Our Sue" chose that moment to push away her glass of milk, spilling it across the table.

"I hate white milk. I want brown!" she said.

"She means chocolate," her mother explained. "She won't drink plain milk."

"Well, we have some chocolate syrup," Trish said, patiently wiping up the spill. "Will that do?"

"I'll mix it," her mother said, reaching for the milk bottle and pouring another glass. "She likes it real chocolatey."

"So, did the ladies next door say anything to you?" inquired the bishop in an offhand tone.

"Nope, but the old one kept mutterin' to herself to beat the band. Put me in mind of a mean old witch, though I reckon I shouldn't badmouth your neighbors, and all."

"That's okay. She's just not real happy with us, right now. I'm glad she didn't call the police."

Hank looked ready to jump and run. "The police! On account of you had comp'ny sleepin' out?"

"She's called them on us for less. But don't worry—if they haven't come by now, they probably won't. Sorry if she bothered you, though."

Hank Lubell laughed. "I gotta admit I felt like doin' somethin' real naughty, just to give 'er an eyeful, but Candy Lee here made me be good. She said no, not in a good Mormon bishop's yard."

"Well, I do appreciate that," the bishop said, nodding in Candy Lee's direction. His appreciation was sincere.

Y

"Here you go, folks," the bishop said, as he loaded the last box of groceries into the van. "And here's a little cash to get you down the road."

"We sure do thank you, sir," Hank Lubell said, climbing behind the wheel. "It's a great thing, to belong to a church that looks after its own, ever'where you go."

"It is, isn't it? Reckon I should tell you, though, I haven't used Church funds for any of this. This is just a friendly hand-up from me to you, because I can see you're in need, but you and I both know you folks are not members of The Church of Jesus Christ of Latter-day Saints."

"You mean Mormons? Why, sure we are! What d'you mean?"

"No, sir. You're not. And you're real easy to see through, so I don't suggest you continue trying to pass yourselves off as members. I think an honest job somewhere would be your best bet. You know, we have a scripture in our church that says that a man who doesn't support his family is worse than an infidel. Now, whenever you're ready to straighten up and do things right, you might want to look into attending our church, where you can learn the truth and how to live by it—and how our welfare system really works. I invite you to do that. Y'all have a good trip, now." He slammed the door and patted it a couple of times before going back inside his market, where he took a scrap of paper from his pocket and jotted down the van's license number.

Y

"So, Dad—these people that are coming, the ones that don't like us—what d'you think they'll do?" Jamie asked Wednesday evening, as they sat side by side on the family room sofa, watching a video recording of the previous Sunday's Nascar race.

"Oh, I s'pose they'll rant and rave and yell and say all kinds of insulting and ignorant things about us, and try to get people not to listen to our missionaries, and to think we're some kind of weird cult instead of a real church."

"What's a cult?"

"That's a good question. One fellow said that a cult's just a religion that you don't like. But usually it means a group that brainwashes its members and takes away their freedom and identity and sometimes their money and property and makes them do whatever the head man says they have to do."

Jamie's face screwed up into a frown as he thought about that. "Well, our church doesn't do that stuff, so why do they call us a cult?"

"Because they don't understand us very well, and they don't believe we need a living prophet in our times. They think having one makes us a cult. They also don't think there can be any more scriptures, except for the Bible."

"Why not?"

The bishop looked at his son, whose face was turned to him instead of to the automotive excitement on the screen. *This, Dad,* he told himself, *is one of those rare teaching moments you hear about.*

"Well, mostly, I think, because they haven't been given any more scriptures, and they don't have a living prophet. But some of them say it's because in the last book of the Bible, the Book of Revelation, there's a verse that says nobody should add to or take away from that book. They think the verse means the whole Bible, instead of the Book of Revelation, itself."

"Huh. But it doesn't?"

"No. I think it just means the book it's written in. You see, Jamie, the thing is that the Bible's actually a whole collection of books, written at different times, and collected into one volume over the centuries. There are still lots of different versions of it. In fact, we don't even know that the Book of Revelation was the last one of the New Testament books to be written. It might have just ended up being put at the end of the Bible because it talks about times to come."

Jamie chewed on this information and turned back to the race. "Okay. Hey, look—Mark Martin's in the lead! Cool. I really like him."

His father smiled. He knew, from the sports section of the paper, that Mark Martin had done very well indeed for himself in this particular race. But he wouldn't tell his son that.

A while later, Jamie's active mind brought forth another question. "Dad?"

"Yes, son?"

"On Sunday, my Primary teacher was telling us about how the old-timey Church members got beaten up and killed and their houses burned, and they had to run away in the wintertime on the icy river and stuff. Are these guys gonna do stuff like that around here?"

"No. We have better laws now to protect us. They wouldn't be able to get away with such things. They'll probably just yell and wave signs and try to get people not to believe anything we teach. But try not to worry about it, okay, James? Heavenly Father will protect us."

"Yeah, I know."

They leaned back and watched the race. The father didn't

know if his son's concerns had been adequately addressed, but he found that his own attention to his favorite sporting event was somewhat distracted. He was surprised at the extent to which Jamie had internalized the news and the threat of the expected unwelcome visitors. His mind was working the material, coming at it from different directions. Other young people in the ward were undoubtedly doing the same thing. He hoped they would ask questions of their parents, and that the answers they received would be reassuring. He looked sideways at Jamie's close-cropped brown head, and reached out and pulled the boy close to his side. Jamie didn't object, but leaned against him as the cars screamed round and round the track, juggling for position. Neither father nor son moved for a long time.

"Here's another poison pen from Maxine, by way of Miss Hestelle," Trish said later that evening, handing him a type-written sheet. "Looks like she knows about the rally."

"Huh! She probably invited them to come here," replied her husband, taking the paper and examining it under the dining room light. He sat at the table, with his Rhys genealogy spread before him. He had been enjoying the spirit of that work.

"Jim—you don't think she might really have instigated their coming here, do you?"

"Probably not. But it's others like her who did. Well, let's see what she has to say."

"To all concerned Christians," she had written. "The time of redemption is surely coming. Those who practice deceit will have their wickedness turned upon their own heads. You can join in the effort to expose their lies and their false religion by coming to the Rally for the True Jesus, which will be held at seven P.M. on the third of August at the Fairhaven Fair Grounds.

Plan to bring your whole family to this celebration of real Christianity. All can be true Christian soldiers in this war against the menace of Mormonism! Come as individuals, come as couples, come as families, come as whole congregations! Simply come, and have your eyes fully opened regarding the river of filth and untruth that is flowing like a torrent through our community! Do not be deceived, and do not let false ideas of religious tolerance stop you from attending this important community activity. Tolerance has no place in this great fight. Evil must be eradicated. Your Christian friend."

"Isn't that disgusting?" Trish remarked.

"Actually, she's a pretty good persuasive writer," her husband replied. "Governor Lilburn Boggs would've loved her."

"She's a person after his own heart, that's for sure. I keep wondering how many people are persuaded by this stuff. And how many read it. I'm sure she must hand these out at her church, whichever one it is, as well as here in the neighborhood. And, for all we know, in other neighborhoods, too."

He nodded. "You almost have to admire her for being so proactive in a cause she really believes in."

"I know. She obviously truly believes this is a way of serving the Lord."

"Well, the missionaries have a saying they often use—'It's not enough to be sincere. You also need to be right.'"

"I've heard that. And I've never seen a better example of misguided sincerity."

The bishop took Chuck Stagley aside in a quiet moment at work.

"How're things going for you, Chuck?" he inquired. "You're sure doing a good job for us."

"Thanks, Jim. Or, I reckon I should say, Bishop."

"Jim's fine. Answered to it all my life. How are you coming with the missionary discussions?"

Chuck smiled. "Real good. They're fine young fellows, ain't they? I look forward to every visit with 'em. And I gotta tell you—I been readin' the Book of Mormon, and I don't care what anybody says, it wadn't no ordinary uneducated guy like me that wrote that! Parts of it are real deep, and you can just feel it's right and true."

The bishop felt a thrill of joy and testimony run through him. "That's exactly how I feel about it, Chuck, and I'm glad you see it that way, too."

"I hatn't never thought much about angels comin' to earth, and God talkin' to people face to face, but the way the elders explain it, it makes sense that it needed to happen. I'll tell you one thing—I do believe it would've come to a young boy like that Joseph Smith, if it come to anybody. It likely would've been harder to convince an older man, somebody already trained and steeped in his church's view of things, you know? I figger the Lord needed a fresh, young mind to train up in his way."

The bishop nodded. "I believe that, too. I believe Joseph was prepared for that calling from before he was born."

"That's another thing I like," Chuck said. "The way your church makes eternity go backward as well as forward. Like I didn't just start when I was born, but my life's a part of a long line of things we all go through, one part building on the other. And Jim, I don't know why, but I feel closer to my mom and dad now than I have since either of 'em died. I think it's on account of what the boys taught me about families being together forever. That thought sure does appeal to me."

"Yeah, it's comforting, isn't it? Especially for any of us who've lost people we loved—or who're afraid we might."

"Yep. So, in answer to your question, I reckon things're just swimmin' along, with me and the elders. And, um—I don't know how to bring this up, but—I've sure enjoyed gettin' to know your secretary, too. She's a fine young lady."

"Mary Lynn's a real sweet girl. Smart, too. You couldn't do better."

"I know, but it ain't like I got anything to offer her, in the way of marriage. No real job, no savings, nothin' to show for all the years I've lived." He shrugged. "I'd be 'shamed to even bring up the subject."

"Now, stop and think a minute, my friend," the bishop told him. "What you've accumulated in all these years may not be material goods or money, but you've had years of life experience, and you've learned to sacrifice and to be honest and faithful and do your best at whatever you do, and that's a whole lot more than some guys have to offer."

"Well, but a girl like Mary Lynn, she deserves that and more! She oughta have some security, and a future, in case there's kids and all . . ."

"Chuck, don't underestimate Mary Lynn. She has plenty of common sense and knows what's important and real. Besides, you have your mother's little house, and that's worth something, either to live in or rent or sell. And I'm confident you can get some kind of steady work. Plus, she'll have her job here for as long as she wants it. So don't discount your feelings, pal, okay? Or hers. Maybe it's time for both of you to have a little happiness."

"I'll consider all that, Jim. I hatn't known her that long, but I'm sure taken with her."

"Well, I happen to know she feels pretty much the same about you."

"You serious?"

"I am."

Chuck's smile was beatific.

The bishop's scheduled meeting with Melody Padgett the previous Sunday had been canceled because little Andi had developed an upset stomach, so he invited them to come to his home on Thursday evening. Trish greeted Melody with a hug, then kept the children, including a recovered Andi, back in the family room while the bishop and Melody talked in the living room.

"Bishop, it's good of you to see me at your home," she told him. "I'm real sorry to inconvenience you like this. It really could've waited till Sunday, what I wanted to talk about."

"No need for that, Melody. Besides, Sunday's schedule is already pretty full. What can I do for you?"

"Well, I was wondering—have you seen Jack, lately?"

"You know, I haven't. I've been meaning to get in touch with him, but things have been pretty busy."

"Sure. Okay. Well, I was just wondering how he's doing."

"Is he still getting money to you and keeping up the house payments and all?"

"Oh, yes. He is. He's always been real good that way. Very responsible about money."

"Good. I'm glad to hear it."

"He does have some good qualities, you know. He's not all bad."

"No. He's not. He has a lot of good in him."

"I reckon he never really had much of a chance, if his upbringing was as dysfunctional as I think it was."

"It sounds pretty dysfunctional, all right. He feels that his parents—but wait, you probably don't want to hear about it, do you? That was what you said, before."

She regarded her slender fingers, clasped in her lap. "I do and I don't," she replied. "Does that make sense?"

"Perfectly. It's normal to have mixed feelings about people you've loved who've treated you the way Jack did."

"Reckon I do have mixed feelings, Bishop. Just a couple of months ago I didn't even want to hear his name. But lately, I've been thinking about how much I missed Andi when she was taken from me and realizing that he must be going through something like that, too."

"He does miss her. It's not quite as bad, now, because he knows you have her back and that she's happy and safe. But still, he misses—both of you. I know that much."

"Will you think I'm crazy if I say I sort of miss him, too?"

"Nope." He smiled at her.

"Maybe you could tell me—just one little tiny thing about his childhood. He never would talk to me about it."

"He couldn't bring himself to talk about it. It was way too painful and too embarrassing. He was supposed to be the big, strong Marine, and talking about his family reduces him to jelly."

Melody stared at him. "Why?" she whispered. "What in the world did they do to him?"

"I think it'll be better if he tells you—if and when you're both ready. I'll just say that they did their best to destroy his trust—in them and in his brother."

"That's awful. Why would they?"

The bishop shrugged. "I suppose they were pretty sad and confused people. But here's the amazing thing—Jack's been working on their genealogy, and I think it's had something of a healing effect on him. I believe he understands a little bit more about why they were like that."

"Jack—doing genealogy? I never knew him to take an interest in that, before! In fact, he was always kind of scornful of the whole idea."

"Right. He had to be, don't you see, Melody? How could he bear the thought of happy, forever families, when his was so totally opposite? He had to reject the notion that it was even possible. I think he knows better now."

"Who got him started in genealogy?"

The bishop smiled. "Well, a man has to have a lot of interesting activities to take up his spare time when he's determined to be morally clean and stay totally faithful to his wife, even in a marriage that only has a fraction of a possibility of surviving what he did to it."

Melody covered her mouth, and tears filled her eyes. "Poor Jack," she murmured.

"And poor Melody," he reminded her. "Much as I'd like to see your marriage mended, please don't rush back into something you're not sure of. Jack's making good progress, but I don't know if he'll ever be entirely healed. I hope he will."

She nodded. "So do I. But Bishop—the Lord can heal all kinds of sickness, can't he?"

"Yes, he can. It takes faith and desire, and has to be the Lord's will, but it can surely happen."

"Then I'll pray for faith and healing—for Jack and for me."

CHAPTER SEVENTEEN

" . . . ALL MY DAILY TASKS FULFILLING"

Early on Saturday afternoon, Bishop James Shepherd pulled a footstool up beside his mother's chair in the sunny, plant-filled family room of his sister, Paula Trawick, in Anniston. Trish and the children sat nearby, and Paula was preparing a snack for them in the kitchen.

"Mama, I've got good news for you," Jim told her, as she nodded and squeezed his hand with her good one. "The family and I took a trip down to Georgia last month to look for records of your father and his family—the Rhys family."

She nodded harder. "Good," she said firmly. It was one of the few words she had mastered since her stroke several years before.

"We were really blessed, Mama. We found a lot about them. We found out that your father, Benjamin Rhys, died fighting in World War One. By the way, the spelling is R-H-Y-S, instead of R-I-C-E."

"Ah?"

"I know. I was surprised, too. We couldn't find Grandpa Benjamin's grave, though, so we figured he might have been buried overseas, wherever he died. We're still researching that part. But then we discovered a Rhys cousin still living in the county and talked to him about the family. His name is Ezra Rhys Jr., but he just goes by Junior." He went on to tell her, with help from Jamie and Tiffani, the miraculous way in which they had come to meet Junior and how they had been led by the Spirit to go back the next morning. Then he showed her the Bible pages that had been snatched from the jaws of obscurity just before Junior had been bused off to his new quarters. He was aware of Paula, stopping her fixing and fussing, standing in the doorway to listen.

His mother's eyes had teared up. "Son—good. Good," she kept saying. He took a tissue and patted her cheeks.

"It was good," he agreed. "It was an absolute thrill for us. And from these pages, plus some deeds and a will and the census records that we've found since we got home, we've got four generations back from Junior on the pedigree chart, and family groups for each couple. I'm not sure they're totally complete yet, but I believe we've got most everybody. See here?" He turned the pages of the group sheets, while his mother looked on in awe.

"Can I get copies of that stuff, Jim?" asked Paula. "I'd like to look it over and show it to Travis, and to the kids when they come."

"I brought you copies, Paula," her brother told her. "And I thought maybe Mama'd like for you to read over them to her, when you have time, so she can get familiar with her dad's people."

"Good, good," his mother affirmed, nodding deeply.

"I sure always thought the name was Rice," Paula remarked, bringing in a tray of cake and milk.

"So did we, and that had us stymied for a while," her brother agreed. "Until a very knowledgeable researcher suggested that the spelling might be different. Some of the family apparently still pronounce it 'Reese,' which is probably the original way, while others, including our branch, pronounced it 'Rice.' Paula, I'll tell you what—we had help from a lot of sources on this project, both seen and unseen."

Paula raised her eyebrows. "How about that," was all she said. The bishop said no more, though he longed to bear testimony to his sister, who had never seen fit to join the Church, but who was a kind and tender caregiver to their mother. He had learned long ago that Paula had a mind and will of her own and wasn't about to be pushed into anything, least of all religion, and least of all by her baby brother. Of late, however, he had sensed a softening in her and wondered if some of that might be due to having visitors from the Church in her home on a regular basis to minister to Sister Velma Shepherd.

"And we stayed at a farm place," Mallory put in. "It had a donkey and a dog and chickens and goats and a cat with little babies. We had so much fun!"

"You come here, sweet thing," said Paula, "and give your old Auntie Paula some sugar."

Mallory smiled and ran to be enfolded in her aunt's embrace. The bishop reflected that as much as anything else, love and acceptance and gratitude might do as much for Paula as any words of gospel truth he might utter. Trish had gone to stand beside his mother, guiding that lady's hand to her abdomen, where, apparently, the baby was making its presence felt. His mother's lopsided smile widened.

"Ah-h," she said, and after a moment, turned her hand to grasp Trish's in a gesture of affection and thanks.

Y

By the wonder of cell phones, Jim tracked Jack Padgett down at his Anniston store and arranged to stop by and visit him for a few minutes.

"I can't stay long—I've got the family with me," he explained, as he and Jack stepped into a small back room that held a table, two chairs, a miniature refrigerator, and a microwave. "How're you doing, Jack? You look good."

"I'm okay. You know. Existing. Well—maybe a little more than existing. Keeping busy."

"Busy's good," the bishop said, nodding. "Business still doing well? Hey, I've got a friend I can recommend whenever you need a new clerk—especially at the Fairhaven store."

"Good. I probably will need one, before too long. I'll let you know."

"Great, thanks. How's the genealogy coming?"

"Stuff gets addicting, you know that?" Jack replied, with a small smile. "Know more than I ever wanted to about people I never heard of before, and I still go after more!"

The bishop chuckled. "Tell me about it. We've been up to our ears in it this summer, too." He took a moment to relate some of their adventures.

"Now, that's something," Jack said. "Feel kinda like I've had some pushes in the right direction sometimes, too—though why anybody from the other side would care about me or my family is more than I can see."

"Well, exactly—you said it right. It is more than we can see. The powers that be, in these matters, can see the whole picture—why people do what they do, who's repented and been forgiven, who's accepted the gospel and wants to progress.

I figure we don't judge the folks who went before us—we just do the research and the temple work and let the chips fall."

"Guess that's the best approach, all right. Latest dude I've found was my second great-grandfather on my mother's side. He was a Lutheran minister, of all things! Didn't think we grew any of that kind on our family tree. Who knew?"

"I expect we all probably end up with a pretty good cross-section of humanity. Well, I'm glad you're working on that, Jack! And how's therapy going?"

Jack laughed shortly. "On and on and on," he said. "Oh, I guess maybe I'm making some progress, though why I want to bother is a mystery to me. I've already blown it with my wife and daughter, and frankly, I don't think I have the heart—or the confidence—to try again with somebody new."

"I wouldn't assume you've totally blown it. I still think there's hope."

"You're a nice guy, Bishop, but I don't know why you'd say that. Just to make me feel better, right?"

The bishop had sworn he wouldn't be any kind of go-between for either Jack or Melody. However, since Melody definitely had not asked him to, he thought he might venture to give Jack a little hope.

"I had a talk with Melody the other night. It may be too early to say for sure, but I believe her heart is softening a bit toward you. She asked how you were doing and worried that you might be missing Andi a lot. I told her you were missing both of them. She actually shed a tear or two and said she missed you, too."

"Oh, right—I'm so sure she misses getting slapped around by her angry brute of a husband. What woman wouldn't?"

"Well, I think she misses the guy she married, before he got so scared and controlling."

Jack stared at his hands, gripped on the tabletop before him.

"That guy got so scared and controlling because he fell deeper and deeper in love with his wife and was crazy about his little girl and was terrified he'd lose them both if he didn't keep them reined in, because deep down he knew—he *knew*—he didn't deserve 'em."

"I think it's a good sign that they haven't picked up and gone anywhere—nor even talked about leaving. What if that scared guy was able to become more deserving of them? What if he's learned a lot about himself in the meantime and made some really positive changes in his life?"

Jack shook his head. "What if he thought he had but then went back to them and started in again on the abuse? What would he do, then? I'm afraid he wouldn't be able to deal with that, Bishop. I'm afraid he'd end it all."

"Jack, I'm not suggesting that you're ready at this point to jump back into family life. I'm just telling you I think there's hope, on both sides, that eventually you will be ready. I think it'll be a long, gradual process for both of you to learn to trust each other, and for you to trust yourself. But Melody's praying for healing, for both of you. That's more than she's been willing or able to do before."

"She is—Mel is? She prays for me?"

"That's what she said. She asked me if the Lord could heal both of you. I told her yes, with real desire and faith, and if it's His will. I can't imagine that it wouldn't be His will, can you, to heal a family?"

Jack didn't seem able to speak. He just nodded, stood up, and reached to shake the bishop's hand. The bishop pulled the former Marine to him for a brief hug.

"I'll keep in touch," he promised, and Jack nodded again, his lips tight against the emotion he didn't think he should show.

Y

"You know," Trish said as they began their homeward drive, "since we're out this way and don't have to get home right away for anything—and since if we turned north before long, we could wind around and end up at Sister Buzbee's place—what if we were to pay her a little visit? It's been a while since I've seen her."

There were murmurings and little groans from the backseat, but the bishop looked across at his wife and blessed her for her suggestion. It had been a while since he'd seen Hazel Buzbee, also—and living alone as she did, without a phone, he worried about her. He had long since left his phone numbers with the young couple up the road who looked in on her, in case she needed him for any reason, but that didn't take the place of visits. As her self-designated home teacher, he tried to bring someone and see her at least once a month, but he hadn't seen her since before their trip.

"Do we have to?" asked Tiffani. "I'm supposed to go shopping this afternoon with Claire. I thought we were just going to see Grandma. Then we had to stop for you to see Brother Padgett. Now Sister Buzbee. I feel like I'm being held hostage by my own parents!"

"You can call Claire and tell her you'll be later than you thought," her mother told her. "She'll understand that you can't escape. Anyway—it's summer and you and Claire can go shopping any day. You don't have to wait for Saturday."

"She has her dad's car this afternoon, and she can't get that during the week."

"I see. Well, maybe I'll let you use ours one day next week."

"Promise?"

"If it's not a time when I need it."

Tiffani sighed gustily, the sigh of a resigned martyr. "All right, then. Dad, pass me your phone, please. And by the way, if I had my own cell phone, I wouldn't have to ask for yours."

"Oh, I don't mind, Tiff," her father said cheerfully, handing back the small instrument.

Y

Hazel's place was flourishing with flowers and vegetables, with some kind of blooming vine growing over the small porch. The bishop thought that if the cottage had a thatched roof, it would have been at home in the English countryside—at least the countryside he imagined from the illustrations he'd seen. Probably things were all different there, now.

A roly-poly bundle of black and white fur launched itself from the porch and bounded toward them as they got out of the car. As if remembering its duty, it skidded to a halt and emitted a series of sharp, high barks, then began to bounce and wag its way among the children.

"A puppy!" squealed Mallory. "I didn't know she had a puppy."

"Neither did I," her dad replied, looking around for Hazel's rangy old hunting dog. "Wonder where her old hound is."

He and Trish climbed the steps, leaving children and puppy romping in the yard. He knocked loudly on the wood of the screened door.

"Sister Buzbee?" he called, at the top of his voice. "Are you home?"

"Well, 'course I'm home—where else would I be, in this here heat?" she answered, coming into sight. "Mercy! It's the bishop. Y'all come on in to where it's shady, at least!"

They went inside and immediately recognized that "shady, at least," was about the best that could be said for the little house. The shades were drawn, but the front and back doors were open, to catch any breath of air that might wander in, no matter how hot.

"Do you have a fan, Hazel?" the bishop asked.

"Do I have a what? A man?" She laughed.

He smiled and made fanning motions with his hand. "An electric fan? Do you have one?"

"Oh, a fan. Had me one of them, onc't, but the dang thing went out on me."

"I'll bring you one," he promised. "It's awful hot in here."

"Reckon so, though I don't seem to feel the heat like I used to," she told him. "But maybe that's 'cause I c'n take it easy in the heat of the day. I don't do nothin' but sleep or listen to the radio or the tapes y'all brung me. I do my garden work just as the sun's fixin' to rise and just when it's gone down in the evenin'."

"That's good. You could get heatstroke out there in the middle of the day."

"Say what?"

"Heatstroke," he yelled. "Heatstroke, out there now."

"Oh, yes. My husband, he used to say how only mad dogs and Englishmen go out in the noonday sun. Well, I don't know iffen I'm any part English, but I sure ain't no mad dog!" She gave a cackle of laughter.

"Speaking of dogs, where's your old hound?"

"My hound? Wal, d'you know, he up and died on me, couple of weeks ago. Had that old dog for fifteen years. The kids down the road come up and buried him for me. They seen how I was a-grievin' over him, and couple of days later, here they come with that silly puppy dog out yonder. Told 'em I was way too old to take on a pup, but they said iffen I was to die, they'd take him back, so I agreed to have him. He's s'posed to be a real smart breed—Border Collie, they called it—and a good watchdog, but so far, he's about as much protection as my old cat. He is good for a laugh, though!"

"He barked at us when we came," Trish said loudly. "That's a good sign."

Hazel held a hand behind one ear, and the bishop repeated his wife's words. "Oh, did he? Good for him. Reckon my ears didn't pick it up."

Trish tried again, louder. "How are you enjoying the tapes we brought?"

Hazel looked uncertain, and Trish pointed to the tape recorder on the kitchen table. "Do you like the tapes?" she shouted.

"Oh, honey," Hazel yelled back, "I purely love them tapes! Makes me feel like I'm back in touch with the Church, almost like I used to be." She cut her eyes toward the bishop. "I still do drink coffee, though," she confided in a slightly lower voice. "It's hard not to, you know? I growed up on the dang stuff, and seems like it's all that can get me goin' in the mornin'. Hope the good Lord can see fit to forgive this old sinner."

The children tumbled into the house, laughing from their exertions with the puppy, who stood and whined at the screened door. Jamie gave in and went back outside, but the girls stayed in.

"You like my puppy dog, sugarfoot?" Hazel asked of Mallory, who nodded enthusiastically. "Then I reckon you'd better give him a name, like you did my kitty cat, old Stormy."

"Okay," Mallory agreed, and sat down to think.

Tiffani perched on a straight chair and fanned her flushed face with a piece of paper. "It is so hot out there," she announced. "Not very cool in here, either, is it?"

Her mother shook her head in reply. "We're going to bring her a fan."

"Good." Tiffani stopped fanning and glanced at the paper in her hand. "Dad?" she said. "I think you'll want to look at this."

He took the paper from his daughter and looked at the printing on it. "So—word is spreading, even out here," he said.

"What is it?" asked Trish. He handed the paper to her. It was an announcement from the Mt. Olivet Baptist Church encouraging people to make time to attend the anti-Mormon crusade and rally on the third of August. Time and place were announced, and the slogan "Strength in Numbers and in Truth" was printed on a banner across the bottom.

"What is that paper, anyhow? I couldn't make it out," Hazel said. "Somebody left it on my door."

The bishop briefly explained to her what the message was. "We're aware of this meeting, and we're having a special fireside that same evening to celebrate the truth and try to generate faith among our people to fight against this kind of thing. These people are full of lies and hatred, and we don't want to tangle with them on their terms."

"Huh! Too bad Mt. Olivet's folks are falling for that nonsense. I c'n recall we had some of that sort of stuff happenin' years ago, with people trying to run the Mormon missionaries out of the county, threatenin' to shoot 'em on sight. We all fasted and prayed, and nobody got shot that I ever knowed about."

"Well, that's exactly what we're doing, so if you'd like to join your prayers with ours, especially on the third, we'd be grateful. I don't know if you should fast, but—"

"I can, for at least one meal. I'll do that, Bishop. You can count on me."

"Thank you, Sister Buzbee."

"Will you leave a prayer, before you go?"

He quieted the children and offered a blessing upon Hazel and her home, thanking the Lord for her faith and determination to do what was right. He felt strange every time he prayed in her home, because of the decibel level that was necessary for her to hear his words. He wished he had a microphone, just for her.

"So, honeybunch, what's that doggie's name gon' be?" she asked Mallory, as they all stood and prepared to take their leave.

Mallory giggled. "What about Bouncer?" she asked. "'Cause he bounces all over the place." Her father duly repeated her words, and Hazel clapped her hands in delight.

"Bouncer he is," she decreed. "That's a good name for a watchdog anyhow, don't y'all think?"

"It's perfect," the bishop agreed. "And I hope he bounces anybody you don't want around!"

Marguerite Lowell was mowing the lawn next door, and her mother was weeding a bed of petunias as the Shepherd family pulled into their driveway. The bishop went to his dining room desk and retrieved the most recent flyer Maxine had created and headed next door before he could lose his determination.

Maxine stood up as he approached and looked as if she might throw her trowel at him.

"Good evening!" he called loudly, to be heard over the mower.

"Marguerite! Cut that thing off and go in the house!" the mother directed.

"Good evening," the bishop repeated, as the sound died away. "I wondered if we might discuss this for a minute." He held up the flyer.

"Where'd you get that?" she asked, frowning.

"Well, they're pretty easy to come by—they're all over the neighborhood," he said. "I know you and I obviously disagree on some points of religious doctrine, Mrs. Lowell, although if we were to sit down and have a rational discussion, you might find that we agree on more than you think. After all, we read and believe the Bible pretty literally, as I suspect you do. But I wonder why you feel it necessary to put out such libelous and hurtful information? There is such a thing as disagreeing without being disagreeable about it."

"Your name's not on that paper and neither is mine," she stated flatly.

"No, but everybody knows who produces them and who's referred to. Believe it or not, we're not your enemy, Mrs. Lowell. In fact, we've tried to be friends, ever since you moved in."

"I don't have friends that are the likes of you people."

"You know, I believe you're mistaken in what kind of people we are. We've always gotten along well with our neighbors, and I hate it that there's been this contention between us. I don't want it to be that way. What can I do to make you feel better about us?"

"Not a thing, unless you totally renounce your false religion, which is of the devil! If all the people in this neighborhood knew what I know about your so-called church, you wouldn't have such a nice, cozy friendship with them, either!"

"Just what is it you think you know, that you find so objectionable?"

"The Mormon Church is a man-made institution—no, I'm being too kind on that point. It's a devil-made institution, substituting another book for the Holy Bible and causing men to trust in a so-called prophet, who's nothing but another sinful man, rather than in the good Lord! It's—"

"Do you believe in a changeable God?" Jim asked.

"I do not. I believe in an unchangeable God, who is all-knowing, all-powerful, and mighty to save."

"Then haven't you read in Amos, chapter three, verse seven, where the Lord says, 'Surely the Lord God will do nothing, but he revealeth his secret unto his servants the prophets?' If the Lord is truly unchangeable, wouldn't he reveal his secrets to prophets in our day, the same as in Old Testament times? Don't we need direction today, as much as the people did, back then?"

"Certainly not. The Lord Jesus was the last great prophet, and his word is all we need. We have his word in the Bible, and it's sufficient. That's made plain in Revelation, twenty-two, eighteen: ' . . . I testify unto every man that heareth the words of the prophecy of this book, If any man shall add unto these things, God shall add unto him the plagues that are written in this book!'" Maxine threw down her trowel, and the bishop felt relieved that it wouldn't be flying at his head.

"Correct," he said. "The Book of Revelation, written by the Apostle John, often called John the Revelator. Tell me, Mrs. Lowell, was John a prophet?"

"He was one of the Lord's disciples. He wrote what the Lord wanted him to write."

"So you believe that the book of Revelation is just that—a revelation from God, or a prophecy, as John himself calls it in the passage you just quoted?"

"I believe it's the word of God, along with the rest of the Bible, yes."

"So John was a prophet, prophesying after the death of the Savior? Then perhaps the Savior wasn't the last prophet."

Maxine Lowell looked momentarily confused, then angry again. "I don't know when he wrote the book. But I do know he warns against adding to the Bible, and that's what you people do, with your phony Book of Mormon and other fake translations!"

"Are you certain he was warning against adding to the Bible, which hadn't even been compiled yet when he wrote, or was he warning against adding to or taking away from the prophecy of the Book of Revelation itself? I'm sure you must know that the books of the New Testament were still just in separate manuscripts, and everybody lucky enough to have copies had a different selection. The Bible as we know it today wasn't compiled until many hundreds of years later. And some versions still don't include the Book of Revelation."

"Well, mine does, whether yours does or not, and I believe the good Lord knew which book would end up as the final one, and told John to include that part about adding to it just to warn people against such falsehoods as you preach!"

"Mrs. Lowell, why do you want to limit the Lord, if He's all-knowing and all-powerful, as you say?"

"Limit the . . . I beg your pardon!"

The bishop shrugged. "Who are you—or any of us—to dictate to the Lord that He can't speak any more of His will to us in our day? That He's said enough, thank you very much!"

"I know He doesn't need to, because He hasn't done! His word as given in the Bible is sufficient, and salvation cometh through his Son, through grace, though I know you don't believe that, either!"

"I can testify to you that prophets have spoken in our day. And actually, by the way, we do believe in the doctrine of salvation through grace."

"No, you do not! You believe in works—foolish works of man that can never save anybody."

"I think if you give a careful reading to all of Paul's comments on faith, works, and grace, you'll see the whole picture—that both are necessary. We do believe we're expected to do certain things, but we also know that they're not sufficient to save a one of us. We have a scripture that says, 'For by grace are ye saved, after all ye can do.'"

"I don't believe it."

He shrugged. "It's in the Book of Mormon. I'd be glad to show it to you."

"Then it was added recently! I know you all keep making changes, to suit your purposes. Now, good night, Mr. Shepherd. You have not convinced me of a single point."

"Just one more thing, Mrs. Lowell. I wonder what you think of the Savior's admonition to us all in the Gospel of John, chapter thirteen, where He says, 'A new commandment I give unto you, that ye love one another, as I have loved you, that ye also love one another. By this shall all men know that ye are my disciples, that ye have love, one to another.'"

"He was speaking to his twelve disciples."

"Just to His chosen apostles? The twelve? Doesn't He want all who follow Him and love Him, to try to love each other? He tells us to love our neighbor as ourselves."

"In the parable of the good Samaritan," she retorted, "the neighbor was the one who cared for the fallen man. I'm only required to love neighbors who do the Lord's will, not those who ignore His will and His word and create for themselves their own scriptures!"

"Then you do believe works are important."

"I don't know why I'm standing here arguing with you! I've been warned how slick you people are at twisting the scriptures. We have no common ground to stand on, Mr. Shepherd. Please get off my property."

"All right, I'll be glad to. But . . ." He held up the open letter she had written. "It's hard for me to believe that a woman with a true love of the Lord in her heart could produce such trash and lies as this. I'll appreciate it if there's no more of these."

"I'm commanded to warn my neighbor!"

He looked her in the eye. "Yes, ma'am. So am I."

CHAPTER EIGHTEEN

"... GIRD UP YOUR LOINS, FRESH COURAGE TAKE"

B ishop, guess what?" came Buddy Osborne's low voice behind the bishop as they headed into the room where the priests quorum met.

He turned with a smile. "Um, let's see—you sold one of your paintings for a thousand dollars?"

Buddy chuckled. It wasn't a sound the bishop had often heard.

"Well, no, but it's almost that surprisin'," he said. "My mom give me my own house key!"

They exchanged high-fives. "Good for you," the bishop told him. "And you're responsible enough to handle it, too. Proud of you!"

Buddy shrugged. "She just don't want me over to Deddy's whenever he's got—you know—comp'ny."

"That's a good enough reason, though I can think of lots of others. It relieves my mind, to know you won't be locked out any more."

"Yeah, and I won't have to keep hangin' out at your place."

"Hmm. If you stay away too much, I just might have to swipe that key."

Y

"So all right, Bishop, have it your way about the visiting teachers wearing trousers like a man," said Sister Tina Conrad. "Your Relief Society president showed me in the manual what it said—or didn't say—on the subject. But I still feel it's wrong, and I'm still going to insist that anyone who visits me in that capacity has to wear a skirt."

"All right," the bishop said mildly. "I expect there'll be sisters willing to do that, if it's really important to you. And I was wondering if you've seen your daughter-in-law, recently."

"I have. Why?"

"How did it go?"

"Fine, of course. I rearranged her spices for her, in alphabetical order. She was grateful. I can't think why she'd never bothered to do that, herself."

"Hmm. And was there any mention of how to fold garments?"

Tina inhaled deeply. The bishop was afraid she might over-inflate. "No, Bishop, there was not, as I took your advice on the matter. I certainly don't know why I should be prohibited from teaching my standards to my son's wife, but I did what you said. I asked her to make a chocolate layer cake for my birthday."

"Wonderful! What did she say?"

"Well, she agreed, of course. And then I complimented her on her patience with the children, just as you said to do, although I practically had to bite my tongue not to scold my grandson for banging the screened door every time he went in and out."

"Did she seem pleased at your compliment?"

"She seemed surprised, but she said, 'Well, thank you, Mother Conrad.'"

"That's excellent, Sister! You just keep finding good things to compliment in that girl, all right? But don't offer any advice unless she asks."

"That seems so foolish to me! The young don't know to ask for advice. They don't even know they need it! Why shouldn't I offer the benefit of my years of experience?"

"If she knows you love her and approve of her, she'll eventually feel safe enough around you to ask."

"Safe! As if I'd do anything to harm her or the little ones—what can you possibly mean by 'safe'?"

"I mean emotionally safe. Relaxed. At home. Not under examination. Then she'll feel free to come to you with questions or concerns. But as long as she feels inhibited or criticized or nervous around you, you may as well forget it. She'll never open up and ask for your help."

"You think she feels that way? What—has she been here to see you? Or have you talked to her? I didn't give you permission—"

"No, no, no, Sister Conrad, please. I don't even know her name or where she lives. I'm just talking in general terms about things that are true in any in-law relationship. Personally, I've had the experience of feeling—well, of knowing—that one of my sisters-in-law was critical of me, and I know I wouldn't have opened myself up to her as long as I felt that way. I'm just talking human nature, here." He paused, and looked at her reflectively. "When you were a bride, didn't you ever feel just a little worried about what your mother-in-law thought of you?"

"My husband's mother died before we met. But she would never have found anything to criticize in my standards, or my housekeeping."

"I'm sure that's true," the bishop agreed. Privately, he thought the deceased Mrs. Conrad might have been the one suffering intimidation, with a daughter-in-law such as Tina.

Tina swung one dainty, neatly-shod foot, today sporting a very pointed toe that the bishop imagined she would like to use to prod him. "Now, Bishop—regarding the instigators of this despicable rally you've been telling us about. Don't you think it would be in our best interests to go and hear what they have to say against us rather than hiding our heads in the sand, here?"

"Well, no, ma'am—I agree with our good stake president that this is our best course. If they're the kind we think they are, many of those agitators will come looking for a fight and a confrontation. We don't, as a church, generally indulge in either Bible-bashing or head-bashing, whichever it is they want of us."

"But wouldn't it be good for people to see that we don't back down and won't allow ourselves to be intimidated by such activities? If we do nothing, won't we be seen as weak and frightened, as if all the things they say about us must be true?"

"We're not exactly doing nothing. We'll be meeting to generate faith and understanding among our members and our friends. We've also notified the police, and they've promised to have a man on duty here, just in case any of the rally folks get ideas about vandalism or such. Then the Reverend Peter MacDonald of Friendship Christian Church has been in touch with a number of other clergymen around the area, encouraging them to warn their members away from the rally. Some have agreed, others have not. So it's not that we're doing nothing— we're just hoping to do exactly those things that the rally people *don't* want us to do!

"The missionaries in our area are bringing all their investigators to these firesides—and they have quite a few, right now— and we're inviting friends and sympathetic neighbors to meet with us, as well. In our ward, we'll be showing a film about Joseph Smith and the persecutions of the early Saints, and Brother Warshaw will be speaking. I don't know if you've heard him yet, but he's an excellent scriptorian and has quite a conversion story of his own."

"Well, I don't suppose anything I say would move you, but I still think some of us should go to this rally, just to see what the opposition is using against us."

The bishop nodded. "Well, of course we can't make anyone stay away—but that's our direction from President Walker, and that's what we're choosing to follow. Every individual, of course, has his or her agency in the matter."

"Yes, indeed. Well—some of us may just choose to exercise that agency."

The bishop shrugged and smiled. "I'll just say that we'll *hope* to see you here on the third, then," he said. He wondered, not for the first time, if Brother Conrad still had *his* agency intact.

Trish's girlhood friend Muzzie Winston and her children—Brad, Chloe, and Marie—had been invited to join the Shepherd family for Sunday dinner. Muzzie had recently finalized her divorce from her husband, Dugie, who had been her high school sweetheart. The last few years had been difficult ones for Muzzie, watching her husband gradually give in to pornography and other abhorrent practices, at first expecting her to go along with his perverted tastes and demands, and, when she refused, leaving her and the children choking in the dust of his accelerated rush into hedonism. Trish, to her credit, had stayed close to Muzzie, encouraging her to build a new life, based on true principles, for herself and her children.

After the dinner, the adults relaxed around the table while

the children went off to their own pursuits with their company. Brad, though older than Jamie, was just as interested in computerized games, and the girls were still young enough to play Barbies with Mallory. Tiffani's friend Claire came by to visit, and the two girls repaired to the patio for a bit of privacy.

"Oh, gosh, that was a wonderful meal, Trish," Muzzie said, leaning back with her hand on her midsection. "I don't know how you can be pregnant and put a meal like that on the table. I never could stand to cook when I was expecting."

"I'm past the point where the smells bother me," Trish explained, "and not quite to the point where I'm too big and too tired to care. So you hit us at a good time."

"Well, that fresh peach dessert was to die for. Thank you."

"You're totally welcome. It's good to have a chance to spend a little time with you. We're all way too busy, aren't we?"

"I know I am, since I've started working. But it's good for me. And I actually think I'll like working in real estate, once I get my license. I was afraid I'd gotten too old and too lazy to study, but so far, I've passed all the tests just fine."

"Good for you, Muzz!"

"I enjoy it." Muzzie played with her spoon, gazing at it unseeingly. "So I saw Dugie the other day," she said quietly.

"Oh, really? Where?"

"He was going into the bank as I was coming out. I know he saw me, but he just looked at the gal he was with and said something to her—obviously something complimentary, from the way she reacted. I didn't say anything."

"Mm. Had you seen the woman before?"

"Somewhere. Looked like she might be a few years older than Dugie. She wasn't bad-looking. Tiny, of course—not an ounce of fat on her, or Dugie wouldn't be interested. Real short dark hair. Fair skin, big eyes." Muzzie shook her own head of streaked-blonde hair. "I can't place her. Not that it matters. It could be anybody. It'll always be somebody. Probably a lot of different somebodies, for all I know."

Trish looked at her husband. They recognized the description.

"What?" Muzzie asked, intercepting the look. "Y'all know who she is, don't you?"

"We think she's someone who used to belong to our church," the bishop said reluctantly.

"Used to? You mean she what—left? Got kicked out?"

"She asked that her name be removed from the records because she said she didn't believe anymore," Trish explained. "I don't know, of course, but it's my personal feeling that she found it inconvenient to believe in a God or a religion that disapproved of the things she wanted to do."

"Well, sounds like she's a girl after Dugie's heart, all right— more ways than one. Now, y'all don't tell me her name, all right? I don't need to know."

"Thanks, Muzzie," said the bishop, feeling a little guilty already that they had said anything at all.

"Just tell me this," Muzzie continued. "Did she leave a husband or family behind, or was she already single?"

"She left a very fine man behind, and they have a grown son and a grandchild," Trish told her. "The poor man's heart is about broken, I can see that."

"Well, then, she and Dugie deserve each other. I wonder which one of them will break the other's heart first—if they still have hearts, that is. I'm not real sure about Dugie." Muzzie shook herself, then looked up brightly. "So tell me—what's all this about a bunch of hoodlums coming to town to harass y'all?"

They told her what they knew, and she shook her head in disbelief.

"What's the world coming to, that people want to travel around the country behaving like that?" she wondered aloud. "I mean, you'd think they could find a better cause to go up against—like wife-beating or incest or pornography or something. I could tell 'em a bit about that one! Why do they want to fight against good religious folks with great family values like you guys?"

"They think we're impostors when we say we're Christians," Trish explained. "They get our beliefs all mixed up with a lot of misinformation, and then they feel compelled to expose us for the frauds they think we are."

"What a bunch of nonsense! I know you're Christians. And what business would it be of theirs, if you weren't? Honestly! So what in the world do y'all do to try to counteract that kind of mischief?"

They told her of the fireside and invited her and her children to attend.

"We're inviting friends of other faiths as well as Latter-day Saints," Trish explained. "Our idea is to generate as much love and faith as possible, to try to neutralize the negative influences they'll be bringing to town. Of course we know some folks will go to the rally, and some will believe their claims, but rather than engage in a shouting match—or worse—we'll just do our thing and have an evening of rejoicing in faith and truth."

"Well, the kids and I will be there," Muzzie promised. "Although I've gotta admit to a sneaking desire to go out and do the shouting-match thing in your behalf!"

The bishop chuckled. "Thanks, Muzzie. We'll accept the thought in lieu of the deed."

Y

The days marched on. Bishop Shepherd tried to keep his mind and heart on the daily work of taking care of his business and ministering to the needs of his family and his ward. He tried to keep a light touch in talking with people about the impending rally, but in his heart, he deeply resented the motives of the organizers and dreaded the influence the visitors might have on his neighbors and their view of the Church and its members. He spent much time in prayer, laying his concerns before the Lord and asking for peace and direction. A measure of peace came, but not quite enough to dispel all his fears. This he attributed to his own lack of faith and prayed more fervently, asking the Lord to throw a shield of heavenly protection around the honest in heart of Fairhaven and the surrounding areas, that those people might not be deceived and misled.

One perfect summer evening, just before sunset, he saw his neighbor, Maxine Lowell, heading up the street with a sheaf of papers in her hand. She passed his house with a triumphant smile and turned in at Hestelle Pierce's gate. The bishop thought he might never have seen such a chilling smile in all his days. He bowed his head and prayed for Maxine and with even more fervency, prayed for himself to have the grace to truly mean the words he spoke.

"Please forgive her for the mean and intolerant spirit she manifests," he prayed. "I know she doesn't understand. And please forgive me, dear Father, for my anger toward her and help me to somehow forgive her and all who believe and act as she does. Please let Thy truth prevail."

"And," came a mocking voice into his consciousness, "what if the truth really is with her, and you're the one who's deceived? What then, Mr. Goody-goody Bishop?"

He knew that voice was not from the One to whom he prayed. In fact, it had an uncanny way of manifesting itself to his mind in the tones of Marybeth Lanier.

"Father, please, in the name of thy Holy Son, Jesus Christ, remove this doubting spirit from me," he pleaded. "I know, from all the experiences I've had and all the scripture I've studied, and the prayers Thou has answered, wherein the truth lies. I know I belong to the Restored Church of Thy Son. But right now I feel led to say, 'Lord, I believe! Help thou mine unbelief.'"

Wednesday evening was his usual time for home teaching and other visits to members' homes, and on the last Wednesday in July, he found himself and Brother Sam Wright at the home of Sergeant and Elaine Forelaw and their three children.

"Well, how's it goin', you kids?" asked Sam, smiling kindly at the three little people sitting in a row on the sofa.

"Good," they chorused, and he laughed.

"I declare, Sister Forelaw, if they ain't the cutest young'uns I've seen in an age! A mighty fine family, for sure. Where's your good husband?"

"I'm just out here in the kitchen," Sergeant called. The bishop had warned him of Sergeant's tendency to hang about in the background, pretending not to listen to the discussions with his wife and the stories told to the children.

"Oh, hello there, Brother," Sam replied. "All right, y'all young'uns, what do you know about a man called Samuel the Lamanite?"

They knew nothing, but they listened wide-eyed while he told them of brave Samuel, the Lamanite prophet, standing on the city wall and preaching about the coming of the Savior to a people who were not inclined to listen—who, in fact, pelted him with stones and arrows that all failed to find their mark.

"And that's how it is, you see, with folks who try to beat up on the servants of the Lord. They shoot their arrows, all right—but they just don't do no damage. Sometimes they seem to hit home, but pretty soon we realize they didn't hit any vital organs at all, and everything's okay."

Elaine Forelaw seemed to realize that these last remarks were for her benefit as much as for her children's, as she smiled and said, "So is that how it's gonna be on Saturday, you reckon? Just a lot of stray arrows, that don't do no real harm to the Church?"

"That's what we're a-hopin'," Sam affirmed. "What do you say, Bishop?"

"I say if we can have the faith of a Samuel, we should weather this attack in good shape," he said. "We all need to pray for added faith and for the Lord's will to be done. Actually, I'm really looking forward to our fireside on Saturday evening. Are you folks considering coming?"

"Don't know yet," Elaine replied. "Kids go down pretty early, and I wouldn't want 'em to disturb anybody. I'll just have to see."

The bishop nodded. "Love to have all of you, if you feel so inclined," he said. He spoke for a few more minutes about having faith in the face of opposition, then Sam gave a prayer and they took their leave.

"Reckon they'll come?" asked Sam, fastening his seat belt once they were in the bishop's truck.

"Sergeant's only been to one meeting, so far. It's hard to tell what he's thinking—but I know he *is* thinking because he's reading the scriptures on his work breaks and lunch hour, according to Elaine. She saw a Bible and Book of Mormon in his truck several months ago, but he only recently admitted to her that he's been reading them. I think the jury's still out, as far as what he concludes about them. I'd sure like to see him listen to the missionaries, but it seems he's a real independent sort of fellow."

"All right now, James," said the bishop's former fifth-grade teacher, Mrs. Martha Ruckman, who was still allowing her young granddaughter, Tashia, to attend the ward and take part in church functions, though she had not yet permitted her to be baptized. "I want to know what you think about the goings-on with this A.M. Sunshine Rally business. Tashia tells me y'all are having a sort of revival meeting that night, to counteract the influence."

The bishop smiled in Tashia's direction, and the little girl smiled back impishly, her eyes gleaming in her dark face.

"Well," he said, "I don't know if I'd exactly call it a revival, although that might be as good a name as any for what we're try-ing to do. We're calling it a fireside—a less-formal meeting than most. We're going to be showing a short film about Joseph Smith and some things that happened in Church history. Then we'll be having a talk by a brother who's very well-versed in the scrip-tures and who himself is a Jewish convert to Mormonism, with lots of interesting experiences to tell. I believe the missionaries will speak, and we'll sing several songs and bear testimony—that sort of thing. You and Tashia are more than welcome to attend— we'd love to have you."

Mrs. Ruckman frowned. "I might drop Tashia by, if I can ask you to keep an eye on her, James. I'm committed, I suppose, to attend that rally with the choir from my church. We've been asked to sing, and Doctor Burshaw accepted for us. A few of us are not so happy about that decision, but I am a member of the choir and expected to participate. Personally, I don't hold with folks picking on other religions like that. I've seen enough prejudice in my day to prejudice me against it!"

"I understand," the bishop said. "And of course I'll watch out for Tashia—she's one of my favorite people!"

Sam Wright spoke. "I'll bet she'll be sittin' right up front with the Arnaud family, won't you, honey? I know they're comin', and I believe you're real good friends with their young'uns, aren't you?"

"Well, Angeline and Tamika, yeah," Tashia agreed. "I mean, yessir," she added, with a glance at her grandmother. "But not Currie. He's too silly, and he bugs us."

"Well, he's a little brother, see—that's his job," Sam explained with a grin. Tashia rolled her eyes. The bishop was reminded of his daughters, who were also good eye-rollers at the outrageous pronouncements of adults.

"Well, now—this isn't such a bad place," the bishop remarked, as they sat down on the cushioned sofa of Dr. Scott Lanier, in his newly-rented apartment. "It's downright comfortable, seems to me."

Scott shrugged. "Only because John and his wife came down and helped me furnish it," he admitted. "I didn't care what it looked like, to tell you the truth, but John's wife has a good touch with decorating, and I think she enjoyed fixing it up for me. They talked me into getting a cushy new bed, too—and I've got to admit that's been welcome. Seems like I'm tired all the time, but I don't sleep well at night, so I suppose I might as well be comfortable while I stare at the ceiling."

"If you can't sleep, maybe you could listen to scripture tapes or some soothing music in those hours," the bishop suggested. "Do you have a CD player?"

"I could pick one up, I guess. I left everything in the house—you know—for Marybeth. But that's not a bad idea, Bishop. It might help."

"Let's get right on it," the bishop advised. "I'll check with you tomorrow. We've got some CDs you could borrow, till you get your own. I don't like the idea of you lying there with only your own thoughts for company."

"It's true they're not very entertaining—or comforting," Scott said with a faint smile.

Y

"How do you tell a man his wife ain't worth the agony he's going through over losing her?" asked Sam with a sigh as they drove away from Scott's apartment. "Woman that'd act like Marybeth's been doin' ain't deservin' of bein' missed, you ask me."

"I know. I reckon he misses the woman she used to be—or the one he thought she was."

"I believe that must be it. I don't see how a woman with any kind of testimony of the truth could just go off the deep end and do like she's done, all of a sudden like that. It must've been festerin' inside of her for a long spell, is the way I see it. I know she ain't one to take advice nor direction from nobody, to begin with, specially if it interferes with her idea of a good time. Then I figger she hit one of them mid-life crisises you hear about and decided to chuck it all and go for pleasure and freedom and what-have-you. What d'you think, Bishop?"

"Much the same," the bishop replied. "Worst thing is, Scott's lying there suffering, beating up on himself and trying to count all the things he might have done wrong, or left undone, to contribute to the situation. That'd drive anybody to distraction. Yet I know I'd likely do the same thing."

"Man, wouldn't that just be the pits? You and me, Jim—we're lucky in our wives."

The bishop smiled. "Blessed," he agreed. "Beyond what we deserve."

CHAPTER NINETEEN

" . . . LET THY CONGREGATION ESCAPE TRIBULATION"

O n Thursday evening, Bishop Shepherd, his counselors and clerks, and their wives arranged to attend the temple at Birmingham. As he sat in the Celestial Room enjoying the quiet and the serenity, Jim felt Trish's hand slip into his as she sat down beside him. She looked beautiful in her temple clothing, and he was reminded of the amazing day when, similarly dressed, she had knelt across from him at a holy altar and agreed to give herself to him for time and for eternity. The thought of it had been humbling to him at the time, and was even more so now—nineteen years and three-and-a-half children later. He thought about the children—how precious they were to both their parents and how different each was from the others, beginning, it seemed, at the moment of birth.

Well, he reflected, *actually beginning long before birth, according to the teachings of the Church. Their remarkably unique personalities were some kind of blend of premortal development, genetic make-up, and earthly experience. And before much longer, a fourth child would join their family, fresh from heaven with a whole set of characteristics of his or her own to be molded and refined by earthly experience.*

He wondered, as he had many times, just when the immortal spirit takes possession of the mortal tabernacle. Was it at conception—early in the development of the fetus, or later—or at the moment of drawing the first breath? It was something the Lord had not seen fit to reveal to man. Was the unborn baby's spirit present when the baby had hiccups, or sucked its thumb in the womb, or reached out and grasped its toes, as he had once seen Mallory do in an ultrasound exam? He had heard stories of people who claimed to have memories of things that had occurred while their mothers were carrying them, but he didn't know whether or not to credit them. There were many things he yearned to understand, but at least, here in the temple more than anywhere else, there was a sense that past, present, and future were inseparably connected—all on a grand, God-ordained continuum. That was comforting.

"That was relaxing, wasn't it, once we got there?" Trish remarked after they had dropped off Dan McMillan and his wife and were headed toward home.

"Very peaceful," he agreed. "I hope I can retain some of that peace for the next few days."

"Likewise. Are you nervous, Jim?"

"I'm—what am I? Let's see. I'm a little apprehensive but also a little excited. I'm curious about what they'll try to pull, but I'm also confident that the Lord will carry the day. Part of me says I'm making too big a deal out of it, while another part wonders if we're sufficiently prepared. So how's that? Maybe what I am is double-minded, and the scriptures say a double-minded man is 'unstable in all his ways.' No wonder I'm a mess!" He chuckled. She reached over and patted his knee.

"You're not double-minded. You're just facing an unknown, and that's got to be unnerving. But hang onto that feeling of peace and faith we felt tonight. That's just as much reality as the adversary and his little helpers."

"And you keep reminding me of that, if I start to get a wall-eyed, glassy stare about me, will you?"

She laughed. "You can count on it." She fell silent for a moment, then said, "You know, I was thinking how we've all been horrified at the terrorists who try to hide behind the shield of an ancient world religion to do awful things to anybody who doesn't see the world exactly as they do—but how different, in spirit, are these so-called Christians? These guys who go around name-calling and threatening and trying to intimidate peace-loving people just because we have a little different view of things?"

"I see your point. Maybe not so different, at all. They just, hopefully, don't have bombs."

"Verbal stink bombs, maybe."

He grinned. "Then the odor will cling to them."

On Friday evening, the bishop made phone calls to various members of his ward, reminding them of the fireside, encouraging them to bring any friends who might be interested, and trying to answer any of their concerns.

"Linda's coming to the meeting, Bishop," said Ralph Jernigan. "Feel I can do more good scoping out the enemy camp. Got your cell phone number, so . . ."

"Ralph? You have a cell phone?" The bishop was astonished.

"Don't trust the things, true, but I've got me one just for this operation—so, um—anything going on that I think you ought to know, I'll be in touch. Just keep your ringer on vibrate and sit where you can slip out to answer. Won't call unless I feel it's warranted. Hope I won't have to."

"Well, me too, Ralph. You know I'd rather you came to the fireside with Linda, but it's your call. Do what you feel you must. Just be careful, okay? And thanks for all you have done, already."

"My duty, Bishop. And—you know. Happy to."

He spoke with Elder Moynihan, having given a part of the fireside schedule over to him and his companion, Elder Rivenbark—and learned that both were planning to give short presentations. He called to check on the music and discovered that more was in the planning than he had anticipated. In addition to congregational hymns, the choir would be singing two numbers, there would be a solo by Linda DeNeuve, and the prelude and postlude music would consist of a piano and organ duet by Sisters Margaret Tullis and Claire Patrenko.

"Wow," he said, turning to Trish, who sat at the dining table working on a report for Relief Society. "I didn't know the choir was singing tomorrow night."

"Oh, didn't you? Yep—we're doing 'Zion Stands with Hills Surrounded' and 'I Saw a Mighty Angel Fly.' We haven't done much this summer because of vacations and such, but we had already started working on those in the spring, so they weren't too hard to pull together."

"That's terrific. I'm so proud of our choir—you guys and gals are sounding great. Do you happen to know what Linda's singing?"

"Um—yes, I heard her practicing last Sunday, after choir, while we were waiting for you. It was two hymns that she kind of wove together. One was 'Though Deepening Trials,' and the other was that one we sing—I can't think how it starts, but it says, 'He'll safely guide you unto that haven . . . ' Remember that?"

He nodded. "I think so. They all sound like perfect selections for the occasion. Boy, I never had heard Linda sing before we called her to direct the choir, but she's good, isn't she?"

"Oh, yeah. She's really good."

He went to bed that night feeling considerably cheered.

Y

"Well, I s'pose we had to see it, didn't we?" he asked darkly the next morning, as Jamie handed him the latest of Maxine Lowell's flyers. "I saw her taking these around the other day."

Jamie nodded. "Miss Hestelle just called me over to the fence and told me to bring it right to you," he said. "She had it folded up, I reckon so that Lowell lady wouldn't know what it was if she was looking."

Tiffani laughed. "Bet she's sorry she put up that high old fence out there. It means she has to go to all that trouble to climb up to spy on us."

"Well, let's see what flavor the latest poison is," her father said, and unfolded the circular with a sigh.

"Rejoice, dear Christian friends," he read. "The time is here at last for the festering wound in our community to be lanced and the ugly infection inside exposed to the fresh air of truth! All you have to do is take your family and friends and attend the rally at the County Fair Park on this Saturday, the third of August, at seven P.M. You will hear horror stories from people who have been held captive by the Mormons and forced to partake of their paganistic rituals! You will hear them witness of their deliverance and conversion to Christ! You will learn of the twisted perversions of their unholy so-called religion, so that you can reject their ambassadors once and for all when they come calling at your door! Come one, come all, to learn the TRUTH about these worshipers of the brother of Satan! Our time has come! Saturday at seven—BE THERE or be sorry! From a true friend."

Tiffani took the letter from his hand and reread it to herself. "Festering wound!" she exclaimed. "*She's* a festering wound! That stupid, ugly, crazy old woman—how can she write such awful stuff?"

"Easy, Tiffi," her dad soothed. "It's all pretty typical of a certain brand of 'anti' rhetoric that surfaces every so often. It almost makes me laugh, though, because it sounds so much like stuff I've seen that was written about us a century or so ago. I even wonder if Mrs. Lowell might not have access to one of those old books or tracts and be copying her ideas and wording from that source."

Trish looked up. "Do you suppose she is?" she asked. "Now that you mention it, the tone does sound a little old-fashioned, doesn't it? I wonder."

"Well, wherever she got it, she shouldn't be allowed to pass stuff like that around our neighborhood," Tiffani declared.

"Freedom of speech, freedom of the press," her father reminded her. "We're allowed to say what we believe and even to try to convince others of it, if they're interested. We have to allow her that same freedom."

"So is that stupid rally going to sound like that, too?" Tiffani asked.

"I doubt it'll be any better," her mother replied. "But we know what's true about our belief and our faith—and that's what's most important."

"I'm just glad school's out for a few more weeks," Tiffani said. "Maybe some people, at least, will have time to forget what an awful religion I believe in, before we go back."

"You and Claire and Billy and Ricky and T-Rex—and usually Lisa Lou—are good representatives of the Church in your school," her mother told her, patting her shoulder. "I'll bet most people won't believe half of what they hear, anyway—at least, those who know us."

Tiffani shrugged. "I guess I can hope."

The bishop went to work at the store for a while on Saturday morning, hoping to distract himself from thoughts of what the evening might bring. There was no sanctuary there, however, as Mary Lynn Connors, who had also come in to work for a while on some pretext or other, handed him a sheet of newsprint.

"You seen this, Jim?" she asked. "I cain't believe people behavin' like this. Never seen nothin' like it around here."

He scanned the paper. The A.M. Sunshine Rally people had taken out a half-page ad in a Birmingham paper, which featured a photograph of the Salt Lake Temple with an illustration of a cross superimposed over it. "Turn to the Lord of the cross," read the lettering. "Learn the truth about the non-Christian sect called the Mormon Church, and the Jesus they claim to worship. Do not allow yourselves or your families and friends to miss this vitally important rally for Christ!" At the bottom of the page, just above the details of time and place, an illustration depicted two devilish-looking young men in dark suits being followed by a couple of girls with scarf-covered heads, long skirts, and longer faces. One of them looked back dolefully toward the other half of the illustration, which showed a happy couple with healthy-looking smiles striding briskly toward a church with a cross on the steeple.

"Well, okay, then," he said with a rueful grin and handed the paper back to Mary Lynn. "Tell me, Mary Lynn—have you seen any people resembling those poor, long-faced women when you've visited our church?"

She gave a small, derisive sniff. "Those happy-lookin' ones, there, they put me in mind of the Mormons I've seen," she told him. "Fact is, I was tellin' Chuck the other night, them Mormons are purt' nigh the cheerfulest people I ever seen. They act real glad to be at church, even for three whole hours, and then they hang around after it's over, just to visit! I never saw the like."

"Oh, you know," he teased, "we're just brainwashed and forced to pretend we're happy. We can't help ourselves—we just don't know any better."

"And you're just full of it, Jim Shepherd! I hatn't known you and your family all these years and not noticed how y'all act. I've, um, I've admired it."

"Thanks, Mary Lynn. I'm grateful for that. So, are you and Chuck coming to the fireside, tonight?"

"Oh, I don't think them cute missionaries would hear of us not coming! Chuck, at least—and he's asked me to go with him, so . . ."

"Glad to hear it. See you there, then. Thanks—I think—for showing me that." He nodded toward the newspaper on her desk.

She folded it and consigned it to the "round file."

"Huh!" she said expressively.

The chapel was full. The divider curtains had been folded back and chairs set up halfway into the cultural hall. Even as the prelude music was being played, the elders were busily setting up additional seating.

The bishopric sat on the stand, along with those who would participate in the meeting, and watched the people come in.

Many shook hands or hugged as they greeted each other, but there was an air of subdued excitement, and the decibel level was noticeably lower than usual. *The piano-organ duet might be partially responsible for that,* the bishop reflected. It was a treat they generally enjoyed only for the Christmas or Easter program.

His own family occupied the third row of the center section of pews, along with Muzzie and her children. Mallory and Muzzie's youngest, Marie, busied themselves, drawing pictures on small pads that Trish had provided, but Brad and Chloe looked around in interest.

Tiffani, he noticed, kept glancing back until she had seen Billy Newton saunter in and take a place on the second row from the front, and to one side. Yep, the bishop thought. That's what he would have done—had done, in fact, when he and Trish had been high-schoolers, before he had dared to admit to anyone besides himself that he was mightily interested in that perky, dark-haired Langham girl. From that vantage point in the chapel, it was easy to glance back casually and catch the eye of the young lady in question, or check her response to something that had been said from the pulpit. He gave Billy Newton points for perspicacity.

Little Tashia Jones, as Sam Wright had predicted, was happily tucked up between the Arnaud daughters. Linda Jernigan slipped into a spot right by the backdoor, as if she might have to bolt, and he was glad to see Ida Lou Reams take a seat beside her and give her a hug. What happened next increased his gladness: Barker Reams came in, looking uncomfortable in a white shirt and tie, and sat next to his wife. She smiled lovingly at him and patted his knee. The bishop was amazed. Except for the occasional funeral, he didn't recall ever seeing Barker at a meeting. How had Ida Lou persuaded him to come to this one?

The missionaries entered, accompanied by Chuck Stagley

and Mary Lynn Connors. Elder Moynihan scouted out a good seat for them and then went back out into the foyer while Elder Rivenbark made his slow, painful way up to the stand. Soon Elder Moynihan reappeared, escorting the mother and young daughter they were teaching, as well as the rosy-cheeked nurse whom the bishop had met at the time of Hilda Bainbridge's passing. The three of them sat together, and he noticed that the nurse, whose name he was ashamed he couldn't recall, looked up to the stand, caught the eye of Elder Rivenbark, and smiled. A quick glance to the side showed him that the missionary returned the smile and gave a brief nod of recognition in her direction.

One by one, the choir gathered behind him, many of them greeting him as they took their places. He counted at least twenty people—six of them brethren—and silently gave thanks for this choir that had been born so reluctantly, but that had made what he regarded as amazing progress under Sister DeNeuve's patient and expert tutelage.

The Forelaw family filed into the back, their three little ones already clad in their pajamas and clutching blankets, ready to fall asleep during the opening prayer, the bishop suspected. The building filled rapidly just before it was time to begin. Even a carload of the Birdwhistle family had made it down from the hills— Ernie and the four children who were just younger than Pratt, their missionary brother. Buddy Osborne spotted them and slipped silently in beside them. The bishop was grateful for the friendship they had shown to Buddy ever since his tutorials to them on computer basics.

As the minute hand of the wall clock clicked into place, signaling seven o'clock, the bishop stepped to the podium and stood smiling at the congregation as he waited for the last few bars from the piano and organ to slow, end, and die away.

"Brothers and sisters," he began, and was suddenly over-whelmed by such love and gratitude for the people present that he had to pause a moment to regain his composure. "We're met here tonight to worship and praise our Heavenly Father and his Holy Son, Jesus the Christ. We will sing and speak and testify to their living reality and their influence in our lives. Now, we're all aware that just outside of town, a very different kind of meeting is taking place. That's fine—let them meet. You know the Article of Faith: 'We claim the privilege of worshiping Almighty God according to the dictates of our own conscience, and allow all men the same privilege, let them worship how, where, or what they may.' As for us, I'm reminded of a scripture in the twenty-sixth chapter of Alma, verses six and seven, in the Book of Mormon: 'When the storm cometh they shall be gathered together in their place, that the storm cannot penetrate to them; yea, neither shall they be driven with fierce winds whithersoever the enemy listeth to carry them. But behold, they are in the hands of the Lord of the harvest, and they are his; and he will raise them up at the last day.' Our present storm isn't a hurricane or a tornado, but I'm still grateful that we're gathered here together, in our place, and I pray that the Lord will not allow the storm of opposition to penetrate to us.

"I'm grateful for the lovely prelude music from Sisters Tullis and Patrenko and the soothing effect it's had on all of us. I'm thankful for all who will participate in this special program tonight, whether in speaking, playing and singing, testifying, or praying. I'm grateful, too, that the police department has seen fit to send one of their men to stand guard outside—not that we expect any trouble—but just to keep an eye on things. I appre-ciate Sisters Ida Lou Reams and Frankie Talbot for arranging the beautiful flowers you see on the podium—and my dear wife, Trish, for growing many of them! We'll begin tonight with a hymn by the congregation, 'Come, Ye Children of the Lord,' number 58, after which our opening prayer will be offered by Brother Robert Patrenko, my first counselor."

The meeting was all he could have hoped for. The film was touching. The singing, both by choir and congregation, seemed exceptional. Thrills coursed over him as the choir sang "the gospel's joyful sound, to calm our doubts, to chase our fears, and make our joys abound." Yes, he thought—there, encapsulated in those words, was the very purpose of this meeting!

Elder Moynihan spoke of the First Vision of Joseph Smith, detailing very clearly the new understanding that had come to mankind of the nature of God, and of the apostasy that had occurred in fulfillment of the many prophecies in the New Testament that such a thing would happen. Elder Rivenbark then approached the stand, set his canes aside, and gripped the lectern. He expanded on the subject of the Apostasy, speaking with surprising authority of the precious truths that had been lost to the early Christians over the first few centuries after the Savior's death and resurrection. He gave several quotes from very early Christian writers, which, as he pointed out, sounded strangely familiar to members of today's restored Church, but which had ultimately been rejected and changed in times past, creating the confusion and disagreement on points of doctrine that existed among the various sects at the time Joseph Smith was searching for the truth. He went on to quote a number of latter-day scriptures and revelations that matched the early Christian beliefs, explaining to the listeners that Joseph Smith could not have known these things except by revelation from God, since the writings of the early Saints he had quoted had not been translated—some of them not yet even discovered—in Joseph Smith's day. It was a powerful testimony from a young man who was universally loved and admired by all those who knew him.

The bishop noticed how intently people were listening— including Muzzie Winston and the new investigators—and was pleased. Sister DeNeuve then sang her arrangement of the two hymns she had chosen, and then Sister Magda Warshaw stood to speak. She gave a brief version of her conversion story and that of her husband. Her accent was much thicker than John's, so that the audience had to listen carefully to catch everything she said. She told of their experiences as Jewish children in eastern Europe during World War Two, being hidden away and moved from family to family—and how, coincidentally, they had both survived and came into contact with kind members of the Church in Germany, long after the war was over.

"So do you t'ink ve could find de truth in such a place, after all dat had gone on, dere?" she asked. "Vould you t'ink that two Jewish kids vould accept de gospel of Jesus Christ, after all vhat had happened to us? And vould you t'ink ve vould go from being Jews—persecuted like no one could even believe—and join a Church dat also attracts persecution? I mean, vhat is dis? Are ve gluttons for punishment, or vhat?" There was a ripple of laughter as she held both hands up in a gesture of disbelief. "But ve did— ve found de truth and ve found each other, and I'm grateful ve had de sense to know it vas real and true. John vill tell you some of vat ve haf learned, but I just vant to tell you dat dis Church is true. Id is true in Germany, id is true in Poland, id is true in Africa, and id is true right here in Alabama! Id is for all people— efen stubborn Jews like us, once ve can see it for vhat it is!"

John Warshaw then took the pulpit, patting his wife's arm as they crossed paths, and plunged into a fascinating talk about the uses of adversity. He spoke of how persecution and adversity had always, from the beginning, been the lot of those who follow the truth, and was to be expected. He told of the troubles of the children of Israel during their sojourn in Egypt and their escape from Pharaoh and how in both the Bible and the Book of Mormon, trouble had followed truth, because the adversary of truth made every effort to destroy it. He reiterated the persecutions of the Savior during His earthly sojourn and of His apostles and followers after His death. He explained that in order for the gospel of Christ to be restored to earth, there had to be a nation set up with sufficient freedom of religion that it could get a toehold and survive and ultimately flourish. And even here in this blessed land, he reminded his listeners, the newly restored Church had barely survived the persecutions of those who didn't believe that angels could visit or that the Lord speaks to ordinary mortals.

"So here we find ourselves," he concluded, "in a small city in Alabama, minding our own business, enjoying our right to worship as we please, and what happens? We are given a turn at being persecuted, too! Isn't that wonderful? It gives us a chance to show of what we are made! It gives us a chance to stand up and be counted, but in a totally different way to those who criticize and make fun of us. If they are rude and abrasive, we can be polite and kind. If they call out insults, we can speak the truth in peace. If they spew hatred and venom, we can show love and tolerance. If they try to push us out of the circle of true Christian belief and love for the Savior, we can reach out and try to show them a better way and draw them in!

"Now, the folks who are meeting at the fairgrounds—they will no doubt be on their way to another place with their ugliness before we have a chance to speak to them. But we will have opportunities to speak with those they are influencing tonight and leaving behind in our community. Let us be true Saints, my brothers and sisters, and demonstrate what we really believe and know to be true! The Lord will uphold us when we honor and obey Him. Let us be not afraid, but take this as the challenge and opportunity it is, to show people the truth. And may we grow in love for our fellowman, reaching out in tolerance and understanding where little of that exists, that our Father in Heaven may be glorified. God bless us to do so, I solemnly pray!"

Brother Warshaw closed his remarks, and the choir stood to sing their second number. They were just singing, "In the furnace God may prove thee, thence to bring thee forth more bright," when the bishop felt his cell phone vibrate in his shirt pocket. He slipped as unobtrusively as possible from the stand and into the sacrament preparation room, where he closed the door and answered. It was, as he had surmised, Ralph Jernigan.

"Yes, Ralph?"

"Nasty people, these, Bishop. Looks like the rally's starting to wind down, and guys in yellow tee shirts have been handing papers around. Picked one up that somebody dropped, and it's got maps to all the chapels in our stake. Ours is circled in red. They may be coming. Don't know what exactly they've got in mind, but it won't be nice. Heard one guy say 'They're all gonna burn in hell someday, might as well start now!' Don't know if he's serious, but thought you ought to know."

"Thanks, Ralph. Be safe. Watch out for yourself."

"Will do. You, too, sir."

The bishop eased out of the small room and out the door nearest to the front of the building, called by some the "casket door" because it was the simplest route of egress at funerals. He jogged around the front of the building and approached the black and white car of the Fairhaven Police Department. The officer got out of his car as he saw the bishop coming.

"Yessir, what can I do for you?" he asked, grinding out the stub of a cigarette on the pavement. "Y'all got trouble?"

"Not yet, but I just received word that they're handing out maps to this building at the rally and that some people are talking about burning, though I really doubt they'd try that."

The deputy raised his eyebrows. "Don't doubt it. Heard it's been tried, other places. Sorry we don't have more men to siphon off, but one's at the rally, and the others are needed other places. I'll give 'em a heads up, though, and maybe somebody can run over here. Thanks for letting me know."

"Thank you," the bishop replied, and headed back to the meeting. Just outside the door, in a private corner of the porch, he paused for a moment in the fragrant summer dusk, thinking about what Ralph had said. Had they done the wrong thing, he wondered, by calling this meeting? Should he have counseled all the ward members to stay safe in their own homes this evening? Would the faithful be brought to harm by being here? A dark blanket of guilt and fear began to descend over him. What had he done?

"No!" he said aloud. President Walker and his counselors had met and prayed and determined that this was the best thing to do. He and his own counselors had felt positive about it as well. He bowed his head. "Heavenly Father, we're in Thy hands," he prayed. "Please bless and protect these good people who love and serve Thee, and keep them safe from harm and evil of all kinds. Forgive me, please, Father, for my weakness and fears. Thy will be done in all things." He closed his silent prayer and slipped back to his place on the stand, giving his wife a quick wink as he did so, as he knew she would be concerned.

In his absence, Bob Patrenko had taken the opportunity to bear his testimony and was issuing an invitation to members of the congregation who felt so inclined to do the same. The bishop thanked him as he sat down, then leaned over and gave his counselors a brief update on Ralph's call as they waited for the first to testify.

In a steady flow, people streamed to the front, waiting to take their turn at the microphone, expressing their tender feelings and their witness of the living Lord and His restored Church. The bishop had one ear tuned to the testimonies and one to any disturbance or sound of increased traffic on the outside of the building.

Eventually the sound materialized. Cars could be heard turning in to the already full parking lot, circling the building. The bishop could see, reflected on the back wall of the cultural hall, the pulsing light on the police car. He wanted to rush outside and assess the situation, but something kept him rooted to his seat. That same something also soothed his fears, so that he was able to smile at those who came forward to testify. He was aware of the elders quorum president strolling out into the foyer with his baby son, but no one else left. Linda Jernigan looked poised for flight, but by some power—probably the same power that held the bishop back—she remained seated. The bulk of the congregation, if they heard the traffic outside at all, seemed to be paying no attention to it. The testimonies being borne were especially fervent and simple, and there was no abatement in the line of those wishing to testify.

A sudden shout outside and the gunning of engines as cars headed out of the parking lot caused the bishop's heart to leap in his chest, but still he was restrained by the Spirit from moving. The elders quorum president returned to his seat, and as the sound of the departing vehicles died away, the reflection of the revolving light ceased. All was calm. A few minutes later, Ralph Jernigan quietly took a seat beside his wife, seeking out the bishop's gaze and giving him a discreet thumbs-up sign.

When all who desired to bear testimony had done so, the bishop stood to close the meeting.

"Brothers, sisters, dear friends—I feel we've been richly blessed this evening—maybe more richly than we know," he said. "Let's express our thanks to our Heavenly Father by singing together hymn number two, 'The Spirit of God,' after which the benediction will be given by Brother Sam Wright."

The singing was powerful—perhaps, Bishop Shepherd thought, because he and his counselors heard it in stereophonic sound, with the choir behind him and the congregation in front. On the last verse, Sister DeNeuve contributed a soprano obligato. It made the bishop feel that angels might be singing with them. Perhaps, he thought, they were.

CHAPTER TWENTY

Y

" . . . OH, KNOW YOU NOT THAT ANGELS ARE NEAR YOU?"

As the piano and organ provided a reprise of one of the hymns they had played for the prelude, people filed from the building with quiet smiles and thoughtful expressions. Mary Lynn Connors touched a tissue to her eyes and smiled mistily at Chuck. Bishop Shepherd shook hands with those who had participated on the program, sincerely thanking each for doing his or her part to invite the Spirit in the meeting. He then moved down to greet the investigators whom the missionaries had brought, but he didn't linger, since he wanted to catch the Jernigans before they left. He also wanted to speak to Officer Ed Bizzell and find out what had happened to cause their uninvited visitors to depart so abruptly.

He needn't have worried about Ralph, as he and Linda were waiting for him in the foyer.

"Ralph, good—I want to talk to you," he said, squeezing that man's arm briefly. "Just let me just grab Officer Bizzell first. I want to hear his report, too." He turned in time to catch Trish's eye and ask her and the children, including Tashia Jones, to wait inside the building until Tashia's grandmother picked her up, or until he could finish his night's business and lock up, whichever happened first.

"Officer, thanks so much for your presence here tonight," he said, reaching to shake Ed Bizzell's hand. "Can you tell me what happened when all those cars drove through the parking lot?"

Officer Bizzell laughed. "Funniest dang thing I ever saw," he said. "They come roaring up here with all kinds of flags and banners hanging out their car windows, with crosses and Bible verses and what-have-you on 'em. I swear, one of 'em looked like he had a pair of man's long-johns flying from his antenna! They was yellin' and honkin' their horns and all, and they pulled in over yonder, drove through the back part of the lot, and come around this way, and I reckon that's when they saw my vehicle here, and they flat-out panicked! Lead guy, he leaned out his window and yelled, 'Place is full of smoke, boys, must be a hunderd of 'em!' And they all gunned their engines and took off. Kinda made me laugh, seein' as how there was only me! Reckon they didn't know that a couple of my buddies from the Sheriff's department had tailed them all the way from the rally, but was just hangin' back to see if they started any mischief."

"You say they were honking their horns as they came through here?"

"Land, yes—didn't y'all hear 'em? Must have good insulation in your church, there."

The bishop nodded. "Reckon maybe we do, at that."

"I don't know exactly who those fellers are, but there was license plates from California, Oregon, Washington, Kentucky— let's see—um, Ohio, and I think I saw one Tennessee. My S. D. buddies are still on their tail and will be until they pull out of the county. Understand they got a couple of buses out at the fair park, as well as all their private vehicles."

"Interesting. Well, my friend, we're grateful to you—and I just want you to know that you were on the Lord's errand, tonight."

Officer Bizzell looked a bit taken aback. "Ain't nobody ever told me that, before," he said. "But I'll say this—if them fellers was Christians, they ain't the kind we got around here—and I was glad to hear that some folks that went to their rally up and told 'em so."

"Oh, is that right?"

The officer chuckled. "Way I hear it, some little old black lady stood up and gave 'em what for and led a whole section of people out of the park in protest—right close to a third went with her, my friend said."

The bishop had to make a conscious effort to close his mouth. He knew, without a shadow of doubt, exactly who that 'little old black lady' must have been. Then he began to smile and couldn't seem to stop. He thanked the officer again and went back into the building, where he found Robert Patrenko and Sam Wright waiting for him in his office. He invited Ralph and Linda to join them.

"Brother and Sister Jernigan, thanks so much for the work you've done to make us aware of what's been going on," he told them. "And thanks for the call, Ralph. Now, if you will, please tell us what you saw and heard tonight."

Ralph cleared his throat. "Saw a division of the devil's army, Bishop. Didn't start out too bad—nice choir, some hymns. But then they tried to disguise themselves as religious men— 'Christian soldiers,' they called themselves—but easy enough to see through, soon as they started talking. Not so much interested in spreading the good word of the gospel, you understand, as in tearing down the Lord's work and His prophets, from Joseph Smith down to the present. Said some awful things about all of them. Vicious, like a pack of mad dogs. Got louder and louder, talked about how the Lord's real followers in the area had the responsibility of rooting out the Mormon devil-worshipers and sending them packing—that they had no place in a good Christian town like Fairhaven. Talked about how our missionaries kidnap young girls and haul them off to temples and turn them into love slaves and thirty-seventh wives of some old codger—and how we worship Adam instead of God, and we think Jesus and the devil are brothers, and not very different, at that—both being sons of the morning, and all. Went on and on—and after a while, I noticed people around me looking at each other, kind of pulling faces, shaking their heads, like they weren't quite buying what they heard—although some were. Some were shouting 'Amen!' or 'Praise the Lord!' and other such things after every sentence, lifting their hands in the air and sort of swaying back and forth.

"Finally, a lady stood up and turned around in the bleachers and yelled out, 'Anybody besides me think these people are full of lies and hatred?' Some folks yelled out, 'Yes!' 'Anybody think true Christians would do better to preach Christ's word than to come here and degrade our good Mormon neighbors?' More people yelled 'Yes!' And she said, 'Then follow me out of here, and let's show these hypocrites what we think of them!' She marched down the bleachers, and a whole bunch of people followed her. She got down on the field, and made a sort of megaphone out of a piece of poster board and yelled the same kind of things to the folks across the way. They got the picture, and a good number of them followed her, too. About that time, the guys in charge got wind of what she was doing, and tried to cover up by passing out maps to our chapel and talking about going to stage a 'peaceful demonstration,' to let the neighbors who live around our church know that we'd be run out of town before long, that they had support, and so forth."

Ralph took a deep breath. The bishop had never heard him open up and say so much at one time.

"Then," Ralph continued, "they all left the rally in a big hurry, jumped in cars and drove over here, honking and waving flags out their windows. Heard one fellow say something about getting us started on burning in hell, and I thought he might try to torch the chapel. That's when I called you, Bishop," he added, nodding solemnly at his church leader. "Thought they'd get out and do some marching around, at least—maybe come in and try to disrupt the meeting, cause whatever damage they could. But for some reason, they just drove through the parking lot and then headed out like the devil himself was after them. Can't say I'm sorry at that—but I was surprised."

"I can tell you a little about that part," the bishop said, and related what Officer Bizzell had reported to him. "I didn't even hear the horns—just the vehicles, and one man shouting. How about you, brethren?"

"I didn't hear nothin'," Sam reported. "Wadn't even aware of the cars comin' through. You, Bob?"

Robert Patrenko shook his head. "I didn't hear them, either. That's interesting. I wonder if anyone did? And you say the guy shouted something about a hundred cops?" He chuckled. "It sounds as if maybe the Lord—shall we say, 'enlarged their vision'—for a moment, there!"

"And insulated us," the bishop added. "Sister Linda, did you hear anything going on?"

She nodded. "Just the car engines, but not loud. Didn't even hear the shouting or the horns. And I didn't notice anybody else in the chapel looking disturbed."

"Folks, I believe a prayer of thanksgiving is in order, here," suggested the bishop. "Shall we kneel?"

Y

When he emerged from his office, having said goodnight to his counselors and the Jernigans, he was greeted by Mrs. Martha Ruckman, holding Tashia by the hand. *Uh-oh,* he thought. *Mrs. Ruckman's going to tell me she doesn't feel it's safe for Tashia to keep coming to church with us. I should have seen that one coming.*

Mrs. Ruckman stood as tall and straight as ever—which was very straight but not very tall—and her brow was beaded with perspiration. Her eyes were snapping, and her lips were pressed firmly together.

"James?" she said. "My granddaughter and I would like to apply for baptism into your church. I assume you're the person to see to that?"

For the second time that evening, he was completely astounded. He looked at Tashia, who beamed at him with pure happiness. Behind Mrs. Ruckman's back, he was aware of Ralph Jernigan trying to signal him that this was the lady with the makeshift megaphone at the rally. He nodded deeply, his eyes shifting briefly to Ralph, so he'd know the message was received.

"Um—yes, you bet, that would be me," he said. "What— what a wonderful thing! But we'll need to talk about it at some length. You'll want to study—"

"James," his former fifth grade teacher interrupted. "Do you really think I would apply to join a church I hadn't studied thoroughly, and made a matter of prayer? Do you think I haven't read and reread every word Tashia's brought into our home? Now, of course I understand that my next move is to be formally taught by your missionaries, and trust me, I have some very pertinent questions to ask them."

He trusted her. He nodded dumbly.

"So, would you be so kind as to have them contact me to set up a time for me to receive these lessons?"

"I—I—yes, ma'am. I'd be more than happy to do that!"

"All right. I'll be expecting their call. Now, Miss Lady, shall we go home? It's been a rather full evening." Tashia nodded, still beaming, and snuggled closer to her grandmother.

The bishop finally found his voice and his wits. "Mrs. Ruckman, I want to thank you for what you did tonight, at the rally. I heard about it—and I knew it couldn't be anybody but you."

"Well, I have to tell you, those were the most despicable excuses for men—let alone Christian men—that I have ever had the misfortune to encounter. But you may thank them—it was their anger and their lying tongues that confirmed my realization that any church they choose to fight so hard against must be approved of the Lord because it was plain to me that they were approved by the devil himself!"

The bishop finally turned out the lights, locked all the doors, and climbed wearily but happily into his car, where Trish and the children were waiting. He backed out and turned to leave, when he noticed a pickup truck parked in the far corner of the lot. Curious, he drove over to it. It belonged to the Jernigans, and Ralph and Linda were relaxing in lawn chairs in the truck bed.

"Ralph?" he questioned. "What're y'all doing, still here? Planning to camp out?"

"Exactly, Bishop," Ralph replied. "Never know if any of those yay-hoos might decide to come back for a second try when nobody's here, before they head on. Knew we couldn't relax at home, thinking about that. So we'll be here till sunup, and then come back for church."

Linda held up a radio. "Got this, got our cell phone with the police number programmed in. And yours, too," she added. "We'll be fine."

He knew better than to argue. Besides, on some level, he was relieved.

"Don't take anybody on," he warned. "Just use your phone, all right, if you need to?"

"Absolutely, Bishop. See you in the morning."

"They are the most amazing people," Trish said as they pulled away. "I mean, it's kind of strange, but really so good of them, to do that."

Her husband remembered what Peter MacDonald had said, when he'd learned of Ralph's devotion to the Church in spite of his disabling paranoia.

"Noble," he echoed softly. "A noble soul."

"A miracle, Trish," the bishop said wearily to his wife as they sat propped by pillows against the headboard of their bed later that night. "We saw a miracle, this evening."

"I'd say so," she agreed. "More than one, in fact."

He nodded. "The fact that most people didn't even appear to be aware of the ruckus outside is the first one."

"I honestly didn't hear a thing. I guess I was just tuned in to the meeting."

"Or to the Spirit—which was very strong in that meeting, didn't you think?"

"Extremely. I've hardly ever felt quite like that—at least, in a meeting. Maybe in the temple."

"Right. And then the fact that our visitors thought there were lots of police present—that's got to qualify, too."

"So much for their 'peaceful demonstration,'" Trish commented. "If that's all they had intended, why would the presence of the police have spooked them so badly?"

"You know, if the chapel had been dark and empty when they arrived, and Officer Bizzell hadn't been there, we might have awakened tomorrow with no building to worship in. There was that talk of fire, by one person, at least. Of course; maybe he was just blowing smoke—no pun intended."

"Well, where there's smoke . . ."

"Exactly. It might have been in more minds than his. Then for Mrs. Martha Ruckman to decide to be baptized! I've never been so surprised."

"Isn't that wonderful? And little Tashia, too, bless her heart. She's wanted this for a long time."

"I think we're going to have a pretty substantial baptismal service one of these first days—maybe more than one—as things progress. The missionaries have several really fine investigators, including Chuck and Mary Lynn."

"These two elders are outstanding, aren't they? They're both so well-prepared and so earnest, it'd be hard not to believe what they teach." She smiled. "Cute, too. That doesn't hurt, especially when the teachee is a young female. I wonder who the pretty young lady was, that Elder Moynihan escorted in with the Simmonses. Is she part of their family?"

"Oh, um—no. Can't think of her name, but I can tell you that she's a nurse over at the hospital, and she helped care for Hilda in her last days. And, come to think of it, I believe I did notice a kind of special smile between her and Elder Rivenbark."

"Well, his smile's special enough to make any girl's heart flutter, in spite of all his problems."

The bishop nodded. "So I've been told," he replied, thinking of Lisa Lou Pope's fleeting crush on the young elder. "But I have enough confidence in his character that I don't think he'd bend mission rules by doing more than smiling and shaking hands, even if there is a mutual attraction there."

"Let's see—how much longer does he have to go, on his mission?"

"About ten more months. Next June."

"Well, a good girl—if she happens to be the right girl—can certainly wait that long to get better acquainted. And he's so absorbed in his work, the time'll pass quickly for him."

He brushed her knuckles against his lips. "You know, babe—we're probably fantasizing. Maybe the young lady just admires the missionaries who are teaching her. Pretty much everybody does that."

"M-hmm. Probably. Let's just watch, though—and see what we see."

"Shoot, I was so dense about Chuck and Mary Lynn that I probably won't see a thing!"

"How's their relationship coming along?"

"Like gangbusters. I expect a wedding shortly after a baptism."

"You really think Mary Lynn will join the Church?"

"No thanks to me, but yes, I do think so. And I couldn't be more pleased."

"That's so great." Trish sighed, finally beginning to relax. "So, Jim—do you think we dodged a bullet tonight, the way things worked out?"

"I think with the Lord's blessings, we dodged a whole bar-rage. But there may yet be casualties. We'll have to wait and see what kind of fallout there may be around town, from all the lies. Some folks evidently bought into what was being said."

"I'm glad for all those who didn't—who walked out. That was wonderful."

He grinned, thinking of Mrs. Martha Ruckman leading the exodus. "Sure was. I'd like to have been there, just to see that."

"Me, too. Oh, feel the baby, Jim—it's really kicking. Right here." She placed his hand on her abdomen. Sure enough, he felt several little thrusts against his hand.

"Wow," he said reverently. "I still can't believe we're going to have another one. We're so blessed, Trish."

"Aren't we? Not that it won't be a challenge. Less than four months, Daddy! We're more than halfway there."

"You know, the other evening in the temple, I was thinking about when the spirit enters the body, wondering at what point that happens, and if it's the same for everyone. Is it at conception, or first breath, or sometime in between?"

"Did you come to a conclusion?"

"Nope. I know it's one of the things the Lord hasn't revealed, and as much as I'd love to know, the more I think about it, the more wisdom I see in keeping that from us. I mean, just think— if we found for sure that it's at conception, then women who have abortions might find themselves in even more serious trouble than if they honestly think the fetus isn't really a living person, yet. But if we discovered that the spirit doesn't come on the scene till first breath, then the abortionists would crow and proclaim their rights and their innocence because they'd say they weren't really destroying life."

"You're probably right. Of course, a lot of people don't even believe in the concept of a spirit, or a soul, as they'd call it. They just think life is all physical."

"I'm grateful we've been taught better."

"Me, too. So grateful." She turned over to her side and

pulled a pillow down to stuff under her tummy in preparation for sleep.

Her husband leaned over and kissed her cheek. He was also grateful for her—and for the miracles that had protected her and the children and their many friends this night.

Monday morning, Chuck Stagley made a point of stopping the bishop at the store and telling him of his feelings about the Saturday fireside.

"I ain't never been to a meetin' that made me feel the way that one did, Jim," he said, shaking his head. "I mean, the services yesterday was fine, too, with all them folks testifyin' like they did, but the night before—man, that was somethin' special. Me and Mary Lynn both felt it."

The bishop nodded solemnly. "Glad you did, Chuck. I believe that was the influence of the Holy Ghost, and it's good you recognized it. Tell me something—did you hear cars and horns honking and people shouting outside, at any point during that meeting?"

Chuck frowned, and slowly shook his head. "Cain't say I did. Why, was somethin' goin' on?"

"Oh, we had a visit from the folks who held the rally—but most people didn't even notice it, and I reckon something spooked them, and they took off."

Chuck raised his eyebrows. "Huh," he said.

"Jim, you're not going to believe this," Trish said, as soon as he came in the kitchen door that afternoon.

"And what would 'this' be?" he queried, bending to kiss her hair. She handed him a typewritten letter.

"Read it and wonder," she told him.

He unfolded the letter and glanced first at the signature. "Well, from Leanore St. John! What is it—did she find something more for us?"

"Mm—no, let's say she found something more for herself. Read on."

"Dear Mr. and Mrs. Shepherd," he read, easing into a chair at the kitchen table. "You will no doubt be surprised at the news I have for you. I believe I told you that I had, on occasion, made use of the Family History Centers of your church, and that I had found the people there kind and helpful, if not especially sophisticated in their knowledge of research techniques. For this reason—and because I was favorably impressed with the sincerity and honesty you exhibited in your approach to running your family line—when two young ladies from your church appeared at my door a couple of weeks after you did, I let them come in and say their piece. (They insist you didn't send them; is that true?)

"They had a similar sincerity in their approach, and they seemed genuinely to care whether I believed what they had to say. I'm afraid I gave them a bit of a hard time, but in the end, they simply challenged me to read, and to pray about what I read and what I had heard from them—much of which was entirely new to me. I can't say what persuaded me to do that, but do it I did. I expect you know what happened then. Against all my training and prejudices and better judgment, I am to be baptized into The Church of Jesus Christ of Latter-day Saints on Saturday, August tenth! I must confess I am as trembly and excited as a new bride—and I just hope the marriage will be a sound one.

"Your friend—and, I suppose, mine—May Hinton, made good on her threat to come see me, and happened along just as the sister missionaries were arriving for a discussion. She sat in on it, but could hardly wait to think of an excuse to get away. I don't believe May is prepared to venture into anything new. She is a good woman, but has always been rather timid, if not rigid, in her outlook.

"Thank you for the update you sent on your genealogy. I'm glad the Rhys name turned out to be yours, and I hope you will have continued success in your search for your ancestors. Let me know if I can be of help in that endeavor."

The bishop let his hand, still holding the letter, fall to the tabletop. Trish smiled at him mischievously.

"It isn't always the people you think most likely who join the Church, is it?" she said softly. "Of the two, I'd have voted for May Hinton, any day. But isn't that amazing?"

"More than amazing," he agreed. "What a season of harvest we're having! The elders called me today to say that they're feeling really good about baptizing at least four of their contacts, soon—and that three new people phoned them this morning, asking to be taught. They all said they had been at the rally on Saturday night and had become disillusioned with their ministers' support of the agitators. It just humbles me how the Lord can turn negatives into positives!"

"I know—and everyone at Relief Society yesterday was talking about how their testimonies had been strengthened by the fireside and by their preparation for it—the fasting and prayer and all. And that's really good. But Jim, I was wondering. Things don't always turn out so well, when the Saints are persecuted. Once in a while, chapels do get burned or vandalized, and people do get hurt, or even killed, for the gospel. And sometimes, members are weakened by the attacks of our enemies and defect to the other side. Why do you think we were so blessed?"

He pondered her question. "It must be a matter of faith being rewarded," he said slowly. "I reckon only the Lord knows for sure. He's the only one who can read all our hearts and gauge our faithfulness. I know a lot of prayers went up to Him, from all over the stake, and you know the scripture—'the effectual, fervent prayer of a righteous man availeth much.' You take several hundred righteous men and women and children, all praying for a good cause, and I'm certain the Lord listens. For whatever reason, I'm mighty thankful he saw fit to help us."

"Me, too—for your sake, as much as anybody's. I know how concerned you've been."

He smiled affectionately at her. "Well, think of it this way: you're the mother of three-and-a-half children. But I have four hundred twenty-one and three-quarters children—of all ages—that I feel responsible for."

"Wait a minute—three quarters! If I'm the half, who's the other quarter? Who else is expecting?"

His smile deepened. "Surely somebody must be," he teased.